GRAVEYARD
OF AN
ANARCHY

ODYSSEY
OF A
CROWN PRINCE

GRAVEYARD
OF AN
ANARCHY

ODYSSEY
OF A
CROWN PRINCE

Bash Bakr

Eloquent Books
New York, New York

Eloquent Books
An imprint of AEG Publishing Group
845 Third Avenue, 6th Floor—6016
New York, NY 10022
http://www.eloquentbooks.com

ISBN-13: 978-1-60693-822-5
ISBN-10: 1-60693-822-3

Book Designer: Bruce Salender

Printed in the United States of America.

HELLO READERS

It intrigues me to inform you and to absolutely guarantee you that you're in for a tremendous ride. The type specially designed to render you glued and glancing at the door hoping no one comes in or goes out interfering your trance.

The African continent is remarkable and resourceful in many ways.

It's vastly populated and large—*indeed, only Asia is larger*. Africa is about three times the size of Europe and extends over nearly 12 million square miles.

The reckoning of time in history is very important. It's by this means that we can ascertain that one interesting event happened before another.

Graveyard of an Anarchy is a fitting title for this precious novel you're about to read, for it attempts to x-ray the realities of events in the past, entwined with the present in the most fabulous and colorful manner.

Please endeavour to visit me at www.bashbakr.com, e-mail me at info@bashbakr.com or write me at Eloquent Books, 43 Clark Road, Durham, CT 06422 U.S.A and let me know how much you enjoyed *Graveyard of an Anarchy*.

Have a nice day

—**Bash Bakr**

ACKNOWLEDGEMENTS

I am particularly grateful to those important personalities who assisted and inspired me genuinely during the long process of traveling, studying and writing this novel.

TO THE
WOUNDED GIANT
... AFRICA

Life is an opportunity of amazing curves, filled with knocks,
triumph and glamour, emptying in vanity.

—Bash Bakr

CHAPTER ONE

1850

Odua trembled with tension, like a man who suddenly found himself in a lion's den. Odua, a kingdom basking in the euphoria of a mellow season crowned with a resourceful harvest, was now engulfed in a nightmare that threatened to rip it apart from its very foundations.

King Jajaha kakah Tobiolah II, king of kings, was second in command to the throne of the gods. His power and authority reigned beyond Odua, extending deep into the Delta boundaries and the vast areas of Equatorial Guinea up to the great lake peninsula.

His Majesty sat alone in his ancient palace, a rare event. He was completely submerged in his thoughts. Until this moment, it never occurred to him, nor would he ever have believed that his people could reject him. It was as if a dense acidic fog hung over his Kingdom. Nothing seemed right anymore. In spite of the cool morning breeze, sweat rolled down his forehead uncontrollably. His ivory chair, an ancient seat of power, the supreme throne of his ancestors had suddenly become uncomfortably hot, like a stone pulled out of a furnace. Worse-still, when he ordered for his favourite dish the day before, the bush-meat tasted dry and the pounded yam was difficult to swallow.

Deeply disturbed, the king shifted uneasily in his ivory chair, seething against his detractors.

'Sango strike you all dead!' he cursed.

He let out a long-held breath and rubbed his red eyes, a result of the grueling nine-hour meeting that ended in the early hours of the morning.

Like his ancestors, king Jajaha was tall and broad-shouldered. A charismatic leader, looking fit at sixty-three. When he walked, he moved smartly giving the impression of an agile man with vigor and strength. Dark with blazing eyeballs, he seemed more like the god of thunder whenever he flared. His only concession to decent appearance was when he was in traditional attire, with large beads on his wrists and around his neck, and matching leopard-skin footwear.

Compared to his predecessors, he has successfully distinguished himself as a king with unique humour. His admirers and enemies alike labelled him a totalitarian, the conqueror of all battles. He was a colourful king who was not easily stung by criticism, especially when it came from inhabitants of kingdoms he had conquered. More so, it was generally agreed by elders and great warriors of different kingdoms that his greatest gift was his mental toughness that had kept the British at bay for more than two decades. For this, he was often compared to 'Sango', the god of thunder, who had battled other imperialists in the past.

King Jajaha was once reputed to have proudly said of himself that, 'If Sango is thunder and lightening, I am fire and water.'

The situation he found himself in at the moment was such that his spiritual arsenal could not provide the appropriate weapon to avert the looming disaster that lay ahead. The numerous kingdoms he had conquered and his immense wealth seemed of no significance, even though in the past they had always smoothed his paths to numerous accomplishments.

The splendor of his magnificent palace was designed far ahead of his generation. It was a triumph of wealth. So much unlike a Zulu king, Jajaha wasn't a skinflint and that indeed reflected in the overall structural outlook of Odua, coupled with his benevolent attitude to all that encountered him. The abolition of the slave-trade sixteen years back was a setback for him, still, the embargo had made the trade more lucrative for the bold-hearted. The large profits from it contributed immensely to the state-of-the-art palace in the heart of Odua, an edifice widely acknowledged to surpass that of his archrivals like King Deng Bor Yorool of the Dinka Kingdom and King Yezid ibn Saud of the Arabian Gulf.

The exterior lay-out of the palace was more beautiful at night when it glowed with light from one hundred and twenty windows and slim torches erected above the fence. It was a fortress surrounded by a river. On its west side was the forest of the gods, and on the east was a cliff on a large stone so massive that it was often compared to the giant Lumo rock on the southern wing. Royal guards could be seen mounted strategically on the rock in full war gears. They were stationed there basically to suppress any invasion from any of the numerous enemies of the kingdom.

* * *

Today was the third day since the news was announced. The sad pronouncement that had kept King Jajaha in a rare depressive mood, one that had kept him away from the company of his family, his chancellors and the elders of the land. His majesty shifted and gazed unseeingly around the hall, recounting the events of the previous night. For long, he would remember the night he struggled unsuccessfully to persuade his Chancellors and the Chief-Priest to support him to defy the order of Ifa Eledumare, the mouthpiece of the gods. Ifa was all-knowing and held in his palms the past, the present and the future.

For a moment, the King jerked from his trance and froze as faint footsteps shuffled along the passage. Its sound increased as the steps drew nearer. He knew it would be no other person than his Queen, Abekeofin. Nobody was more devastated than the queen who had vented her anger at the Chief-Priest and the Chancellors for denouncing her newborn child as *Abami-eda*, a strange creature. Nevertheless, her strength of character had enabled her to perform her duties to the king. She kept his meals coming in spite of his loss of appetite. The king's declining winsome smiles was evident on his sour face. He had also become cranky, querulous, petulant, and temperamental. His predicament had not only transformed him, but had also created a huge state of emotional disorder and confusion among his Chancellors and the people at large.

As the queen approached the grand-hall in calculative strides, she adjusted her headgear. She was decked in her traditional regalia and in her hands was the king's crown.

'Good morning your majesty,' she greeted on both knees. Odua's tradition required every woman, no matter how influential or old she might be, to be completely submissive to her husband. It was the soul of the people's cultural and traditional heritage.

'Good morning,' the king replied with deadpan dryness. His blazing eyes seemed larger than ever.

'Can we bring your food here or you prefer the backyard?' the Queen asked. There was no response. Instead, the King indulged in a slight frown and then his eyes flickered down, looking appraisingly at her smooth ebony face. Suddenly, he caught sight of his crown in her hands and promptly reached for it.

'Where did you get it?' he demanded in a tensed accusing tone.

'It's been lying in my room for the past three days,' she informed. He squinted at it, bringing it closer to his face.

'Is there anything wrong with it?' she asked as her heart sank in fear.

'I wished you'd call my attention to it much earlier than now,' he said, passing her a curious and dispassionate gaze. 'I'll eat later,' he stated bluntly and waved her away. Slowly, he adjusted the crown, placed it on his shiny head and gazed aimlessly around the hall.

'Your majesty,' the Queen cried in an anguished voice, moving closer and placing her heavily jeweled arms on his thighs. Her voice was gentle with depression, 'for how long will this continue?'

In a rare move, she looked straight into her husband's eyes and pleaded, 'at least for the sake of the family and the kingdom, you should get out of this depressive mood and try to....' That was as far as she got before the King growled.

'Woman, bother me no more!' Slowly, the anger welled up from deep inside him. His frustration was obvious. 'Can't you understand anything? Can't you see I need some peace to think this thing out? To think a way out that will not jeopardize the sovereignty of the kingdom of my ancestors under my time.' He looked away from her for a moment and then spluttered, 'Abekeofin! You have to go now. I wish to be alone for now. I must find a way to deal with the plots of my enemies.'

The Queen closed her moistened eyes with a despairing sigh. She rose effortlessly and headed for the exit. Suddenly, she stopped as if she remembered something. She turned and faced the king, looking boldly into his eyes. Then in a flash, she departed the king's presence.

King Jajaha felt a spasm of tremor run through his heart. The expression on his wife's face was odd. Gone were the hurt, her pleas and even her worries and in their place was cold determination.

'*Oya,* deliver us from your daughters,' he mumbled.

* * *

Hours after the queen's unceremonious departure, King Jajaha stretched lazily in his seat. He could hear the aggressive pounding of yams from the backyard which filled the air with alternating thuds that presaged the arrival of a second meal even while the first remained untouched.

Slowly, he stood up arching his back as he stepped on the tiger skin foot mat. With a truculent expression on his face, he whirled around the hall with arms akimbo. He could feel the imaginary tremor of the earth under his feet. His majesty could not help guessing that this just was not an ordinary quake. It was his world, his kingdom crumbling under him.

'Oluwa mi o!' he had cried to himself when he heard from Ifa. At first, he found it absurd and asked several questions, leading to other questions. However, it soon dawned on him that Ifa's decision is beyond compromise, a price to be paid for a smooth reign, a very huge cost emotionally.

Tensed, he paced about the hall, stopping at the centre. He swayed momentarily and smiled amidst the silence that filled the hall. Then he raised his head and cast a haunted glare at the ceiling. He felt abandoned by his ancestors.

'Why me?' he shouted suddenly. 'Why me? I, King Jajaha Kakah Tobiolah, *Igbakeji Orisa,* the mighty iroko that towers over all black coasts!' Realizing he had raised his voice, he checked himself and surveyed his surrounding to make sure he was alone.

'Meee,' he thumped his chest thrice beneath the thick fabric of his Aso-Oke.

In a rasping voice he continued. 'Me, the conqueror of the throne of thunder and fire. How come it's me? Where did I go wrong? Is it my father, Aare Kakah the greatest warrior of all time? A warring king that conquered seven empires in seven days; man like men, tagged with braveness and spiritual prowess, an immortal for generations unborn.'

King Jajaha drawled for a moment, his beads jiggled across his chest as he knelt holding up his hands in supplication.

'Distinguished royal highnesses, the ancestors of Odua, do not sit-back and watch the royal family collapse. Protect your son from the plot of his enemies. Deliver me from the evil that men concoct in the hours of darkness. Test me not with that which is far beyond my capability, so that your favour will forever glow over thy people and thy land.'

Satisfied, he lowered his hands and his face broke into a huge smile, assured he has been heard. Again he thought of his enemies and mouthed curses at them.

* * *

Meanwhile, away from the palace, activities throughout the kingdom were dull. Its entire inhabitants looked less euphoric and sweltered in unaccustomed breeze. Few went to their farms to plow the soil or harvest crops. There was the ever presence of young virgins at the riverbanks, some busy washing, others fetching drinking water. Many, including the elders of the land, were however held-up at their homes, awaiting words from the palace.

* * *

It was later in the evening that the king decided to call-off his self-imposed hunger strike. He ate alone in the hall. The same bush-meat was served, but unlike the previous day, the food tasted better. Satisfied halfway through it, he pushed aside the plates and washed his hands in a gold plated basin of water placed beside him. He felt heavy, filled with pounded yam, and his back arched for a rest.

'Sleeping at odd hours of the day is a plot from enemies to get at you,' he muffled, unwilling to trust his own feeling. Reluctantly, he rose gently and moved towards the exit, hoping to catch some sleep after all. As he walked along the decorated passage leading to his bedroom, he glanced at the giant mirror fixed to the wall. Memories of his friend, Sir Franklin Gordon crept into his mind. Vividly, he could still remember the day the British knight presented him the mirror on behalf of the government of the United Kingdom, for his unrelenting effort and cooperation in the sales of human property, as slave trade was labeled.

For a fleeting moment, he stood frozen before the mirror, admiring himself. He smiled in satisfaction, pleased with his reflected image. At sixty-three, he was full of life, tall and good looking. Though, there was no denying the fact that he had aged rapidly within the last three days. Abekeofin was always right when it comes to matters about his health. She had even mentioned that he was going grey by the minute. He took a step forward and felt the cold surface of the mirror with both palms. Again, as he had done several times before, he wondered at the creative and imagination of his white associates. The large mirror was about one of his most valued property in the palace, his source of pride. Above all, he cherished his status as the only African king that possessed a mirror of such magnitude. Still fascinated with the glass, his thoughts went to his very first encounter with a mirror.

It was many years back when a group of white men, wearing steel hats and boots, presented a small sized mirror to his father on the occasion of the new yam festival. Curious and suspicious of their colour, he had crawled out of bed that very night and slipped into his father's bedroom. He quietly opened the king's safe-box and removed the wrap over the small mirror. When he saw his image in the glass, he was stunned. Gripped by fear, he dropped the mirror on the concrete floor and it split in two halves. When his father discovered the damage the next morning, he blamed the action of his son on the plot of his enemies to turn the Prince against him. Thereafter, he ordered sixteen traditional head-baths for the young heir, fourteen more than was usual.

On a sudden impulse, king Jajaha turned away from the large mirror and he sighted one of the palace maids hurrying-out of the room occupied by his eldest son, Prince Dada. The sadness, the pain and the humiliation threatened to overwhelm him.

'Why am I a disaster?' he growled in a heavy depressive voice, as the sickening knowledge of his son came pouring into his mind. His vision became suddenly blurred and he became breathless. Briskly, he turned away from the mirror and hurried down the far end of the passage, leading to the Prince's bedroom. He paused by the window and peered through it. Then he moved over to the door and opened it a crack. The light from the passage shone into the room. Two fire torches beamed down on his face as he stepped inside gazing at the sleeping Prince. He moved closer and was startled by the Prince's stillness.

'May the gods grant you recovery,' he said solemnly, staring with disbelief at his first child. The Prince lay-still like a human ready to be sacrificed to an oracle. He had been seriously battling for his life ever since the return of his mother from the United Kingdom. He'd remained in a dim semi-consciousness and several native doctors had been invited to heal him, but none had come up with a solution. Gently, king Jajaha placed a hand on his son's face and tried to wipe away perspiration dripping down his forehead and cheekbones.

Suddenly, a baby howled shrilly and shattered the silence causing him to draw back his hand. He reached out again and this time held the Prince by the hand. And for a moment, the king's sadness was deepened by his discovery. The Prince's temperature was at its highest, almost like a stone extracted from a furnace.

'My ancestors,' mumbled the king, shaking his head in despair as he headed for the door. Outside, he looked up at the yellow glow of the fire touch and rained curses on his enemies before he closed the door gently behind him.

* * *

King Jajaha's bedroom was in darkness when he entered. He did not bother to light a touch. He moved majestically across the room and sat gently on the edge of the bed, feeling like a commoner. Breathless, he closed his eyes for a moment. When he opened them, he immediately felt the intense silence and darkness. Nothing in the room was visible, nothing seems worthy, maybe nothing will ever be again, he thought.

The sweet smell of his royal bedroom had evaporated in the past three days, leaving a strong sense of unhappiness and confusion. He groaned as he lowered himself on his large bed and started re-assessing his life as a king blessed with five official wives that disappointedly bore him fifteen daughters. Abekeofin remains the exception. He had married her when she was just sixteen and she remained his true love and mother to his eldest son, Prince Dada. Most recently, queen Abekeofin had given him yet another son. It was the birth of a new Prince, an

17

event that should naturally call for celebration, but had instead become a nightmare, tumbling the kingdom into an endless abyss. The impending calamity was quite obvious from the very beginning when for the first time in the history of Odua, a prince was born far-away in a foreign land. Worse-still, it occurred in the land of a strange race.

The queen had gone on a trade mission to the United Kingdom when she was already three months pregnant. Her journey had lasted longer than expected due to a slight delay of the Royal Atlantic Ship. Her assignment was simply to accompany the human cargo of ten thousand heads of slaves to Liverpool, United Kingdom. As it turned out, the baby came before its time through a caesarean done by an unpopular white witch, named Amos Caesarian. When the queen arrived home with baby in hand, the Chancellors and the Elders of the community raised eyebrows. The people of the kingdom suspected foul play, and rumours began spreading like forest fire. The consultation of the Ifa-Eledumare by the Chief-Priest finally hammered the nail into the king's heart.

The next day, the chief-priest declared his discovery at the market square.

'O people of Odua Kingdom, open your ears wide and hear the word of Orunmilal! Let those who are present inform those that are not here! Our gods are always there to bring forth happiness, prosperity and stability unto the land of our ancestors. Now they have once again ordered a sacrifice. A sacrifice to wash away our atrocities so that our women will continue to deliver in peace; that our farmers will reap the fruits of their labour and that our hunters will not be hunted down or be short of animals to hunt in the forest; that our young will not die young, and our infants will not die in the cradle!'

The Priest paused to catch his breath. His words hung in the air for a moment, as he paced in a circle. He was impressed by the huge crowd and could even see more heading towards him. At that moment, he knew he had got the attention of everyone in the market place. He cleared his throat and continued.

'The demands of our gods cannot be toyed with, for if their words do not come to pass at present, it will surely come to pass in future. Our gods own us and we are theirs to deal with as they like. We should not allow our emotions to enslave us. There should be no sentiments when it comes to giving the gods what is due to them.' The priest paused again and made a sniffing sound of disgust. Each person wondered at what could be the latest demands of the gods.

'Orunmila has requested for the blood of a strange child, a child brought into our royal family. This child, together with his mother, Queen Abeke, and seven beautiful virgins are to be sacrificed at the river bank in seven days from today!'

The crowd was stunned but the old sage pressed on completely unperturbed.

'Long live his majesty, King Jajaha Kakah Tobiolah II. Long live Odua kingdom. This is my message to you. This is the message from our gods, your gods, the gods of your ancestors.' He concluded, and turning slowly, he carved a path through the crowd towards the direction of his wooden cottage. He was known to be a man of few words. It was a family trait. His great grand-father, Kumalo used to say that a man of many words is nothing but a liar and a devil in shades.

CHAPTER TWO

Two days to the appointed date for the sacrifice of mother and child, the Chancellors and elders of the kingdom finally received the much awaited invitation to the palace. They gathered in the palatial compound to hear the last appeal to Ifa-Eledumare. The chief Priest had not received any news to the contrary that the sacrifice must be performed.

Each of the seventy members of the council and elders was handed a traditional staff at the entrance by palace servants as they took their seats on the carved stool arranged in a semi-circle in front of the throne. Acceptance of the staff signified their continuous loyalty to the King. The noble Chancellors of the seven black coasts could be distinguished from the elders by the leopard skin worn across their shoulders over their garments.

It was the day of decision and each person harbored feelings of hope as the entrance of the king was awaited. King Jajaha, humble and cultured was not the type that kept his people waiting for long. Promptly, he made his usual ceremonious appearance, flanked by his royal drummers who showered him with praises with their talking drums. When he finally walked into the gathering, a loud voice announced his presence and all prostrated.

'Kabiyesi oooo!' All greeted. King Jajaha raised his staff in the air in a warm response, giving the members an avuncular smile, the type he created to baffle his detractors on such occasions. He jerked his head around and the drummers got the signal and left through the nearest exit.

King Jajaha sat on the throne of his fore fathers, looking rather sober and derailed.

Seated by his right, was his chief-priest and on the left his Balogun. He was a fearless veteran and third in command to the throne of the gods.

Without further ado, the chief Priest who recently turned seventy-two, rose slowly to his feet with the aid of his walking stick. An old brown raffia bag dangles around his shoulder. He was the speaker of the day and undoubtedly the wisest and most experienced. He greeted the king once again, bowing respectfully. He cleared his throat, paid homage to their ancestors, and finally welcomed the nobles to the royal palace. As Chief Priest, he commanded a lot of respect, especially among the Chancellors and elders who regard him with a mixture of awe and fear. He was a man whose character can hardly be faulted, for he never hid behind a finger. He was adored by all as a pillar of culture with an encyclopedic knowledge of their past.

'May Odua not come to ruins,' he began in a pinched voice as he sat with his legs folded under him on a lion skin spread on the ground. Gingerly, he pulled out from his hand-bag a long beaded thread together with Ifa's divination board. He laid it gently on the board and looked up in the direction of the king.

'Kabiyesi, may the crown remain on your head for long and may the royal shoes not leave your legs. State your intentions to Ifa.'

King Jajaha bowed his head in silent meditation for a while and then nodded at the chief-priest. The chief-priest raised the beaded thread and cast it on the board. He stared at it for long minutes before picking it up and repeating the actions. He extended and retracted his neck intermittently like a tortoise in his search for Ifa's revelations. Everyone, except the king looked on with anxiety and hope, as the chief-priest consulted the gods. The expression on the king's face was like that of a child lost in a sea of hopelessness. Though, he knew Ifa would never compromise, he held on to a thread of hope.

All through the ritual, a deep and uncomfortable silence descended on the gathering.

Occasionally, the king shifted in his seat trying to dislodge the tidal wave of thoughts that was sweeping over him like a rippling sea. He struggled inwardly to dominate his thoughts. Why the gods should expect him to fold his arms and allow his most loved ones to be wasted baffled him. What was he the king for, if he could not decree what can be done and what cannot be done in his kingdom? No one would lay a finger on either of them. Not while he remained the king. No one would dare, Ifa or no Ifa! These thought raced through his mind while the old priest performed his job.

All eyes lay on the chief-priest who looked tensed and completely enraptured in the worlds of the spirits pouring forth incantations. His reddened eyes at times lit-up like the sunrise, and at other times dimmed with depression. For several minutes he was in communion with the gods, his face a mixture of fear, veneration and awe. After what seemed a lifetime, the chief-priest returned to earth with a triumphant smile that could have cracked the hardest rock. He looked around the large gathering, there was anxiety in the air and all eyes were fixed on him full of expectations. He gazed upwards as though he were watching spirits depart to their abode. Slowly, he turned to the king who met his gaze and the aged priest spoke in a matter-of-fact voice, reverent with conviction.

'Kabiyesi, may your reign be long,' he announced.

'What is it?' asked the eager king.

'The gods of your ancestors are always on your side,' the priest replied plaintively.

'They directed me to tell you that there are sixteen spiritual principalities that lord over men. The gods will never deceive anybody and so you will not tolerate deceit from anyone too,'

he stated emphatically, looking away from the king. Spontaneously, he packed up his bag, staggered to his feet and rested his
weight on his walking stick. Thrice, he hit the ground with the
staff, casting his gaze at the king.

'They want you to panic no more, for they have heard you
aloud and in silence. They've heard your grievances and the
worries of your family and your people, and have decided to
offer you an alternative,' he pronounced. The gathering reacted
immediately by curtsying joyfully with the greeting, 'Kabiyesi
ooo!'

They were delighted over the unheard news, perhaps due to
the warm and reassuring smile on the priest's face. Balogun
rose swiftly from his seat, singing a famous traditional song,
swaying left and right in calculative dance steps. Soon, everyone joined him in singing. Gone was the sour mood, and in its
place was jubilation.

While the joyous mood spread like wild fire, the Priest
blinked rapidly at his people until his eyes finally rested on the
king. The king felt slightly mollified to hear that the lives of his
wife and her child were about to be spared. Amidst the excitement, the priest hit the ground thrice again with his walking
stick and an expectant hush followed. He smiled sagely to himself and raised his voice so all could hear him.

'Kabiyesi, my grand-father, Gbajabi crowned your grand-
father. My father Agbamoye crowned your father and you
Kabiyesi. By the powers of those whom Eledumare had given
possession of the days and nights, of life and death, and those
who were present before humans, I shall live to crown your
son. Kabiyesi, may we never witness any sort of calamity beyond our capability,' he prayed, and all intoned, 'Asheeeee!'

The Priest shuffled closer to the king, resting his whole
weight on his long staff with each step. He stopped a few paces
from him and stared into his eyes.

'Kabiyesi, listen and listen very well. First of all, the gods
of Odua want you by mid-night today to submit for rituals,
seven able-bodied men from numerous slaves, for sacrifice at
the riverbank.'

There was heavy silence in the Palace.

'Second,' the old priest swept his eyes over the heads trying to make sure all were attentive. 'You are also to provide seventy-seven bulls and sixty ducks to be buried alive tomorrow evening at the junction leading to the forest of the gods.' He paused again and grinned at the ground.

'Third, they want you to provide twenty kegs of honey, one hundred and twenty baskets of kola nuts, eight hundred and forty kegs of palm-wine and five hundred and eighty kegs of palm-oil, all for cleansing rituals at the grand shrine tomorrow morning before the cockcrow.' The priest paused again and regarded the people languorously.

'Lastly Kabiyesi,' he began with a frown. 'The day after tomorrow which marks the seventh day of Ifa's initial pronouncement, the gods of Odua want you to provide fried soyabeans for distribution to every house in the kingdom, and beyond. However, Kabiyesi, the newly born Prince alone, I repeat alone, must be banished from our land forever.'

'Haaah!' The people shouted. In the silence that followed, many cast furtive glances at those around them. The king raised his hands to his face, closing his eyes for a sad moment. The Priest was silent for a minute, gazing at the king and then the amazed congregation.

'That is Ifa's message to you, Kabiyesi,' the Priest said and took his seat obviously unshaken. For a while, the numbness in each person made it appear as if the blood in all had been drained by fear. They all knew Ifa's words were binding and there was absolutely nothing anyone could do about it.

* * *

A curfew was imposed at mid-night after the meeting. At exactly twelve midnight, king Jajaha with his Chancellors and some elders, including the chief-Priest, filed-out in two straight lines. They walked bare-footed, bare-chested and wrapped in sparkling white traditional robe around the waist. Some wore hand-beads made of seashells and beads. Their destination was the bank of the Osun River, the place for the rituals. Already awaiting them at the riverbank were seven able-bodied men, lying naked on the red sand. The slaves were bound in chains, looking completely dazed, the effect of charms used on them to render them totally submissive.

When the king and his entourage finally arrived at the scene, they were already exhausted. Notwithstanding, they set about the occasion that brought them there. By custom and tradition, it was the duty of the Priest to slaughter the condemned men and drain their blood into a special calabash. Thereafter, he would escort the king into the river, cleansing him with the blood and water from the river. Once the cleansing was over, all would proclaim loudly an ancestral veneration until a shadow is cast upon the river. Then the Yeye Osun, the goddess of the river would glow in her majesty upon the river in pure white garments, except for her falling black hair. She would grimace, speaking no words, raising her left hand that bore a smoky pot dripping with human blood. Her appearance signified success, a sign of spiritual accomplishment and communication, meaningful to those who were skilled in the language of the spirits, among the twenty-one members of the inner circle, headed by the chief-priest.

Expectantly, after the completion of necessary rituals, she would laugh so long that her voice would resonate as if it would engulf the land. Yeye-Osun was the most venerated among the goddesses in Odua. In her hands lay the peace, success and harmony of the kingdom, hence, the respect she commanded in the land.

* * *

Day six

The sun was at its peak in the afternoon, causing the green plains of the land to flourish beautifully. King Jajaha woke up exhausted, glad that he has completed the demands of the gods with every sense of responsible leadership. Obviously, he was succeeding in uprooting the plots of his enemies. Having cast strong curses on his return from the river the previous day, he was deeply convinced that the end was near for those that did not wish him well.

He had just eaten his lunch, when his trade adviser, chief Aremu rushed into the palace announcing the arrival of two new ships from overseas. The ships were owned by two powerful companies, which loaded their cargoes in the waters of Odua.

'Your majesty, they are here with better bargains and lots of oriental products,' reported Aremu. King Jajaha forced a smile. He knew better and was getting wiser with each transaction. This time, he simply refused to be deceived by their exotic offers in exchange for his slaves. In the past, he had been cheated more than a dozen times by new companies. The painful experiences had expanded his scope, creating a strong sense of awareness in him as to how crafty and dishonest his white-associates could be when it came to profiteering.

They were full of shady habits many African kings were ignorant of. In fact, what disturbed him most was their religion. They were busy all over the coast-line, preaching a strange god just like the Arabs. The thought of the latter disturbed him the most. They had nothing to offer him unlike the Europeans. From their lands in South-West Asia, they often sailed across the Indian Ocean to East Africa, forcefully seeking slaves and ivories obtained from tropical Africa. Those who were able to escape their clutches sought refuge in Odua and in the depths of the Congo forests. Wherever the Arabs invaded, like their European counterpart, they introduced a strong network of slave-trading, alongside their faith. They had turned Zanzibar and Pemba into a huge market centre for slaves. Undoubtedly, it was no longer a myth that they dreaded the west-coast of Odua throughout their conquests.

His knowledge of these events had strengthened his resolve never to allow any of them step foot into his territory. He was also determined to resist them if they should venture into the Niger and the Benue. He knew the Europeans were formidable with their weapons which spewed fire. But *Sango* and *Esu lalu ogirioko*, and the powers of his ancestors would ensure their firesticks had no effect on the great warriors of the land. Should such confrontation arise, Sango, the god of thunder and lightening would pursue them to the other side of the ocean where they would be feasted on by wild beasts.

To the disappointment of Chief Aremu, King Jajaha shoved away what he considers a great opportunity. Instead, he ordered an immediate meeting with his British and French traders in his waters that evening.

'A devil you know is much reliable than the devil you don't know,' he said, grinning at Aremu.

* * *

Later that evening when the sun seemed totally shaded by clouds and the air subtle with the kingdom's natural breeze. King Jajaha stepped gracefully through the crowd amidst drummers, Chancellors and loyal subjects, all heading for the junction leading to the forest of the gods, where seventy-seven cows and ducks were to be buried alive.

The mood was joyful and the royal drummers were at their very best, churning out words of praises with their talking drums. The King was gay as he waved cheerfully at the teeming crowd. The catastrophic situation in the land had been swept far away by Ifa's renewed decision. He had also successfully struck a deal hours ago with his British and French traders. A deal that would fetch him numerous oriental products and a posh palace in the nearest future. And for the first time, the British introduced him to an American business entrepreneur that came along with them. The American is said to be a member of the renowned American colonization society. He revealed some classified information of his government's intention to construct a large commercial vessel capable of enhancing the smuggling process of slaves from the West African port to North and South American ports, without the usual hassles of human-right agencies along the Pacific Ocean. He announced to the king's delight, the death of the renowned anti-slavery radical, John Brown.

King Jajaha wholeheartedly welcomed the smuggling idea and agreed to trade with the Americans as soon as the ship became sea-bound.

* * *

As expected, all preparations had been made before the king's arrival at the junction.

The rituals went accordingly and at sunset, the large canal was covered smoothly with sand. It marked the end of seventy-seven bulls and ducks, breathing twelve feet below the ground. Satisfied, everyone began to depart with that inner mind of security, fulfillment and actualization. The king's eyes glowed with enthusiasm. For him, the next day was the d-day, the day of the child he would live to remember for the rest of his life.

* * *

When he returned to his palace that night, he went straight to bed and slept off almost at once. He dreamt of his enemies and his final triumph over them. Later in the wee small hours, his eyes were wide open. His sleep had not been smooth and his body seemed totally drained of vigor. Unable to bear the stress, he crawled out of bed to have a word with his wife, whom he suspected would be going through a worse state of nervousness. He reached for his wrapper, tied it around his waist and thrust his feet into his leather slippers. He moved to the queen's bedroom next to his, knocked on the door gently and slipped inside. At the foot of the bed he stood with his mouth agape. The queen was sound asleep, without a care in the world.

'Abekeofin! Abekeofin! Aina!' He slapped her on the foot. 'What kind of a mother are you in deep slumber like a she-goat?' Her chin came up and she stared at the king fearfully.

'They are banishing your infant child tomorrow and you're here sleeping like the happiest woman in the kingdom. Is that child, my child?' he asked doubtfully.

'Of course, he's your child,' she retorted with a yawn. 'What kind of question is that at this hour?'

The king's expression turned aggressive. He looked down at her with disbelief on his face. Then he lowered his weight on the edge of the bed, pivoting his head with both hands.

'Your majesty, what do you expect me to do?' the queen demanded sitting up on the bed. 'You and your people have decided to show us your might. You people decide who should live and who should not,' she accused tearfully.

'Imbecile!' The king exploded. 'What nonsense are you saying? Are you sure you're fully awake? Perhaps you are under some kind of spell for you to be talking to me in such uncultured manner. Who am I to give life and take life? Isn't that the work of Eledumare and Esu lalu ogirioko? I'm talking to you woman, answer me! Talk!'

The queen remained calm and quiet, like a true daughter of Orunmila.

'Is it me who also asked them to banish your child?'

'You wouldn't do such a thing,' replied the queen.

'Then why?' he demanded with his hands spread out before him. 'Why talking nonsensical talk I just heard from you?'

She shifted uncomfortably and said, 'At least you could do something about it in our favour.'

'Something such as what, woman? Such as what exactly are you implying?' he drew his face closer to her, as if to make sure she was fully awake.

'Are you trying to advise me to defy Ifa's orders when you know fully well that it is because of Ifa that we have no disaster on our land? Are you saying what I think you're saying, or am I mistaken? Answer me woman!' he commanded. The queen said nothing. Instead, she lowered her head in regret.

'Abekeofin, I thought you're more intelligent than this. The statement coming out from your mouth clearly shows you're a moron after all. Certainly, the clans of your father are not senseless lots.' He finished in a voice laden with anger. Though his face was in the shadows, the frown on it was quite vivid to the queen. Hurriedly, she jumped out of bed and knelt before him, placing her arms on his thighs.

'Please do not be so angry with me over what I just said, I spoke according to my understanding of the issue, I did not mean to upset you in any way. I'm very sorry, Kabiyesi…'

'Enough!' He passed her an unreadable glance and took a deep breath. Gradually, his anger subsided. When he spoke again, his tone was more sober.

'We married you because of your family's background of wisdom and bravery. You are not just an ordinary woman. You must know this fact today if you don't know before. You're the queen of the land, the forewoman and my closest companion. This fact alone means power. And I've told you times without number that you should see yourself as a warrior. You must be ready at all times to support me in tribulation and battle." He paused with a sigh and passed her a resentful gaze. Slowly, he leaned towards her as if to whisper a secret and spoke softly.

'Now woman, listen very well to what I have to say. I'm not sure if your eldest son Dada will live. His illness remains a mystery to me. In view of this…' he paused and caressed her hands affectionately. Then he arched his eyebrows and starred at her amusingly.

'I know a white man once, Franklin, a noble man, a man of principle who served his kingdom with honesty while on our soil. My idea is this: I shall send your new-born baby to my dear friend, Sir Franklin Gordon in the United Kingdom. I'll ask him to take your child as a son and if he so desires, he may give him their type of education. I've this feeling that we will be doing that child much good by sending him back to Britain, where he was delivered.' He paused again. 'It's fair that way than allowing him to wander aimlessly in a far-away forest, to the delight of my detractors. Never! I'll always prevail over my enemies, home and abroad, dead or alive, for the gods are for-ever on my side.'

Stunned, the queen retrieved her hands from his grip but said nothing.

'My friend, Sir Franklin Gordon is of a weak blood. He made this clear to me long ago that he's incapable of bringing a child into the world. He might love your condemned child and take him as his real son, so he may live a fulfilled life,' he concluded.

'But your majesty," the queen protested. 'How do you expect a white man, a slave dealer for that matter, to take care of a black child and give him the true love of a father? Will this man not add the prince to his numerous slaves?'

'Abomination!' The king cried out. 'You do not give what belongs to humans to dogs. He wouldn't do such a horrible thing. A prince is far different from a slave. And point of correction, Sir Franklin Gordon was never a slave owner. He's just a middleman in the business. He's the most decent white-man I ever traded with. He's calm, modest and unassuming. I can only liken his decent way of life to that of the Zulu king.' He grinned knowingly, wiping his mouth with both hands.

'I shall arrange provisions for your child, so that he won't have to depend solely on Sir Franklin.'

'I've a question, gestured the queen. 'Will our child be able to visit?'

'Your child will never visit you again. Never! Ever'! The king declared. 'It's hopeless to assume such possibility.' He cast a quick glance in her direction, trying to read the expression on her face. In a cracked voice, he muttered, 'This expulsion is a journey of no return; your child shall never meet you ever again, ever.'

The words struck the queen like a dagger in the heart. Sadness enraptured her, weakening her knees and causing her stomach to rumble silently. She looked away from the king in order to hide her tears, but he noticed.

'This is no time for crying, Abekeofin. You don't cry over spilt milk, do you hear me? What is bound to be shall be. His destiny is quite different from ours. It is by mistake he came into our lives,' the king said in consolation. In a show of affection, he held her cheeks in his hands, his fingers moved to her temples, then her shoulders, rubbing and soothing. Then he pulled her up by the hands so that she could sit beside him.

'How old is your child?' asked the king.

'One month and six-days,' she replied tearfully.

'Your child will spend the first five years at the Gold-coast, thereafter he will be taken to Gordon in the United Kingdom. I'll send a message to the Ashanti king,' he assured her.

His hand slid downward from her cheek to her neck and shoulder with a steady gaze of affection and pity on his face. She wiped off her tears after a while, and they starred at each other for a long moment.

'Abekeofin, you're so much more than a woman should be and never in my life have I respected any woman the way I respect and adore you. Do I have the honor tonight to nest in her royal bed? It's been a while,' he said, as his mouth curled into a suggestive smile.

'Your majesty, you'll always have the honor to shed-off all that is veiled, as you wish,' assured the queen. His smile broadened and slowly his hand found the knot of her wrapper. It fell to her waist, revealing ripe girlish breasts of the most influential woman in the kingdom. The king smiled with pleasure and they later made love the way culture and tradition deemed fit.

Day Seven (Expulsion)

That evening, the clouds basked in bright sunshine. It was the seventh day after Ifa's pronouncement. The Prince named Ifashanu Majek Abedi Tobiolah was banished at cradle from the land of his ancestors, to a journey of no return. Indigenes and strangers alike gathered silently to bid farewell to the infant prince. Amidst the huge crowd was king Jajaha, his wives, the Chancellors and elders. There were also emissaries from Odua's neighbors. Some of these kingdoms, especially the most powerful ones are the Berbers, the Anglo-Egypt-Sudan, the Buganda kingdom, Dahomey, Fulani Empire, the Bantu empire, Songhai empire, the Mandingo and the Zulu kingdom, had all met in private with king Jajaha, expressing their willingness to grant Prince Ifashanu a permanent residence in their renowned kingdoms.

Unknown to them all, king Jajaha has plenty of ideas in mind for the future. His main focus for the future was to conquer two-thirds of the kingdoms in Africa, with the support of his British, French and American allies. He had thought it wise to send prince Ifashanu to a distant land, away from regions that would soon turn into a battlefield for his conquests.

* * *

Waiting at the Kingdom's town gates were a dozen Ashanti horse-men, sent by King Akofi Kojo II, a close loyalist. Immediately after the rituals to expel the child of the royal family, king Jajaha had the responsibility to hand over the baby-prince to the leader of the horse-men, en route to the Ashanti kingdom. The Ashantis began to treat Odua with great respect after the conquest of the Alafin, backed by the Alake, a century before. The Oyo-mesi and the Egbas, assisted by Sango, had waged an unforgettable war to suppress the advancement of the Phoenicians in the Songhai Empire, Dahomey and Ashanti kingdom, at a period when the Gold-coast was growing in influence and trade in the continent.

During the handover, the queen stood frozen and watched her baby nestled in the arms of a foreigner. The sadness in her eyes was palpable. She resisted the urge to shed more tears, but deep in her heart she knew she would not rest until she sets her eyes on her child again.

CHAPTER THREE

UNITED KINGDOM 1860, Ten years later

Saturday is a splendid day for a birthday, especially that of a loved one. It was Lord Franklin Gordon's habit not to leave his bedroom before Romana's arrival. The fixed obligations were, early morning greeting, breakfast in his room and instructions for the day's duties. Fully awake, he gazed at the ceiling, feeling the faint streams of sun-rays escaping the shades of his wool curtain and hitting directly at the centre of his mattress.

'Goodness,' he whispered.

Summer had come and gone. It was autumn with the temperature hovering high above 19-degree-Celsius, although subtle breeze still blew from the west to the south as it did all seasons. He shifted in bed looking through the window and admiring the beautiful blue sky of London. Lord Franklin smiled. What a nice day. Simply the type of day when one would want to dance in the park, or take a long walk down the aisle, he thought.

Effortlessly, he rose and sat on the edge of the bed, rubbed his wrinkled face with both hands and gave a slight groan. It was the groan of a tired old machine that was once a master of politics, with complete dedication to the Conservative Party for thirty-two years. Unlike the Lords who inherited their seats in the House of Lords, his was granted as a reward for his long time service to the Kingdom of his birth. He was a patriot who by virtue of his position as a Lord was highly regarded and connected across the continent. Lord Franklin was acquainted to all those that mattered in every region of the world, ranging from Dukes, Marquises, Earls, Countesses, Viscounts, Barons and Baronesses, Kings and Queens, Field-marshals, and a host of other world shakers. All were people concerned with world politics, trade and religious maneuvers.

Today however seemed a blessed day for Lord Franklin. He had no doubt that, if he failed to turn up on time, Duchess Kimberly would be greatly disappointed. Amusingly, he gazed down and his thoughts shifted to his feet. Once they had been young and smooth. He gazed forlornly at his hands. They were all wrinkled. Funny though, he wondered what his face would look like. Not expecting much wonders, he stood up lazily and shuffled to the front of a full length mirror mounted on his closet.

'Jesus,' he mumbled. At seventy-one, he looked smart and buoyant. God knows how many Brits of my caliber maintain such fitness at such a dead age, he thought. Halfway through his self-examination, the image of the beautiful Duchess Kimberly appeared. He winked thrice at it and the image disappeared. It had been like that for months. He sighed deeply. Wonderful, he thought. He could never be able to differentiate between likeness, fondness, love and obsession for a woman. Perhaps till the very moment of my death, he thought.

The duke had died more than a year before, yet they had both decided to keep their affair very discreet, just as they did when the duke was diagnosed with Parkinson disease and a failing heart.

Still standing in front of the mirror, he placed a hand under his jaw and gently pushed before taking a final glance of approval. He reached for his wristwatch on the bookshelf, determined to break his routine and started for the door. He held the knob before a gentle knock made him take two steps backward.

For an instant, he thought about Ifashanu, whom he called Ifash.

'Come in,' he said. Romana stepped in with a tray containing milked-coffee, sliced bread and cheese.

'Good morning, your Lordship,' she greeted meekly.

'Good morning Romana, you're pretty late. Is everything alright?'

'I am sorry for my lateness your Lordship. The cylinder was empty and I'd to rush to get it refilled at Robin-avenue,' she said with a regretful expression as she placed the tray on a small table beside the bed.

'It's okay. I was just a little bit worried,' he said and waited for her to leave the room before he closed the door gently behind her.

* * *

Halfway through his meal, Lord Franklin was not sure if what he was feeling inside was hunger, anxiety, or old-age fatigue; but whichever it was, he must eat a little more to strengthen himself. He ate a few more mouthfuls and gave up. His breakfast never lasted for more than fifteen minutes. So also was his morning shower, another quick routine. This morning, however, he decided to be more relaxed, taking his time to wash every part of his ageing body. He would like to be at his best when he's with the duchess later in the day.

After a thorough bath, he opened his wardrobe and selected his favorite suit. He felt the inner-pocket of his black tuxedo for a handkerchief, but found a fitting bow-tie instead. He returned to the mirror and adjusted the tie. Satisfied, he reached for his walking stick, placed vertically beside the largest of the three bookshelves in his large bedroom. He held the stick in the air and remembered something precious, his perfume. He searched through the closet, found it and sprayed it roughly over his suit. He eyed the silver liquid admiringly. The bottle labeled 'Royals' was a special birthday gift to Princess Margaret in 1617 by the designer Giorgiano Salvatore, from the Roman Empire. It was amazing that the silver liquid still ranked among the very best in the world and remained in the possession of a privileged few.

Nevertheless, the reason he cherished the perfume was because it was his 70th birthday gift from Duchess Kimberly. Idly, he scratched his jaw and smiled.

Hardly free from his thought, another gentle knock came from the mahogany door, jerking his Lordship back to reality.

'Yes, come-in,' he said.

'Good morning Pa,' Ifash popped his head through the door and flashed a reckless smile at his father.

'Close the door,' beckoned Lord Franklin. The little boy closed the door with both hands and pressed his back against it.

'What are you up to, awake at 6:00am,' the six-foot tall Lord demanded and bent to meet Ifash's height, pulling his left cheek. 'What are you up to this time around?'

'Pa,' Ifash smiled, fumbling with his bow-tie. 'I smell that scent. The one you always kept in the inner closet. I'd to quickly rush out of bed and wear my sweat shirt,' he piped before changing his expression. 'Are we not going to that old-woman's house together?' he asked innocently and staring into his father's assessing eyes.

'Ifash, you surprise me,' Lord Franklin said, straightening himself and placing a hand on the boy's head. He raked his young hair with long wrinkled fingers and smiled into his handsome face.

'So, are you saying, you smelt my Royals, and you got the gist and that was it. You didn't even bother to take a shower, no toothpaste, didn't say the Lord's Prayer, and no breakfast. You thought it wise to invade my privacy in a rumpled sweat-shirt, right?' he scolded and waited for his response. When he did not get any he continued.

'I thought I mentioned it over dinner yesterday that it's a gathering for adults, kids are not invited. Come, let's have a sit,' he said gently and carried Ifash to a rocking chair while he sat on a reading chair.

'At dinner you said children will be allowed in later in the day,' Ifash reminded him.

'I see, did I really say that?' Lord Franklin inquired calmly.

'Yes! You did. You also said Tina and her mom will be coming too. You said so Pa, you did. I can swear!" Ifash stated. Lord Franklin smiled knowingly.

He shifted his gaze from Ifash to the big history book on the table and opened few pages, faking concentration. He reflected on his fading memories and about Ifash in an all-white party.

Duchess Kimberly knew the little boy, but definitely not her guests. She had once joked about the thousands of white kids at the Hampshire's Home for Motherless Babies looking for decent fathers like him. She had wondered endlessly why he had opted for a black kid among a pool of options.

'Pa!' Ifash interrupted his trance. He took his eyes off the book and faced his son. He noticed the disappointment in the boy's expression.

'Alright, alright,' he said. 'You don't give me that look today of all days. You must promise me you'll be well-behaved,' Lord Franklin said with a finger in the boy's face. Ifash grinned, raised his thumb and nodded in agreement.

'Good, that's very good!' Lord Franklin stood up. 'All's said and done,' he said and stretched a hand to Ifash and led him to the door. 'Tell Romana that you're escorting me to Duchess Kimberly,' he directed the boy as his face melted into a smile at the mention of Kimberly.

'Thanks pa,' Ifash jumped. Lord Franklin bent to receive a peck, patting him on the back. 'Off you go,' he said and closed the door behind the boy.

Lord Franklin returned to a quiet corner in his room where he relax with his rock chair, ritually enjoying a solitary pipe. He curled his fingers together into a fist and drifted into a trance. In no time, his thoughts went to five years before when Ifash arrived at his ranch house with bags full of antiques, raw gold and cocoa. The king's note was very brief. His friend King Jajaha Tobiolah II was a charismatic leader he met thrice at the west of the Atlantic. His majesty in good gesture unbelievably sent him a prince to be considered a son. King Jajaha's major concern in his short note was to give the child all that he desires, including education that will make him fit properly into the society, no more, no less.

1855 was the year Ifash came to London and was enrolled into Elton nursery and Primary. That same year, Lord Franklin opened a fixed deposit account in the boy's name, thereby insuring his university education at Cambridge, where he once taught as an associate Professor of Political Science. However, in a world filled with obstacles, all had not been so silky smooth for Ifash. There were a number of occasions he had sought for a transfer to another school, where black discrimination was less. As the only black kid at Elton, life was difficult for Ifash for lack of love and respect from his mates. The white kids saw him as a privileged slave child who deserved no respect and friendship.

Most importantly, with all the racial challenges that surround Ifash, Lord Franklin had gradually developed a strong love for him. It was a love so dear that he allowed his heart to fully accept him as his only child. Ifash was a gift from God, a source of pride for a man who had totally lost hope of raising a child. Since the little boy came into his life, his beliefs on racial issues had changed. He had become a strong supporter in the campaign for the total eradication of slavery in Europe. The scope at which he presently viewed the black community had been redefined. He came to realize that the black communities, especially in the United-Kingdom had been deprived of so many basic rights. Though they were not all monolithic as such, but many blacks could now have access to education. Also recently, many African kingdoms were doing quite well on the political spectrum, and were now crying for total independence. It was a development black empires could never have thought of some ten years back.

His thoughts returned to Ifash and Duchess Kimberly's birthday-gala. He remembered initially that taking a mere stroll with Ifash, let alone taking him out to a special gathering, had been very dreadful. His society was quite hostile, but with time he personally developed a great fatherly affection for the boy, without care for what people around him said. It was no longer a secret that people were wondering with irritation what a dignified statesman like him was doing, hanging around with a slave-child. The English being who they were could not bolster enough courage to confront him about the issue. It all remained a hot gossip every now and then. Interestingly, he was familiar with gossips. His whole life had been built on gossip ever since his mother, Rebecca Gordon, committed suicide the day she found her controversial younger sister, Aunt Susan, in bed with his father, Simon Gordon.

As the clock chimed the hour, Lord Franklin got impatient and made his way downstairs. He opened the front door of the house and found Ifash already dressed in starched long-sleeved white shirts with stripes, a blue cap and matching brown shorts. His white stockings were pulled up to the knees.

'You look handsome by the way,' Lord Franklin said smilingly and tapping his cap with a finger.

'Thanks pa. You look lovely too,' Ifash said.

'I hope so,' Lord Franklin murmured under his breath, reaching for Ifash's hand.

* * *

The wagon-wheel was ready and parked a few meters away from the main gate. Lord Franklin had informed the wagon captain three days earlier of the importance of the day's ride to the city-hall. Hand in hand, he crossed the lawn with Ifash.

Romana looked through the kitchen window, as she placed the plates in the rack. Instinctively, Ifash looked back and caught her gaze. She spared him a brief smile and waved.

The wagon captain was busy inspecting the wheels as Lord Franklin helped onto the vehicle.

'Everything alright?' he asked.

'Perfect sir,' replied the captain doffing his cap slightly. Lord Franklin climbed in from the side of the metallic red-wagon and settled in the most comfortable angle. He beckoned to Ifash to join him and the boy did, nestling close to him.

The captain prompted the horses and the wagon pulled away. They surged ahead at a fast pace raising dust behind them. Lord Franklin's attention shifted to the dusty road and he indulged in one of his usual trances. This time, he thought proudly of his past. Indeed, he was an accomplisher contented with the simple way of life he led. Despite being financially outclassed, he never felt inferior among the wealthy. Having made his mark on the continent and beyond, he cherished his position as a Lord in the world's strongest Kingdom.

His thoughts soon shifted to Duchess Kimberly and his heart skipped a beat. He could not possibly be falling in love at this stage of his life. Could he, he wondered. He had always been a strong advocate for those groups of men who totally dislike the idea of wedlock, because he never believed in love and had never found one. He saw no great value in living with a woman, pleasures apart. He had turned down several marriage proposals in the past in order to fully concentrate on his service to the government of the United Kingdom. Till date, he valued his days as a top British protocol officer in Africa. He served for more than twenty years in various parts on the African continent. At a later stage of his sojourn there, he got involved in the slave trade business which he had self-consciously dreaded for years until he met king Jajaha and his fabulous offers.

He was a middle man for six years, and the gains were instant and enormous. The fact remained that he never knew any business as lucrative as slave-trading in his entire life. It was such …

'Pa! Pa! Pa! Are you alright?' Ifash's voice broke into Lord Franklin trance.

'Yes, yes, I'm with you, what can I do for you son?'

'I'm alright pa, what about you?'

'I'm alright too, maybe a tobacco will be a brilliant idea,' he said, tugging his hand in his side pocket from which he extracted a long stick of tobacco and lit it. Ifash looked on, fascinated by the thick smoke. He wondered why people smoked. Could tobacco be sweeter than chocolate candy? He had this strange urge to ask his father, but he thought otherwise. He knew well now that anything said against tobacco could annoy him. Tobacco was his father's best companion. No contest.

Another forbidden topic was his mother. Lord Franklin had informed him that his mother was black. She was married to him for years until she went to live in Africa but had died unexpectedly when he was just a year old. As doubtful as it seemed, Ifash nonetheless loved his old man dearly. Anytime he was in his presence, he felt comfortable, loved and reassured. The love the world outside his home could not offer, he got in bundles from Lord Franklin Gordon. As their horses bumped along the dusty road, Ifash gazed at a heavy wagon with different colors of horses, lumbering towards them on the other side of the road. The wagon was pulled by two oxen and loaded with freshly cut woods. He was struck by the countless numbers of slaves walking along behind the wagon. And moving closely behind the slaves were group of white men in large steel hat, holding riffles and making calculative noise with the whistle in their mouths. Ifash had seen slave wagon in the past but never as large and strictly co-ordinated like this.

'Ifash,' Lord Franklin called through coiling smoke, diverting his attention away from the road. 'Tell me about Elton nowadays, anything new?'

'It's beautiful, nothing new, just the old stuffs. Can I tell you about my best-friend?' Ifash asked excitedly.

'Ah, who do you refer to as best-friend?' Lord Franklin asked, leaning forward to smile into his young face.

'Wise up kid,' he teased. 'There is nothing like best-friend in this clime. Don't lean on anyone, I assure you that you'll soon be caught off guard and disappointed. The word 'best' isn't meant for humans. Most people you think are human are actually beasts,' he fumed.

'Who is it meant for?' Ifash enquired, puzzled.

'Jesus Christ! None of that created from flesh. The word actually died with Adam in the Garden of Eden and was buried in the Roman Empire,' Lord Franklin said with a shrug.

'Alright pa. Let's say, my favorite friend,' he gestured with a hand.

'Wise up Ifash, that also doesn't really exist. Spill it out and give me the right word,' the lord challenged.

Depressed, Ifash looked on with folded arms. Lord Franklin smiled at the expression on the boy's face. A stirring of panic, puzzlement, and amazement seized Ifash, and he looked deep into his father's eyes for a clue. What other expression can be used instead of best friend, he thought with effort, gazing at the roof of the wagon. In tensed concentration, he ventured another one. 'My friend,' he blurted out.

'That's better,' remarked Lord Franklin, putting a hand around Ifash's shoulder. 'Don't ever be caught unaware that friends do become great enemies, and if by chance they both happen to live long, like seventy years just like me, they may eventually become best friends,' he said and smiled faintly. 'Like marriage, a successful friendship is simply the union of two forgivers, but in truth humans aren't forgiving, do you understand?' he asked puffing out heavy smoke, as if to express his disgust with the word 'best.'

'Now, what about him? What did you want to say? Let's hear you,' he asked. Intrigued by his father's enthusiasm, Ifash began fervently.

'His name is Adam McCarthy, from Leeds. He's going to be fifteen years old this autumn. He lives at East-Sussex, house no 0139. He lives with his mum, because, his dad is dead. He died in a War. He was a young soldier in the Republican Guard. Adam's favourite food is potato-chips and macaroni-sauce, and his favourite drink is ginger. His favourite sport is boxing and wrestling. He is the champ and also...'

'Stop there!' Lord Franklin interrupted sharply. 'Did you say boxing and wrestling, combination of two most violent sports?' Ifash grinned, sucking in a harsh breath. He did not notice his father's rough expression. When he did, he was taken aback. He saw the redness slowly spread over his face, and Ifash knew what that meant.

'Are you alright pa?' he asked chokingly. Lord Franklin's face had altered with fear and hopelessness. His dream for Ifash was grand. He wanted him to be the best he could be in a very cruel world, and that essentially meant his keeping the right company. His eyes flickered down, "Ifash," he called emphatically. 'A kid that boxes and wrestles other kids must be aggressive in nature, and too soon, he's going to be very capable of anything that will endanger human life. That isn't the sort of person I expect you to call a friend, let alone a best friend. You know I will not tolerate any act of indiscipline in…'

'No pa, no. You got it all wrong,' Ifash interjected with a stricken expression. 'He's intelligent. He wants to become a politician in the future. Adam said maybe one day, he could become the Prime Minister of England, you see?' he gestured with both hands.

'Oops!' Lord Franklin gasped. 'That could only mean having a thug at 10 Downing Street,' he said clearing his throat of nicotine.

'Most Prime Ministers and Secretaries that I know today enjoyed swimming, tennis, snow-games, and pebbles or such when they were kids. Many of them don't even engage in sporting activities. Take Walls Truman for example, he was a loner. Not for once did he get to represent his school at the local council competition. I did. I your father did,' he said grinning proudly and poking a finger into his chest. 'Walls actually tried but he just wasn't good at any sport. So you can see, you'll know them by their features; it's always in them. If you're smart, you won't miss noticing it,' he said shrugging his shoulders.

'Adam is intelligent pa,' Ifash protested.

'I did not say he's not intelligent,' Lord Franklin said pulling the boy's flat African nose. 'To wrestle and box other kids requires some level of intelligence and accuracy. What was his score last term?' he asked sarcastically.

'62%,' Ifash was quick to answer.

'I see,' said Lord Franklin with a deep sigh. The tobacco dangled between his fingers.

'That's cool for a kid that boxes and wrestles,' he said. He took a last drag from his tobacco and reached for a handkerchief from his chest pocket with which he wiped his mouth.

'Here,' Lord Franklin stretched forward, handling over the remaining tobacco to the wagon captain. The captain grabbed it gladly.

'Thanks your Lordship,' he said enthusiastically without taking his eyes off the dusty road.

'So, Ifash, tell me what other amazing gifts your friend possesses,' inquired Lord Franklin, sitting back comfortably.

'He's got a good idea,' Ifash shot-back excitedly.

'And what's that good idea all about,' Lord Franklin starred suspiciously at him and then forced smile on his face. 'Giving you the benefit of the doubt, what's it about?'

'He wants us to go on an adventure and discover the 18th century lost ship that belonged to Robin of Shire wood. He said it contains gold, ivories and diamonds.'

'Jesus!' Lord Franklin exclaimed. 'Where on earth is that lost ship? he asked, faking a serious expression.

'It's our secret,' Ifash responded proudly, feeling he had scored a sweet victory over his father. 'We won't tell anyone, until we are ready to leave.'

A momentary silence passed between them before Ifash continued. 'We will need large bags; each one should contain enough sweat-shirts, canned-beef, and jams, and lots of candies, assorted biscuits and diet fruits and sweet ones too.'

'Your friend is a very clever brat. He'll make a good politician after all. He wants you to go after the spoil of a rebel,' stated Lord Franklin. 'I am just hoping he won't turn out a rebel leader one day,' he said and smiled tremulously, turning Ifash's cap backward.

'Tell your friend to include me in the team. Discovering a ship filled with gold and diamonds could be wonderful at seventy-one. That certainly will be breaking news around the world,' he chuckled.

'It's alright pa,' Ifash said and flashed a triumphant smile. 'We'll take you along, but you won't smoke when we get there. Adam said spirits don't like smoke, but we intend to fight them later with fire and smoke. Then you can smoke to scare them if they try to attack us, got it?'

'I concur, no trouble at all,' Lord Franklin said cheerfully.

Something at a distance caught his attention and he leaned forward. It was a signboard with a bold inscription: ***Niggers are maggots, pay for one and take two***! He sat back, obviously disturbed.

'God have mercy on the king,' he mumbled and draped a hand over Ifash.

'How many hours left to the city hall, captain?' he shouted so that the wagon team could hear him clearly.

'It could be forty minutes, your Lordship,' the captain replied.

'I can't wait, we've got to get there on time. It's a lunch party, remember?'

'I do remember your Lordship, I'll venture speeding up a little.'

'That'll be fine,' encourage Lord Franklin. He sat back and relaxed.

'Pa,' Ifash tapped him on the lap. 'Pa.' he called again.

'Yeah,' he held the boy's hand and wiped his mouth with the other hand.

'I'd like to make a guess,' Ifash said slowly, arching an eyebrow inquisitively. Lord Franklin drew him close to his chest.

'Go ahead and make your guess,' he said.

'Em, will the old woman one day live with us?' Ifash asked looking up to meet his father's changing red eyes. Instantly, he realized there was something wrong in his choice of words. Smartly, he sought for an alternative, but it was too late.

'Okay pa, we'll have to pack to her place instead.'

Lord Franklin felt rattled by Ifash's assumptions. He dug his hand inside his inner pocket for another tobacco but he found none. What he actually needed was a stiff drink. Ifash's lousy conclusion caught him by surprise and what upset him most was his usual description of Duchess Kimberly as an old woman.

'My goodness,' he mumbled, taking a deep breath. 'Ifash don't forget we have an agreement. You promised to be well behaved where we're going. But what you've just said is an indication of bad manners and disrespect to an older person,' he stressed, trying to sound calm. 'I've told you times without number that Duchess Kimberly, should not be referred to as 'the old woman' or 'that old woman.' It's horrible to call someone such and I think I've warned you enough,' Lord Franklin affirmed emphatically pulling Ifash by both ears to drive home his point.

'Whoops!' Ifash cried out in pain, but Lord Franklin did not yield to his plea but pulled harder.

'For the last time, Duchess Kimberly is going to be your step-mum someday,' he warned and froze at the reality of what he just said. 'She's forty-nine years old and I'm seventy-one. She's still young and full of life and so am I. From today, you must refer to her as 'mum' or 'aunt', or better still, 'Kimberly.' Do you understand or may I repeat myself?' he demanded, pulling at the boy's ears once again. Ifash squirmed in pain.

Lord Franklin released him and watched as his son struggled to hold back the tears. Ifash turned away from his gaze and sulked while trying to contain the pain in his ears. A few minutes later, he was fast asleep with his head on his father's thigh.

CHAPTER FOUR

The merriment did not begin until 1:30pm, London time. More than five hundred guests were invited, but only two hundred and seventy-eight turned up. Lord Franklin held Ifash by the hand as they approached the main entrance that led into the Rose garden, where most of the guests converged.

'You welcome Lord Franklin, this way please,' greeted an attendant. 'Should I get you a drink right away?'

'Scotch, shaken not stirred and a juice for the boy,' he requested. He was quick to observe that, more than half of the guests in attendance were those that mattered in the United Kingdom. Everyone held wine in glasses and were chatting animatedly. Most were seated. Among the few that were standing, he spotted the Duchess and his heart missed a beat.

* * *

With the fluctuating two-hours difference between London and Africa, the time zone in the Odua Kingdom read 3:30pm. King Jajaha Kakah Tobiolah II suddenly woke-up to find the sun bright in the sky. He rolled over in bed and sat up in surprise.

'Sango o!' he cried. It was strange indeed. He never slept this long for fear that his enemies might take advantage while he lay unconscious. He blinked and forced a silent groan in response to his arching bones. With a little effort, he managed to stretch both arms. As he stretched, the rays of the sun hit his forehead and his eyes flew wide open.

'Abekeofin! Abekeofin!' He shouted, but there was no reply. A sudden panic seized him and he stood rock-still lips compressed and looking around suspiciously, swaying from left to right. Slowly, he opened the door, and walked along the passage with stunning agility for a man of seventy-three.

A decade had gone by, a decade that had witnessed several events including the expulsion of a prince. Wars had been fought and won by brave warriors of the land. More slaves had been acquired and more had been sold. Kingdoms had risen and more had fallen. Life in Odua had since resumed its rhythms. In the evenings the young virgins of the land would gather at the village square to enjoy the breeze, drink pure undiluted palm-wine and later engage in long, often passionate folk-tales. All in all, it had been a prosperous decade for king Jajaha and the entire people of Odua Kingdom. He had sealed many trade agreements with his European associates as there were more white men on the African continent seeking greener pasture. Many of them came with new ideas and innovations. Few were still preaching and forcing people into the new faith, a faith that has no legitimacy, nor made sense to King Jajaha.

The British colonist and armies, unlike other European countries, continued to treat Odua Kingdom with great respect. Never for once did they try to venture forcefully into Odua, by the virtue of king Jajaha's wealth, strength and territorial control. The bilateral relationship between the two kingdoms remained stronger than ever. The British fulfilled their promise to the king, building him a befitting palace of modern architectural design. It was the first of its kind on the continent. They replaced the mud bricks and sand with concrete blocks. The bamboos and mats were replaced with mattresses, leather-chairs and cashmere rugs.

King Jajaha was so impressed by the generosity of the British that he sought for a way to repay them. So, he consulted Ifa-Eledumare for a clue. But to his astonishment, Ifa-Eledumare warned that the white men coming from the other side of the Atlantic Ocean were his worst enemies. Ifa warned that he should fear them the way he feared the spite of a woman, stressing that despite the generosity of white men, they were still direct agents of *Aburu*, god of disaster.

With this piece of information, king Jajaha braced-up and changed all his regulations and style of dealings with his white associates. Among other restrictions, he put an end to the idea of discussing trade in his palace. Instead, all trade negotiations were to be sealed outside the borders by Aremu, his trade representative. He no longer wished to discuss with them face to face.

* * *

Later on, the king sat on his throne in reflection, awaiting the arrival of Abekeofin. Life had indeed taken a dramatic turn over the years. Life had been good, kind and full of surprises. The child, Prince Ifashanu was a gone and forgotten episode in his life. The only person from whose mind it seemed the memory refused to depart was queen Abekeofin.

During those early years of Ifashanu's departure, she had requested for a yearly anniversary in honor of her expelled son. But the king stood against such move.

'It's a taboo of the first order to honor anyone dishonored and condemned by the gods,' the king declared. She did not raise the issue again; however, in her mind, the child remained unforgotten, especially as he was her second child.

On the other hand, Ifashanu's elder brother, prince Dada had grown fully into a responsible man. He was slightly built, soft spoken and was an intensely anti-colonialist speaker. He married Agbekele, the daughter of a loyal chancellor to his father. She had borne him two children, a prince and a princess.

With abundant successes through the years, king Jajaha gave all thanks to his ancestors and the gods of the land. His new reputation as one of the most powerful kings and merchants, had won him a great deal of respect across the globe. His next focus was on his biggest trade deal in months. He intended to send Prince Dada with ten thousand heads of slaves to Rome via the Mediterranean Sea, where he would join his Italian associates on a voyage to America. The Americans had assured him of huge rewards in returns. Rewards far in excess of what he made from the British and the French put together.

For the first time, he asked them to include in his payments a large supply of weapons. Should everything work out the way he planned it, he would be very rich and powerful to be the sole ruler of Africa. He planned to extend his tentacles even beyond that. That would mean attacking the entire nomadic Arabs in various parts of the continent. Then he would proceed gradually to the Arabian Gulf and ensure that more Arabs were held in captivity. They would surely serve as fashion slaves to rich Africans who could afford them. In order to fully secure his grip in the Arabian Gulf, he would seek the support of his European associates, especially the Jews. Hopefully they would provide him with weapons of mass destruction. Predictably in the near future, he would even be stronger to attack and capture two-thirds of Asia, he must go after the Chinese and the Indians, so that when he died eventually, he would be remembered in history as the king who conquered eight continents. It was a feat his father, Aare Kakah, with all his greatness and might, could not have thought possible to achieve.

CHAPTER FIVE

Two months after the Duchess' Birthday

The Mercury-Testacota lurched roughly through the first gate of the ranch. At last, Duchess Kimberly breathed a sigh of relief after a long tiring journey to the countryside. She did not consider it a casual ride as speculated by her lover. The bumpy road still stretched on for another mile after the signpost that read: *Lord Franklin Gordon's Residence.* She glanced at her gold wristwatch. It was 12:45pm, four solid hours on the road. The house of someone you love is never too far, she thought. She was almost certain that her feelings for Lord Franklin were nothing but pure undiluted love. She always felt young and reborn whenever she was with him or she thought of his presence.

She examined her make-up in a small mirror. All was intact. Inside, she bubbled like an anxious princess about to meet a handsome prince on a weekend rendezvous. The two had not met face to face since her birthday bash, though they remained in contact through mails and occasional phone conversation.

It was her first time at his ranch and had never been alone with him since the demise of the Duke. They either met at a friend's cocktail, state sponsored galas or at the cathedral occasionally. Their romance began immediately after John, the Duke of York, was diagnosed with Parkinson disease. Franklin's casual visit to John, for whom Kimberly regrettably had no child, soon took a different direction altogether. Had she not made the first move by asking him to stay back for dinner at that late hour in June, Franklin would not have ventured asking her out. To her, he was that type that was light-headed and disciplined, and whose reputation came first before any other thing.

That particular night, after little persuasion, he thought it wise to spend the night in the castle guest room because it was already too late to embark on a long ride to the countryside.

It was not until later in the wee small hours that the Duchess slipped out of bed while the Duke was fast asleep. She opened the door of the guest room where Franklin was taking his shower before going to bed.

For her, it was an action that yielded the desired result. It was an action that gave birth to the beginning of a sweet romance. Ever since that night at the castle, she lived in a state of bliss, and her days of sexual deprivation with John were over.

A looming structure diverted her attention and the driver brought the Testacota to a stop in front of it.

'Here we are Ma'am,' he said. She removed ten shillings from her purse and paid him.

'Thanks Madam,' he said appreciatively. She was convinced that the Negro did not know her true identity. If he did, he would have said, thank you, your majesty, she assured herself. From the back seat, she took a quick glance around the ranch. Franklin's house was a moderate brick house, constructed with polished timbers on the sides. It had a wide porch and a narrow front steps. Her eyes settled on what seemed an old plantation with surrounding flowerbeds and trees like a boulevard. At an angle of the house, she noticed a pond covered by green micro-organism, evidence of negligence.

In her view, Franklin's place was just as simple as he always appeared. She smiled delightfully at her luck, stepping out of the car one leg at a time. The car drove away slowly on the granite track. She loved fancy cars, fancy places, and fancy dresses. For a moment, she stood gazing, admiring the simplicity of Franklin's house. A wistful expression appeared on her face the moment she spotted Franklin opening the front door. He wore a simple striped shirt and trousers. Lord Franklin's heart missed a beat immediately he set eyes on her and he smiled broadly.

'Welcome home, Duchess of York,' he pronounced delightfully with out-stretched arms, as he walked down the steps. He held her on the shoulder and kissed her on both cheeks. She inhaled his strong masculine smell with warmth, bringing her mouth closer to meet his. She surrendered her body into his fold and smiled happily at him. Cheerfully, he led her towards the door, their hands inter-locked. Her thick golden hair brushed her cheeks as she moved. Quickly, she pushed them back each time, giggling and smiling brightly. The smile revealed how she felt inside; the brightness in their eyes and the joy in their hearts displayed all. They were both suddenly filled with sparkles and life.

The sitting-room reflected more accurately Lord Franklin's personality. There was a chimney on her far right, facing clusters of comfortable leather chairs. His rug was thick green, and the wall-unit stood some distance away from the dinning table. There were short tables at every corner, and some bound books on the large central table. The sight of books everywhere made her wonder if she was in his study. In all, she summed her lover's home as, a simple old-fashioned house, with lots of elegance and warmth, much like the lord himself.

'Take a seat Kimberly,' he gestured with a hand, and they sat facing each other.

'So, how was the journey,' he asked, looking at her in an amusing way. He noticed her smiling face looked more youthful than he ever imagined.

'It wasn't much of a stress, knowing I'll be meeting you,' she giggled.

'That sounds lovely,' he said and winked at her. She could hear soft music oozing out from an aged gramophone stationed left to the chimney, with a radio machine on the right. She looked triumphantly at him, a symbol of gentility, success, her knight in shining armour.

'Thank you Frank. Thanks for allowing me visit you. Really, you gave me the first opportunity of seeing the country side alone,' she said hoping her words would sustain the mood.

Lord Franklin stood and took a bow before he responded.

'It's my utmost pleasure having you around, your majesty,' he said. She looked graciously at him and smiled.

'Don't know what I'll do without you,' she remarked, charmingly flustered by the fact.

'Your designer must be good,' he observed with a grin and bowed again in an effortless and graceful manner.

'You like my dress?' she exulted and touched her stomach to indicate her dress.

He eyed admiringly at her navy-blue gown that reached down to the ankle and cut to a short-sleeve, exposing the upper part of her breast. To him, the Duchess possesses that body chemistry that could compete in any beauty contest in any part of the world. With her well manicured fingers, she unraveled the light-blue veil around her neck, flinging it to the chair beside her with a smile.

At that moment, the sound of sloshing water came from the direction of the kitchen. Romana soon appeared with a tray bearing a bottle of wine and water, with two glasses. She placed it down gently on the large table between them.

'You're most welcome ma,' she greeted softly.

'Thank you very much Romana,' the Duchess responded and the two women exchanged bright smiles. Romana happened to be the only one in the United Kingdom that is aware of the flaming romance between the Duchess and her master, Lord Franklin. After placing the content on the table, she walked briskly into the kitchen with a tray and a napkin.

'You must be tired I believe,' Lord Franklin said, looking the Duchess over while bending to pour the wine in the two glasses on the table. He handed her a glass.

'Toast to our togetherness,' she said.

'For as long as there is forever,' he said and they toasted each other with long sips.

'Um, completely Russian," she acknowledged delightfully.

'You're amazingly perceptive; you seem to know the taste of every wine on the continent. Does that skill come with being a Duchess or it's just one of your sweet qualities?' he replied huskily.

'Imagine. Very funny, it's not all about being a queen, a duchess, or a knight. It's pure instinct. I hadn't expected you to find my guess brilliant, anyway. But you know how suspicious Scotland Yard is of Kremlin and Berlin,' she raised a brow, looking into his eyes inquiringly.

He stared back at her in such a way that made her lips tremble with smile.

'You look tired,' he whispered.

'Not as tired as you probably assume,' she corrected between sips. 'To be honest, I haven't had a real rest for the past few days, have been too occupied from one function to the other. Oops! It's been a boring week,' she said in a voice filled with distress.

'You need not worry, I've got it packed and ready,' he said and smiled brightly at her as if she were a school girl returning home for the summer break. 'I hope you'll love the arrangements,' he said in a matter-of-fact tone.

'I should, dear,' she said and grinned, studying his face with a knowing smile lurking at the corners of her mouth. His eyes were bright with affection that really touched her, and she wanted to reach out to him, to curdle him.

Lord Franklin broke the silence with a deliberate sigh.

'For now let's finish our drinks and then take something light for lunch,' he said and took a sip from his glass. 'Once the food is digested, we go for a ride with grand-marshal, the greatest horse in the U.K. Then, there is this special scotch, locally made though. I want you to attest to its quality and tell me if U.K is making a breakthrough in the liquor industry or we are just one of the crowds,' he said and downed the remaining wine in his glass.

'I can see you've really got it all wrapped up,' she said and applauded with a thrill. She felt light in the head. It was one of those rare occasions she felt like dancing in the rain, challenging the sun, and embracing the moon.

He continued to look caringly into her soft green eyes filled with love. His forehead furrowed as he refilled his glass.

'I made ready a casual wear upstairs for your riding comfort,' he said pointing towards the stairs.

'That is absolutely fabulous!' The Duchess exulted.

* * *

The heat of the sun was at its lowest when they got outside. They rested their arms on the porch bars and watched with fascination as the barn master marched Grand Marshal to the front of the yard.

'She's beautiful,' whispered the Duchess and Lord Franklin grinned.

'My dear, you've not mounted him yet,' he said with pride.

Their eyes locked in a moment of intense feeling. She allowed a shy girlish smile to curl her lips.

'My patience is slipping,' she muttered quietly. He gave her a tender smile in response.

He was aware how completely vulnerable she had been in the past weeks. Obviously, she craved for the closeness, touch and love of a sensitive person; a person of his outstanding qualities, he thought confidently.

* * *

Some minutes later, Lord Franklin went to Grand Marshal on the granite track. The barn master begged to take his leave having explained the steps for a smooth ride on the luxurious horse.

'You've done very well,' Lord Franklin said and discharged him promptly. With his right hand he patted the stallion on his hairy head and felt his tensed muscles began to relax.

'Good," he murmured and held up a hand to Kimberly who was seated on the porch. She dusted her pants and went to him. In her eyes, Lord Franklin saw the desire and the safety she felt from being with him. He also noticed the sun in her eyes as she closed up on him in a faded jeans and an oversized shirt.

'We're going to ride together on Grand Marshal and experience those grand slides,' his voice trailed off as she pulled him close to her body.

'That sounds great. Let's see if I'll be very impressed,' she replied softly. They went round the horse, inspecting, touching and feeling his massive muscles till they were both satisfied and ready for the slide.

Lord Franklin felt a tingling sensation rising from the pit of his stomach. What had started between him and the Duchess had inflamed into genuine attraction. Or is it obsession? It seemed to have taken him to a height he has never been before and had never hoped to reach.

'Alright, here we go, let's feel the thrill,' he gestured, reaching for the bridle and helping her onto the saddle. He climbed up behind her and held firmly to the rope. The Duchess giggled excitedly.

'Want me to take the lead?' he asked and gave her body a squeeze. She grinned,

'I'd love it if you do,' she whispered into his ear. Tickling her on the sides, he jerked the ropes upward and the horse dashed forward in calculative steps as if it were at a circus.

'Oops! She's excellent! You'll know a brilliant horse from its first steps,' Lady Kimberly observed and her eyes shone with excitement.

'You're absolutely correct,' Lord Franklin said, nodding proudly. 'Like I said before, she's the most beautiful horse in the Kingdom. He's excessive, the dream of every rancher. She's called Grand Marshal, hired from Lord Christopher Chisel from down town Dublin. Lord Chisel has everyone knows, sure raised some of the finest horses in the Kingdom.' he boasted while the Duchess rubbed her hands on the horse's hairy neck.

'She's lovely,' she said sweetly. 'How thoughtful of you; I do like her mixture of black and white spots,' she said and felt the warmth diffuse inside her when he leaned forward to kiss her cheek.

'She's a sophisticated beast. I knew that the moment I set eyes on her,' he affirmed in a husky voice, placing a hand on her thigh. 'When I saw her, I knew instantly she's what we deserved for this special weekend.'

"Um, you're a very special, sweetheart," she said and let her golden hair dangle sideways as she turned to receive another perk on the cheek.

A short silence passed between them as they rode. Only the echo of the woods and birds intruded the serene countryside. They were preoccupied with studying the horse as he paced gently along the edge of the pond, which was part of the front of the ranch. It ended in an artificial lake commissioned recently by some environmentalists who named it after Queen Victoria.

'How's the kid doing? Haven't seen him since my arrival,' the Duchess asked with concern, turning briefly to meet his gaze. Lord Franklin squeezed her waist affectionately before returning his hands to the ropes and concentrating on his grip on the horse.

'He's doing quite well,' he said tartly. 'He's with the other kids not far away from here. I prefer him there. Don't you think we need some private time alone, after two months?' he enquired.

'Imagine. Indeed I agree fully, we need more and more private time alone,' she teased, twisting slightly to receive a kiss on the mouth. She melted in his fold, unaware that the rider was no longer in control of the horse. His mouth crushed her lips, causing her whole body to convulse in ecstasy. Grand Marshal proved his worth steering himself while the lovers explored each other's desires on his back. He gently maneuvered through the muddy paths that led to Lake Victoria. His turns and steps were accurate and fascinating, as if he was aware of his riders' age and the feelings they shared. He avoided a large pit, and another which could have sent his riders tumbling off him. The moment Lord Franklin realized the ropes had slipped off his hands, he panicked and let go his lover while hastily reaching for them.

The Duchess adjusted herself to maintain her balance on the stallion even as her body still trembled from the sensations that engulfed her moments before. She wished Lord Franklin had allowed the horse to continue on his own. He swung the rope, mumbling instructions to the horse. She could sense that his breathing was just returning to normal because his voice trembled while directing the beast.

Lord Franklin eyed the Duchess focusing on the side of her face that had no make-up; her beauty was purely natural. She needed no make-up because her face shone even brighter without mascara. He wondered idly what she had looked like at sixteen. A faultless sweet sixteen for royal grab. He thought briefly about her life with John, the Duke of York, his friend. Were they happy together? Was their marriage full of regrets? Did having no child mean depression for John? These questions raced through his mind before her golden hair diverted his attention as it flew about in the country breeze, falling about her shoulder.

'Good heavens,' he murmured under his breath. She looks absolutely gorgeous from behind. The faded jeans hugged her lush fish-like contours, the shape that always made his heart race. Suddenly, something stirred deep inside his heart and a faint tremor shook his leg involuntarily. Could this be it? Could this be love? The love he had never known, he pondered. His inner intellectual mind that should have corrected the notion and rebel against such feeling was however blissfully silent.

As Grand Marshal slid along independently, their confidence increased. They began to chat, laugh and gossip about the House of Commons. They talked about the future plan for the European Union, the visit of the Prime Minister to Kremlin that weekend, and the agenda of the royal family for the rest of the year. They felt joined by their common understanding and affection for one another.

About an hour later, fatigue set in and they decided it was time to return to the ranch.

The return journey was equally exciting for the two and they found Grand Marshal a unique horse. Duchess Kimberly silently concluded in her heart that he was a horse that fully understood the plight of aged lovers. In her early years as a young Duchess, she recalled her believe in riding a horse simply for fun and sport. She had ridden on countless horses, but never has she encountered one with such perception.

* * *

At sunset, Kimberly emerged from the bathroom and changed into fresh clothes. She brought out a deodorant from her bag, sprayed her armpits, the sides of her neck, her back and finally her waist down. She picked her wristwatch from the chair and discovered it was 7:15pm. Frank must be wondering what was taking her so long for supper. She had been hanging upstairs for over an hour, she thought and reached for her veil on the sofa, then she went down the stairs.

A delightful smell engulfed the living room as she descended under the watchful eyes of Lord Franklin who had changed into a black suit. For a moment, he stood frozen. Watching her was like watching an angel descend. His face furrowed with the warmest smile he could produce. He regained his composure and stepped forward to reach out to her from the bottom of the stairs. Then he led her to a large dining table full of assorted dishes, especially her favorites. Romana had just set a hot trencher at the corner of the table while they sat facing each other.

'A night worth more than a thousand nights,' Lord Franklin said, cutting the silence between them and watching her smile without a word.

'Kimberly,' he called. His husky voice startled her. He hardly called her by her name. She followed the direction of his pointed finger.

'Eat,' he encouraged with a broad smile. Effortlessly, he reached over and began to cut the large piece of meat into two halves. He placed one part on her plate.

'Here you are,' he said. First, she tasted the fried potatoes and eggs.

'Um, can't be better,' she said after taken a slice from the meat. She looked up at Lord Franklin who was staring at her and remembered he had once told her he sees the sun in her eyes. She had responded then that she sees the sky and the moon in his.

'I'm glad you're enjoying the meal. Romana is one of the best,' he beamed. She smiled and bowed mockingly.

'Agreed, Your Lordship,' she said.

Unlike her, Lord Franklin seemed to be more interested in the fried fish and meat. She glanced at him in surprise at the size of his appetite. No wonder he looked like a handsome and fleshy guy in his forties, the Duchess thought. She knew he would always hold her passions captive as if he had cast a spell on her. She had not realised how much she loved him, until he had left so early on the night of her birthday. His departure left her miserable throughout the night in spite of the over one hundred distinguished guests in attendance.

A smile appeared on her face and she decided she needed to tell him about herself. She would tell him tonight as soon as he finished eating. She had waited too long, she thought.

As she looked him over, she made up her mind to ask him to marry her.

On the other hand, Lord Franklin gazed curiously into her eyes, causing her to blink rapidly. She smiled broadly in order to diffuse the tension building up inside her. Uncertainty, fear and happiness all mixed up ricocheted through her heart.

'What are you thinking with that royal brain?' he asked, smiling. She labored with determination to calm down.

'Nothing, just enjoying my meal,' she replied calmly.

* * *

After supper, they moved to the leather chairs. On the table between them, a bottle of champagne stood untouched. Lord Franklin extracted a handkerchief from his pocket to wipe off the perspiration on his face. When he spoke, his voice took on a peculiar softness.

'You look marvelous tonight,' he said. She did not say a word, but she winked her approval and realised that what she felt for Frank was similar to what she had felt for John some twenty-six years before. As usual, her face became colored and animated anytime her imagination evolved to reality. With hope of suppressing her feelings, she started serving the champagne. Her hair fell over her shoulders, but she tossed them backward and handed a glass to her lover. Then she filled her own glass while her mouth longed for a taste of the wine. She savored the taste long after she had taken a sip from her glass.

'A strong champagne, it must be one of those French imports,' she observed. 'Did you also hire this one for us,' she said with an expectant laugh.

'What you're drinking is the latest brand from Seaman's and sons,' he corrected her. 'Aren't we making headways in the industry?' She offered him an agreeable smile.

'I knew from the onset that with all the thousands invested in a single industry, it's bound to storm Europe by surprise,' he said.

For a short while, they sat in silence, sipping their champagne until Lord Franklin broke the silence once again.

'How about some music?'

'Nice,' she replied softly. He downed his drink and went over to the turn-table. He placed the pin on the plate and in few seconds, sentimental sax filled the room.

They danced locked in each other's embrace, feeling each other's warmth and desire while he turned her from side to side. The Duchess fought desperately to restrain herself from declaring her love for him. It was the second time in her life that love would outwit her, catching her off guard and subjecting her to restraints. She felt slightly embarrassed that her mind was no longer in control of her body; and to her shock, she felt herself yielding to his touch like a candle in a desert sun. At a point, she became unsure if her feet were still on the ground, or somewhere in the air winged by the newfound love Frank had aroused in her.

After about half an hour, she finally felt her foot touch the ground, and by then, she was tired and dazed with passion.

'Frank,' she whispered seductively into his ear. 'I am uptight, I think its time I have my rest.' He released his grip around her waist and glanced at his watch.

'I didn't realize it's this late,' he lamented, smiling into her face. He strolled across the room and switched off the light, leaving the candles burning on the dinning table. As they climbed the stairs, he felt the familiar skip of his heart, the one he experienced whenever he gazed at her curves. He felt her hands around his waist and he stopped in his strides. He turned slowly to meet her gaze.

'I love you Frank,' she said honestly.

'Kimberly,' he said with frustration and tingeing his voice with disappointment. Not with her, but with himself because he had planned to tell her first; to say those three words to her in bed. But she had gone a step ahead of him. He wondered what else he could say to her in bed that would make sense to them both. Looking into her green eyes, he could see into her heart and knew she meant what she said.

'My love,' he said softly cupping her face with his hands. 'May I call you love?' he enquired.

'Imagine. You already did and it sounds great,' she said with a smile.

'Should we get married?' he asked in a strange voice.

'Well, that sounds great too,' she said and raised a brow before she placed her hand on his. 'I guess that will be the epitome of the true love we share,' she added and her smile broadened. She realized they were both engaged in a kind of staring contest because their eyes remained locked for long minute until he arched his eyebrow. His eyes probably narrowed from the effect of alcohol. She looked away, bringing her gaze down to his chest and conceding victory to him. Lord Franklin felt that with her by his side, he would always be a winner.

'It's going to be alright Frank,' she declared softly and raised herself on toes to meet his eyes. She saw in his eyes a burning passion and she sought his lips with hers. The warmth of his arms wrapped around her waist with his chest pressed against her breasts stirred sweet sensations in her body. Her nipples hardened through the fabric of her expensive material. Her body was in flame and her breathing quickened as they kissed hungrily for several moments.

Thereafter, he led her in his arms into the bedroom.

The room was dark so she could not see much. Only a single candle illuminated it and it smelt masculine. The large bed at the centre was covered with white satin sheet and an aged rock chair was at a corner, beside a book shelf. Gently, he pushed her down on the bed after undressing her and climbed into bed with her, still dressed. She unzipped his trousers and pulled it down his thighs. Sensations overwhelmed her as she caught glimpse of his erection. He kissed her on the lips and nestled his head in her bosom.

Energize! He took both nipples into his mouth, one at a time. Moving further down, he kissed her on the navel, something he had never done to her. She felt certainly that there was magic in the night.

Lord Franklin undressed fully and stretched his body over hers, resting on his elbows. Her lips found his once again and they kissed passionately with urgency, with desire and longings that enraptured their tangled limbs. She dug her fingers into his shoulders as his weight crushed down on her. Affectionately, his fingers stroked every part of her body causing her to blush. She gasped and moaned intermittently at the delicious spasms shooting through her body and settling between her thighs. She had never thought Frank had such expertise, and she had never felt so intensely aroused in her life.

She let her hand slip under him reaching for his erection. His voice was hoarse with excitement as she stroked him with the lightest of touches. When she noticed that he was past the limit of arousal and needed the final fulfillment, she opened up to him. Her legs went around his waist as his lips brushed faintly across hers, and then her cheeks and her eyes. She moaned with pleasure and kissed him on the eyes, the nose and the lips. Her hands seemed to be all over him, in his hair, on his back and his butt. Slowly, she further explored regions of his shoulders down again to his waist exerting more pleasure from their union.

Lord Franklin's breathing came in quick gasps as every touch set off spasms of pleasure. He willed it never to end and was determined not to let her down. She deserved the best always, he told himself. He lowered his head and tasted the skin of her breast. At that point, her response was fast and shattering. She wrapped her legs firmly around him engulfing the whole of him. The pleasure running through the Duchess made her gasp, then a growl of ultimate pleasure soon escaped her lips and she cried out her fulfillment for the world to hear.

Fulfilled, she rubbed his neckline with both hands and gave him a full kiss on the lips. Her vision was poor in the dark as she struggled to regain her breath after her eruption. She couldn't have seen Lord Franklin in distress. The sensation that was fast spreading inside him was more intense than passion. It seemed a thrill of pleasure had been suddenly replaced by a piercing pain inside his heart. Yet, he felt the final wave and spilled the content of his manhood in an involuntary gush, shrieking above her. A strong feeling of elation settled on the duchess face. She was glad at the thought of him experiencing the full wave of his climax. She held him steady, buried inside her, her hands rocking the back of his head. Randomly, Lord Franklin fought for breath in the darkness; he fought for his life in the heat of intense passion. All of a sudden, he jerked, rose and fell, collapsing over her and throwing up on her face.

CHAPTER SIX

It seemed forever before the Range Rover ambulance reached the Queen Alexandra Hospital. With luck, the Duchess thought, they might still escape the headlines of every newspaper in the United Kingdom, which might read: *'Lord Franklin, the elderly statesman slump atop Duchess of York.'*

However, the leader of the paramedics had assured the Duchess that what transpired at Lord Franklin's country home would not get to the press through his team. Kimberly had got out through the back door of the ranch and had earnestly instructed Romana to follow the ambulance. She advised her to make necessary decisions on her master's care, promising to surface at the hospital the next day, like any other sympathizer.

On the hospital's lawn, three doctors and six nurses were waiting anxiously with a gurney for ambulance serial number L.R.H52. When it did arrive, they rushed Lord Franklin inside with utmost urgency.

'Will he make it?' Romana asked one of the doctors.

'I honestly don't know, it's hard to say at the moment,' replied the doctor, stealing a quick glance at the devastated lady in old fashioned Victorian skirt and blouse.

'Are you his next of kin?' He asked in a regretful tone.

"No, Yes, I'm his niece." She replied with much fluster.

The doctor was in his mid-fifties, short and plum. He looked at Romana curiously. He did not know what to make of her because he was not sure if what he was feeling for her was sympathy or suspicion. Whichever, someone's life was at stake; there was no time for questions. When they reached the door, he turned to Romana.

'Okay lady, this is as far as you can go, you'll have to wait outside, we go in alone,' he told her and Lord Franklin was rolled into the emergency room.

'Where are you taking him?' Romana asked, but no one answered her. They entered while she stood by the door with tears in her eyes. She felt dizzy, weak, and exhausted by the thought that Lord Franklin might not recover.

* * *

After about forty-five minutes, one of the doctors emerged. It was the same doctor she had spoken with earlier. He did not hide his surprise at seeing her standing by the door where they had left her.

'What's the name?' he asked impatiently. 'Would you mind taking a seat over there?' he said pointing to a bench at the corner.

'How is he doctor?' She asked desperately. The silence that followed before the doctor replied made her almost fall apart; her whole body pulsated with aches.

'He's alive and responding to treatment,' he said calmly, holding her by the hand, he led her to the bench. She sat reluctantly beside him, watching feverishly as he dug a hand inside the large pocket of his ward coat and brought out a stick of cigarette. He struck a match and lit it.

'What exactly is wrong with him sir?' Romana asked.

'He suffered a cardiac arrest...heart attack as u would call it,' he replied blankly, without looking at her face.

'I'm sorry,' he apologised when he saw the distress on her face. 'There are other complications involved,' he continued seriously. 'But madam, I believe this is no time to start discussing details about facts you can hardly understand. But I'd like to ask you something. Was he into any sort of exercise today, or did he experience any crash of late?'

'None that I know of; he was quite healthy but he was with a friend when this happened,' she affirmed, moving her hand to her face to wipe off the tears.

'And where is that friend of his?' he asked, gazing at the smoke of his cigar, watching them curl into the air.

'The chief paramedic can explain it better,' she replied gently.

'Alright, if you say so,' he said, nodding, as if getting the answer to his question. Sometimes the sweetest things do kill, he thought silently, trying to recount how many similar cases he had encountered in the past. He recollected three and all of them, extra-marital affairs, adultery. Troubled by his line of thought, he inhaled deeper.

'Alright Mrs., you said you're a next of kin,' he asked. Romana nodded silently.

'As I told you earlier on, his condition is critical, he experienced a cardiac arrest and all we can do now is watch and see if he's responding to medication,' he said and paused to examine her expression. He could see her face was dried of tears and now expressionless.

'We are not some mystic revealers,' he said further. 'But I and my colleagues suspect a possible myocardial infarction.' Romana fixed the doctor with a steady gaze, looking at his mouth, like a moron.

'That's all there is for now,' the doctor said and stood up to leave.

'You're a believer right, a good Church goer?' he asked when she kept staring into space. Romana swallowed, she was short of words.

'Then show some faith,' he said. Everyone wants to go to heaven, but no one wants to die, he thought. She responded with sobs and desperation. 'Please doctor, please, don't let him die,' she begged hysterically, breaking down again.

'It's going to be alright, madam,' he assured and stood up. 'We are surely going to do our utmost best,' he said, putting out the cigar and depositing the stub in the ashtray.

'I will send a nurse to you right away,' he said as he hurried back into the emergency room, hands in his pockets.

* * *

It was three hours later when the doctor re-emerged. This time, he wasn't surprised to find Romana sprawled on the long bench in deep trance.

'Mrs. Gordon! Mrs. Gordon!' he called and glanced at his watch. It was 2:25am. 'Mrs. Gordon!' he called again and touched her on the shoulder. Her eyes opened slowly with uncertainty; she blinked and gazed at the doctor with sleepy eyes.

'Yes,' she answered clearing her throat.

'Lord Franklin is responding to treatment and I'd like to suggest you go home,' he said. Romana's gaze sharpened for a moment before the tears returned to her eyes. Her heart soared because she thought it miraculous that her master would recover. He that God gives long life no one or action can shorten it, she thought religiously. Recalling how broken-hearted she had felt seeing him lie unconsciously in the ambulance, at no time throughout her fourteen years of service to him had she seen him look so helpless.

'I think it's high time you go home and rest,' the doctor said leaning forward to console her with a pat on the shoulders. 'You must be as exhausted as I am. You shouldn't leave yourself irreparably damaged. You still have time to catch some sleep as it is still early,' he advised. His gaze shifted to Romana's face. He looked straight into her eyes and saw how sad she felt. Romana's mind was far away from there. She thought of distant places and other events, of good times and bad ones with her boss. She regretted she was not the praying type but decided she was going to start. She resolved she was going to praise Jesus at the cathedral, almost nine years since she last set foot inside a church.

* * *

On Sunday morning, the day after Lord Franklin suffered from an acute myocardiac infarction, the news broke all over Europe. The circumstances leading to his condition however remained unclear. The pen pushers were still unable to dig up the details, keeping their fingers crossed in solving the puzzle. Meanwhile, Romana arrived home at half past three in the morning in a chattered taxi. She rested for five hours and was out again accompanied by Ifash.

On their way to the hospital, they stopped at the cathedral. She was surprised when the evangelist called for a minute of silent prayer for the quick recovery of Lord Franklin Gordon. The news had spread like a flood, a small world we live in, she thought tearfully as she prayed with all her heart.

At noon, when the sun had fully registered its authority over the clouds, Duchess Kimberly arrived at the hospital with some politicians and personal friends of Lord Franklin, including his attorney, Mark Barnes. She entered the ward through a special door reserved for important personalities. She was met by a team of doctors. After warm handshakes, she was directed to the office of the chief paramedic in charge of Lord Franklin.

Alone by herself, she walked briskly down the lobby like a common visitor. She was much calmer than the day before. Immediately after the incident, she had been so shaken she could barely coordinate her actions.

At the door, she took a deep breath and entered after knocking.

Although deep inside she would have loved to cry out her anguish, to tell the world about the tricks destiny was forcefully playing on her, she could not just come to terms with fate's cruelty towards her. So unkind and completely heartless it had been to her in disregarding her happiness. First, it was John and now Frank. What did she do so very wrongly to deserve heartbreak each time she was near happiness, she asked in her heart. She drew a seat before the doctor, watching him dismiss a nurse and her files. He was a robust man, mid-height, with thick mustache and an Irish accent probably in his early fifties.

'Your majesty, you're welcome,' he greeted and shook her hand bowing respectfully. 'Please sit,' he gestured. 'I'm really sorry about the event of yesterday. I hope you'll be able to get it off your mind as soon as possible,' he said, placing both hands on the table.

'Thank you, I hope it will end well and be over soon,' she stated nervously, removing her coat and laying it on her lap.

'What can I offer you, tea or coffee?'

'No, thanks,' she said. 'I'd simply like to know the latest. How's he responding to treatment?'

The doctor raised a brow and sat back comfortably.

'About Lord Franklin's condition you mean?' he asked. 'Your majesty, I'd like to ask. Was it just coitus or did something else happen that you've not told me? I can understand there was really no time to discuss in details yesterday. We have all the time now; and of course, it will remain confidential, classified,' he said and nodded smiling.

'Look doc,' she said, her voice shaky and desperate. 'There is absolutely nothing to add to what I already told you. He passed out on me in bed,' she stated blushing with embarrassment. 'In the evening, we rode a special horse; we drank exotic alcohol, and danced. Nothing more, that was it,' she stated further, obviously angered by the doctor's lack of trust. 'For Christ sake, I mean how could you possibly think I'm hiding information, when he lies in bed seriously sick?' she asked.

'From what you've said, it'll be an accurate guess to conclude that he actually gave more than his system could tolerate', the doctor stated frankly.

'How's his condition?' she asked ignoring his rhetorical question and passing him a penetrating look.

'He's under intensive care,' he answered dryly. 'His age is a non modifiable factor contributing to his condition and a serious disadvantage to his quick recovery.' Her green eyes turned brownish-red, heavy with tears. They shifted away from the doctor as he tried to look into them.

'Do you think he'll make it at the end of it all?' she asked not expecting much luck.

The doctor gave her question a thought before he responded.

'If I must be honest with you, I'd rather say I'm not so sure of what will happen at the end of the day. His situation is unpredictable; some people survive it, some don't. It's an open battle, sort of. But I can assure you we've done all we could, and we are still bent on doing more,' he explained.

He picked up some papers on the table and put them in a transparent file. Through the corner of his eyes, he caught a glimpse of her depressed mood.

'Your majesty lets be hopeful. Pessimists dominate our world and they've made a mess of it, but everyone in this profession is an optimist. We've got self-confidence in what we do and that is to say that the percentage of survival is becoming higher by the minutes. After all, despite the fact that he has suffered from a massive stroke, his response is quite impressive. These are enough signs that he'll make it somehow,' the doctor said hopefully.

'What do you mean by stroke?' She asked with a frown licking her lips, a habit she indulged in when under stress.

'It's a condition that may render a man paralyzed losing some of his normal functions like speech, hearing and so on,' he explained calmly.

'Can I see him?'

'It's not advisable at the moment. The nature of his condition is no good sight,' he said shifting uncomfortably. 'It is better you check on him later around 9:00pm. By then we expect that his situation might be better,' he said and began scribbling on a piece of paper.

'Another fact I should let you know is that Lord Franklin is actually totally paralysed. Even if he eventually makes it, he'll be confined to a wheelchair, a vegetable case,' he said with a deep sigh, dispensing any false hope.

Kimberly was startled. His statement was like a knife pushed through her stomach. She hated the doctor instantly and restrained the urge to stand up and hit him. He must be a fool to refer to Frank as vegetable.

Irish bastard, she cursed. She looked away from him to hide her disgust at him. For a moment, she prayed in her heart silently for Frank to recover. Then remembering where she was and who she was, she faced the doctor.

'Okay doc,' she stood and began to put on her coat. 'I have to leave now. I'll be back tonight,' she stated and glanced at her wristwatch as she headed for the door. 'And don't forget,' she said turning abruptly. 'Not a word to the press!' She stared hard at him and hurriedly left his office before he could get around his L- shaped table.

* * *

Lord Franklin did not wink until later in the night. It was his third day in hospital; he was still having difficulty breathing and his coughs were terribly deep. A gas mask delivering oxygen extended from his nose downward. Two intravenous lines for administering drugs were fixed on both arms, and cardiac electrodes connected to his heart extended to an electrocardiogram to monitor the rhythm of his heart. He had spoken with one of the doctors complaining of diminishing sight and body aches. He then requested to see his son, Ifash and Romana. The doctor granted his request.

* * *

At 8:25pm sharp, a nurse led Romana and Ifash to Lord Franklin with an instruction from the doctor that the meeting should not exceed ten minutes.

Lord Franklin, in spite of his condition, recognised Romana and Ifash the moment they stepped in.

'Christ, here you are! How long have I been here?' he asked faintly, turning to Ifash.

'Since Saturday pa,' Ifash replied in a very small voice sitting on a high stool beside the bed. He gazed intently at the intravenous tubes, the oxygen mask and the machines. His eyes rested on his father's chest that bore unfamiliar marks.

'Ten minutes,' the nurse reminded them, closing the door behind her.

'How're you Romana?' Lord Franklin asked faintly.

'I'm fine Your Lordship,' she said sullenly, standing beside Ifash for support.

'And you Ifash?'

'Great pa,' Ifash answered.

'I hope you're feeling better, Sir?' Romana asked hopefully.

'I don't think so, Romana. I feel terrible, I must confess,' Lord Franklin replied with a faint smile. The tears she had been holding back spilled over at the mention of 'terrible'. She staggered and found a seat away from the bed. She could not bear to look on the helpless state of her master and she felt she was going to pass out seeing him so bedridden. The silence in the room was cut short by Ifash.

'Pa, you having fever?' he asked and sat gingerly on the edge of the bed. Lord Franklin attempted to laugh but settled for a faint smile. There seemed to be no energy left in him and he felt completely drained of blood, perhaps of life itself.

'How I wished it was fever? The doctor said it's something more severe.'

'Like what?' Ifash pressed on, leaning over him and straining hard to hear what he was saying. Fever was the most talked about illness in school. It was the only illness that took his friends and their siblings to hospital; it went with lots of get-well cards and messages. Nothing could be more severe than that, he thought.

'It's an attack, I believe,' muttered Lord Franklin.

'Attack?' blurted Ifash. 'Who attacked you? Did she attack you?' he asked, puzzled.

'No Ifash, you've got it mixed up,' Lord Franklin said. 'Not the type your friend McCarthy enjoys; not a wrestling contest. This has nothing to do with brutality. It's a failure of my heart,' he said and coughed deeply. He could hardly control it, as he breathed with difficulty and mucus dripped from his nostrils.

Ifash reached over and wiped off the mucus with his bare hand and wiped it off on his Khaki shorts.

'Thanks,' murmured Lord Franklin. 'Men will not get irritated by you,' he prayed, attempting a broad smile at Ifash. He saw something in the boy's eyes that stirred his heart, something that made him feel the necessity to reveal his true background to him before it was too late. Lord Franklin was a realist and he could imagine the reality of his destination from the hospital. Though, he hated to admit his fears, but no one ever fought nature and triumphed. He was battling fate, a battle he did not expect to win. Above all, he could feel them looming around, waiting for him to prepare his home before the inevitable.

He turned his head to the side so he could see Ifash clearly. A forced smile dented his wrinkled face. He wanted to say something but his mouth was heavy with burden and his vocal cords failed to release any sound. He saw the tears in Ifash's eyes. The boy could never have imagined seeing his ever buoyant father in a helpless condition. Lord Franklin fought desperately to regain his voice as saliva drooled from his mouth.

'What going on kid? Sons of great men don't weep. Wipe those tears on your face,' he said. Ifash obliged and drew in his breath. He removed a handkerchief from his breast pocket and wiped off the saliva and sweat off his father's face.

'Ifash,' Lord Franklin called breathlessly as blood rushed to his head making him dizzy for few seconds. 'I have something important I should let you know,' he said and his cough deepened.

'What's it pa? Ifash asked tearfully.

'You listen carefully and promise me you won't forget my words tonight.'

'I won't pa, I promise, I won't.'

'Good. Remove this mask from my face,' he commanded.

'No pa, no I can't,' Ifash protested. He peered closely at his father and shook his head. 'No pa, I won't. I'm not a doctor and i don't know how to do that, am not a doctor pa. Don't know how to do it,' he said shaking his head sobbing and wiping off perspiration on his forehead.

'Come on Ifash, don't be naughty. Papa knows better than you do,' he said and paused to recover his breath. With determination he opened his mouth again and faced his son.

'I want to be able to talk better to you, son. Come on...,' Lord Franklin encouraged the boy he had trained to appreciate obedience as a virtue.

Reluctantly, Ifash stood up and removed the oxygen mask with shaking hands. At that point, Lord Franklin saw that Romana had slumped and wondered how long she had been lying on the floor. He turned back his attention to Ifash.

'Nice, sit here,' he said indicating a spot on the bed. Ifash moved over there and wiped the tears in his eyes.

'I feel much better now, Ifash,' Lord Franklin said. 'Now listen carefully Ifash...,' the cough he had struggled to restrain forced him to stop. After he had recovered, he looked up to Ifash.

'Education is the best I can offer you. My attorney, Sir Barnes will see to it that you will never be in need of anything for long till you finish your college education.' As he spoke breathlessly, he could feel blood moving up to his head. At a point, he thought he was going to explode any moment.

'I'm sorry I lied to you,' he said regretfully. 'Those lies were important for your psyche, considering your age. Forgive me if my assumptions were cruel. A man is a product of divine calculations. Your biological father is from Africa, a king at a region not far from the Atlantic. I do remember the people of the west coast are by no means all of one tribe. Often they are found in different areas having arrived at different times with different social-cultural groups. Certainly, your ancestral home can not be far from the people of the Plateau or in the Jlah and Casamance.' He paused and took a deep breath before he continued.

'Ifash, all my entire life, I have never known generosity that surpasses the action of your biological father. He is the king who gave one of his children, a prince, to a barren Lord in Europe. It is kindness so unimaginable,' he said with strong emotion.

Lord Franklin remarked tearfully without expression, fixing his gaze to the ceiling. 'Son,' he said, 'I can't talk much. Each breath I take is awfully painful. Can you hear me?' he asked in a changed tone.

'Yes pa, I can hear you,' Ifash answered between sobs. His responses could no longer register in Lord Franklin's foggy mind.

Already, Ifash was crying like a bereaved child.

'Son, why don't you do the rest of the talk? Ask me concerning things you've never been able to ask me before, talk to me,' he said with effort, gasping, waiting and hoping that Ifash would talk rather than weep.

Ifash said nothing and continued to cry. Just when Lord Franklin had lost interest and hope, the boy stood and attempted to replace the mask.

'Don't leave me pa, I love you pa, I love you,' he sobbed. 'Teach me now, Teach me how to replace it pa,' he said and struggled to put back the mask. Repeatedly, the child's voice echoed through to Lord Franklin. He took a deep breath and tried move his arms but could not.

'Get going, I will be alright. Call the doctor, Romana is very sick,' Lord Franklin mumbled. Ifash turned around and his crying seized abruptly. He was stunned. How could she be very sick just now? With this thought he dashed out in haste.

Lord Franklin's breath was degenerating and his sharp eyes were now glazed. He thought of Kimberly and he smiled. He felt some sense of fulfillment; but on the other hand, he was sad to have been separated from her so early and unexpectedly. A deep cough shook him and he felt it through his entire system. While he regained his breath, he heard the footfalls of people along the corridor outside the room. The nearer they got, the fainter they sounded to him. Gradually, he drifted into sleep with his mouth agape by the time help arrived.

Two doctors and four nurses went to work on him. One of the doctors reached for the gas mask and fixed it. The other was applying the defibrillator on his chest when one of the nurses noticed Romana's body sprawled on the floor. She alerted her colleagues and they rushed her out of the room.

The battle to save Lord Franklin's life proceeded effectively. The doctor kept on applying the defibrillator, trying to get some response. At a point, one of the doctors glanced at the cardiographer screen. Shocked, he fixed his gaze on it hoping for a miracle. No miracle was manifested. The medical team stared helplessly at the lifeless body of Lord Franklin Gordon.

'Damn it,' swore the senior doctor in frustration. 'He slipped, put me quickly through to the office of the Prime Minister,' he said and hurried out of the room soaked with perspiration.

Meanwhile the duchess was waiting in the doctor's office for an appointed meeting with her lover now proudly referred to as the late Lord Franklin Gordon, the knight of the British Empire. He was buried with pomp and pageantry, and decked in the colors of the union jack.

CHAPTER SEVEN

Odua Kingdom 1877 (27 years-later)

For two days the storm raged, non-stop in Europe. By night of the second day, the ice had claimed several small ship, including a large one, the largest ever constructed by man. It was shortly after dawn on April 12, 1877, two months after the wreckage of Roma Explorer. The sad news finally got to the palace that the largest ship ever constructed by a white man, on its very first voyage had been hit by an unexpected storm that measured over 5,000ft in the Indian Ocean. The Roman ship meant so much to king Jajaha. Not only for the 3,000 slave heads tucked beneath the ship, but for the loss of the heir to the throne of the gods, Prince Dada and his nuclear family aboard the wrecked ship.

When the king heard the news from a team of elders, he slipped into a water of grief, a deep turbid river of sorrow. Afterwards, he was responding to all around him with little animation than a flower responding to subtle breeze. Later on, he suffered a strange shock that resulted to a stroke in matter of days. He'd remained in a state of coma ever since. It took the queen some extra affection and skills to comfort, feed, bathe and dress the king daily. The Ifashanu saga was nothing compared to the present situation. King Jajaha was barely holding on to life, like a fish on the river banks. His dreams and hopes had been shattered by the wreckage of a single ship.

The queen unlike her husband appeared much stronger in dealing with the blow unleashed by the misfortune. Though it has become a routine for her to hide in the backyard every evening, squatting on a pile of bricks with her hand clasped tightly below her chest, she often stared into the blue sky, saying a thousand prayers in grave silence. The real damage she seemed to feel, was not just the death of the prince, or the huge commercial loss, or even the unconscious state of the king; rather, it was the collapse of the royal family altogether.

Ten Months Later (1878)

By the 15th of February, the condition of the king changed from bad to worse. It became clear to all that the centre could no longer hold. King Jajaha had lost grip of the kingdom and things were falling apart like a pack of cards. More disturbing, disaster seemed to be pilling upon disaster, sorrow upon sorrow, and other calamities were being witnessed.

Their king remained deaf and dumb and his spirit appeared to have departed from his body long before the night the queen tried unsuccessfully to wake him for supper. Queen Abeke knew instantly when she entered his bedroom, judging by the position of his arms, and the rigidity of his body and his exposed teeth.

'Here lies king Jajaha, my husband and a brave man. Man like men, enroute the home of his ancestors. May the gods of our land grant you all that you will require in heaven. Do not discriminate, eat with them whatever they eat, rejoice with them at their moment of joy, curse that which they curse. Till we meet again, may your gentle soul rest in peace,' she lamented with deep sorrow and a heavy sense of lost. Then she wailed aloud and roused the kingdom.

King Jajaha Kakah Tobiolah II, aged ninety, must have given up the ghost that night because of his failure in life's endeavors. The sad news spread to every corner of the land, the continent and beyond. Even though the chancellors and elders saw it coming, there was little they could do. They could have given anything to avert the death of their king, but death being what it was would not negotiate or compromise. Whenever it arrived, it was simply the end as it was for Jajaha, son of To-biolah.

It was end for a king whose tenure made the Kingdom the strongest and wealthiest on the continent.

'The passage of our king to the abode of our ancestors should not mean that life must stop for the living. Let those who worship and adore Jajaha know today that Jajaha is gone forever; gone to a greater place of our ancestors. But our heritage, culture and tradition remain an integral part of us. We must continue as a people to remain firm in periods of adversity. Let us think of what next we shall do and which direction to pursue in order to receive the favors of the gods, for they live on forever more.' All these the chief priest had stated at the gathering of chancellors and elders.

Seven days after all rituals were completed; the king was buried in the north wing of the palace. The ceremony that followed was flamboyant. It was a colorful occasion that brought together kings and queens, the rich and poor, wisemen and fools, great spiritualists and brave warriors. Every living soul that was once friends and enemies of the king were all present that day to pay their last respect to a legend that ruled the seven coasts with an iron fist.

A Fortnight Later

Two weeks after the ceremonies that graced the burial of king Jajaha, queen Abeke together with the king's chancellors and elders, gathered as early as they could and deliberated on the successor to the throne of the gods. It was a known fact that King Jajaha died leaving five wives and eleven legal children, fifteen grand children, and a banished son.

The meeting that began that early morning at the palace was tension-soaked. They agreed and disagreed on pressing issues concerning culture and tradition in line with the situation at hand. There were hardliners among them who took the hard lines. They refused to agree to any solution contrary to tradition. The liberals, however, sought for flexibility in applying the traditions of the land. They argued about changes in their contemporary society, which were not traditionally inclined and they suggested the need for wisdom and new initiatives.

Queen Abekeofin supported the liberals as pre-planned before the meeting. In private, she had promised selected Chancellors and elders riches and positions should everything go accordingly. When it was her turn to speak, she spoke emphatically about the importance of giving trials to one another in life.

'The lack of trial, trust and confidence in one another is a serious negative factor affecting the progress of most kingdoms on our continent,' she stressed. She went further, asking the gathering to come together on terms and seek a bargain with Ifa-Eledumare to accept whoever the majority desires. 'Ifa should for once consider the person we feel is most suitable for the throne and bless that individual for the good of the land,' she emphasized.

The hard-liners were led by the Chief *Balogun*. He understood the plight and plot of the queen. But, the effects of her statement were strong and convincing. Somehow, it softened his nerves and inflamed his heart. Undoubtedly, she was a woman with unmatched intelligence and strength, coming from a strong family background. She was a force to be reckoned with, not only because she was the queen, but chiefly because she was the overall leader of the women occult group with spiritual powers dating back to the time of Iyemoja, the river goddess, and Ogun, the god of iron.

At long last, it was Chief Balogun who finally calmed down the nerves of the hardliners because of his admiration and respect for the queen of the land.

According to the tradition of Odua, promises made on an empty stomach are null and void. It was after a delicious breakfast in the palace that the gathering conveniently reached a joint consensus. The consensus was to appease Ifa Eledumare.

The queen took the glory and was assigned with a mission that was specific and time-based.

CHAPTER EIGHT

United Kingdom, 28 Years Later

Sheriff Adam McCarthy picked up the phone on his desk with tobacco flaming between his fingers and dialed a number. The phone rang a couple of times at the other end.

'Gordon's residence,' said a sleepy voice.

'It's me.'

'Adam?' Ifash enquired angrily. 'Confirmed, you're totally messed-up in the head. Don't you ever get any sleep your whole life? Anyway, that's left to you; but why won't you allow someone else have a good rest in his house. What's all this for, show a little respect for other people's right and comfort at least…'

'Shut the fuck up and listen!' Adam shouted at his end fumbling with a pile of files on his table. 'What right has a nigger? Don't trail on that line again and listen carefully to what I've got to say. It's vital information for you,' he said.

'I don't want to hear anything from you! You can stick the information up your white ass!' Ifash retorted.

'Nonsense,' said Adam. 'Your bitch, that sleazy ass, she's here again and this time around I think she's in for it for good. She isn't going to get away with this and if she does, her legs

will be right in the air. You've ever seen a ghost catwalk?
You'll know what I'm talking about in few hours,' he concluded ominously. He spun the dial of the radio beside him and
a newscaster's voice came through the speaker.

'Already she's all over the news. I got a report that your
dumb ass bitch just knifed an asshole in a goddamn all-night
club down town, a bitch's heaven. The doctor said he's one leg
in, one leg out. He might not make it. Precisely, he will not
make it! He's fucking drunk to the maximal and his situation
resembles that of...'

'Cut the Crap, Adam,' Ifash interrupted angrily. 'You and I
know she's just a novelty, no more no less.'

'Christ, what's my fucking business in all these, what's my
ache,' he sniffed reprovingly, resting on an elbow. 'Do I look
like her father or some next of kin? Am I white? What's the
connection after all? I don't want you ever calling me at mid-
night about some attempted murder. Do I look like some fucking cop? Adam, are you drunk on duty?'

'Listen,' Adam plunged in softly. 'Yes, you're no cop. I
haven't also forgotten you're a nigger with no self-restraint.
You're the one who walks about town with his cock in his
mouth,' he said and puffed out thick smoke from his tobacco.

'It seems you've forgotten so fast about your identity. I call
to inform you because I owe you that. We've been homies for
God knows more than twenty fucking years, and I'm not the
type of gent that enjoys sitting back and watching his buddies
being spanked publicly. But mind you, I will watch gladly once
I have hinted you about the impending trauma. Are you still
there?'

'Talk!' Ifash snapped. Adam waved away an officer who
poked his head through the door. 'Well,' Adam continued
roughly. 'You think you can pour it around as you so wish,
hanging out with rated sluts you so desire? It's a free world you
always say,' Adam said and giggled. 'It is a free world for a
freelance mother fucker!'

'What's your point?' Ifash found his voice. 'I'll sleep on
you any moment; you're not making any sense as usual.'

'The point is simple. Get up and save your ass, save your reputation if you still have any, especially if you still wish to maintain your family ethics,' he replied plainly. 'You're of a prestigious British family; no one has forgotten about Lord Frank of the British Empire and his adopted black kid. You think we all have? Not so fast. No one would easily forget such an odd tangle. Truly, you know I have always been nursing this feeling that your cock will drive you to your grave someday. But, what I'd never figured out is that, it will be driving a whole lot of people along with you. You've been a threat to decency and basic morals. You've even become a threat to the integrity of the empire. Now that the law has caught up with you, what I can advise you is to face it like a man. I don't see this as her fight alone from the scope I am looking at it. It's more of your fight. It's more of the Gordon,' he said.

Another officer poked her head through the door with a bunch of files in one hand. Adam jerked his head, dismissing her. 'Tell you what; I don't have much time to spare either. Do your sleeping and I'll do my laughing much later. But then, I've this expensive advice, really expensive, but I'll give it to you free without a shilling. After all, what are friends for?' he puffed expansively.

'Your bitch needs a lawyer, a damn good attorney. The press will soon be here; maybe they are on their way already. And you can bet she's going to be intimidated and forced to sing some dirt; filthy statements that won't go down well with some dignified Gordons. And you can guess the caption in *The Time* mag, *The Sketch*, and *The Mirror*, all of those voices screaming alike, "The whore world of Lord Franklin's black kid!" Can you fathom that?' Adam demanded.

There was a momentary silence and then Ifash burst into laughter, a lengthy one for that matter. Ifash's laughter was not convincing and he crawled out of bed and began pacing the room in rage.

'What's your problem Adam? What's this all about? What do you want from me? Are you drunk again?' he demanded angrily. 'You've been taking too much drink, too much of those shits when you should be making sure everyone in this town is safe and in bed. Now listen, I've lost enough sleep and I don't intend to lose more. Get the hell out of my life! Feed that to the birds and I'll see you at the other end...'

'Wait, hold on, don't drop on me yet,' Adam said and put out his tobacco in the ashtray while licking his lips. 'I have one last word to say. You're going down with her, believe it or not. Don't forget to buy the dailies in the morning. Piss-off nigger!' Adam shouted and banged the phone. He indulged in an ominous smile as he reflected on the imminent downfall of yet another close friend.

Ifash mused at the phone in his hand, hissed and placed it gently on the cradle. Shuffling back to bed, he tried recapturing his smooth sleep. But his mind was heavy, pre-occupied, and his eyes remained wide open. As he lay in bed trying desperately to draw some sleep, his memory sailed, slipping to the first day he met Jane.

Vividly, he remembered the graduation night at Cambridge. The night all graduands came with loved ones. Over three thousand graduates converged at the large auditorium. It was in a period when racial discrimination was at its peak. Cambridge was a predominantly white college. The blacks made less than one percent. There was not a single black female on graduation day. The public felt education was of no major importance to black African women, judging by their low status in the society.

That night inside the main hall, the fact that he was a Gordon and had passed out with excellent degree in social studies did nothing to boost his ego. None of the white girls paid any serious attention to him throughout his four miserable years at Cambridge. Most would not even return his greetings and that night was no exception. They avoided him the way rats avoided cats.

Suddenly, Ifash sat up on the edge of the bed and sighed. Reflecting back to his days in college, where he first set eyes on Jane. It was at Cambridge that he fully digested the extent of discrimination against blacks by whites, who relegated them almost to the level of orangutan. He cupped his head with both hands allowing his mind to sail further. He remembered sadly how frustrated he was that night. Everyone was ignoring him on a day meant to be his happiest day, his day of great achievement. No one said a sincere 'hi' to him; it was a hopeless situation for him altogether.

However, just towards the end of the send-off, he made one last attempt before crying home. It was not as if he was not charming that night. He looked smart in a well-tailored black suit, a blazer and a bow tie. To be or not to be, he thought and confidently walked up straight towards a section, where Jane was seated with crossed legs among her colleagues.

'Do you mind if we step on the floor for a second?' he whispered into her ears. Unlike previous failed attempts, he met his luck for the night. To his utmost surprise, the lady rose, clinging to his arm. At first, he thought she was drunk because alcohol had flowed freely throughout the day. They began to dance, holding each other affectionately. Her words were well coordinated. They danced like old friends, a duo who had known each other for donkey years. With gratitude that surpassed his excellent results, he realized she wasn't drunk. She was as sober as he was.

That night at Cambridge, it was Jane Wool who had damned all the consequences. It was her who had stooped low to dance with him in front of a large white audience. This could be partly because, apart from being a graduating student, she was one of those 15th avenue flirts who considered trading their bodies to the highest bidders a means to an end.

'I'm indifferent, whether you black, you white, you red, it makes no difference to me. All I know for certain is that, you guys are all assholes,' she had said to him.

* * *

Still in trance, his thoughts drifted hastily to the day he brought her home to the ranch. She had been very surprised.

'Is this where you live?'
'Yes, this is my home.'

'Are you sure you are telling the truth?' she pressed.

'Of course I'm saying the truth. You expected a slum?' he replied sarcastically.

That was three years ago. So much had happened since then. They had remained friends. He went frequently to visit her at her 15th avenue apartment, having succeeded in building a relationship with her. He did not have to pay for sex like others and he grew more sensitive to her desires; and so did she. She would visit him once in a blue moon at his country home with a basket full of roses, snacks and iced sodas.

* * *

Ripples of swirling air rose from a distance of about twenty thousand miles. Soon a band of rain began to spiral towards the country side. A sudden thunderstorm with lighting jerked him back to reality. He heard raindrops falling on the roof and the glass windows, and the cold breeze made him more alert. Abruptly, he got up, moved across lazily to the open windows and shut them.

Immediately after his graduation, he had moved into Lord Franklin's bedroom. He enjoyed the front view that looked directly into the Lake Victoria. Lord Franklin had willed the ranch to him on condition that he stayed in England under the watchful eyes of Romana. A strange will it was. Where else did he expect him to go, he had wondered. The ranch was just about the only vital property lord Franklin possessed, apart from a ten-acre farmland in Dublin.

The rain beating against the glass windows reminded Ifash of aunt Romana. She never slept without making sure the windows were open. He hurried into his pajamas and walked out. Her room was downstairs. He knocked gently on the door and waited anxiously for a reply. All he could hear was a snoring sound of someone deeply asleep. Slowly, he turned the knob and stepped inside. It was completely dark, though he could figure out her shape on the bed. He closed the windows soundlessly and left the room leaving the door partially closed for ventilation.

Ifash returned to his room and stood innocently by the window with arms folded. He watched with less interest as the rain did justice to the grassland and formed little pools elsewhere. Strange feelings were bombarding his conscience and he glanced at his watch. He realized he had been standing by the window for well over twenty minutes. Sighing deeply, he braced up and entered the bathroom. Like his adopted father, he came out hurriedly in less than ten minutes and began dressing in simple shirt and jeans, and a pair of brown suede shoe. The next moment, he was running down the stairs, taking it three at a time. He had left a simple note: "*Morning aunt, I'm out early. I will be back soon. Take care and don't forget to see doctor Mosun. She returns to the U.S tonight, love.*"

A faint smile crossed his lips as he walked out. Aunt Romana was so predictable. He knew she could not complete a day without dusting the piano. She cherished two things in her life, the Starlat piano and her sleep. That was why he had left the note on the piano.

* * *

It was drizzling when he got outside. A summer rain was a sign that a lioness was in labour. He assumed the rain could not hold on for long and did not bother for an umbrella. Across the newly constructed road, he flagged down a cab and popped in while it was still in motion.

'Sterling island station, fast,' he said settling beside the driver.

'Right on brother,' replied the black driver who put the jaguar through a swift u-turn.

He turned on the radio and a familiar voice at the B.B.C was on air reporting the weather. Ifash hated news because it was all about politics, wars, and lies. Precisely he hated mindless politicians. Through the window, he noticed once again with huge sense of emotion as different groups of slaves move out into the large field which is strategically located miles before his country side home. As usual, they were carrying long cotton sacks while a few others prepare the mule teams and wagon that would convey the cotton to the gin in Chelsea.

The ride to Sterling Island was fast and comfortable. The rain had stopped the time they got to the station, meaning the lioness had delivered peacefully. The early morning sun was now making its challenge gradually, he noticed through the opened window. He tucked two coins into the palm of the driver and hastily got out of the car. He entered the police station through the back door under the drizzling rain. It was the first time he would visit Adam at his new post. He had been transferred from Leeds station, an area with a low crime rate when compared to Sterling Island, a mixed neighborhood. He turned to his left because on his right was a notice that read: *"Officers only."*

As he moved along down the hallway, the white uniformed policemen eyed him suspiciously. None passed him without a second glance. He found a woman receptionist on the right. She was fat and was busy arranging files. He wondered idly what an obese woman was doing in the force. He moved closer to her and smiled broadly into her fat fueled face. She did not take his polite smile as a compliment and her hand moved towards the gun in its holster. Ifash saw the movement and reacted quickly.

'I'm Ifash Gordon. I have an appointment with Sheriff Adam McCarthy,' he said. Her hand dropped to the side, she looked behind her and pointed.

'Thanks officer,' Ifash grinned.

'Get lost,' she growled.

'You bet,' Ifash nodded as he walked to the door labeled, **Sheriff A. McCarthy, District commissioner.'** He knocked briefly and did not bother to wait for a reply. He slipped inside and slammed the door behind him.

Adam raised his head and glowered at him.

'If it wasn't that you're a Gordon, I would have had you incarcerated for slamming my door that way, like a tout,' the police boss threatened, twisting in his chair. A fresh stick of tobacco was glowing between his fingers.

Ifash leaned against the door, watching as he puffed thick smoke into the air. They stared at each other for couple of seconds like two boxers in pre-match confrontation. It was Ifash who lowered his gaze at his watch which showed **5:55**a.m. He drew a seat to himself and sat back comfortably in it, facing the sheriff.

'Would you like to smoke?' Adam asked offering a fresh cigar, but Ifash declined with a shake of the head.

'You look tensed up; you met a ghost on your way here?' the sheriff asked vaguely, puffing deliberately into his face and hoping he felt intimidated. Ifash knew Adam better than anyone in the U.K and the world at large. So he kept his gaze calmly on him, never taking his eyes away from his long nose which reminded him of the beast in him.

Adam stood, taking off his suit and exposing his shoulder holster. He took some calculative steps around Ifash, like a detective trying to drill a charged suspect or a criminal for that matter.

'Ifash, you may be a pussy freak, but most time you remain wise. You don't get too carried away, too intoxicated. I like you for that, I'm proud of you nigger. Besides, how's your aunt, the immigrant. Did I ever tell you that witch scares me to death, with those popped out eyes of hers? I don't like her. And I am sure she doesn't like me either. Is she still of the opinion that I'm a bad influence to a decent kid like you?' he asked seriously, bending to meet Ifash's gaze.

His hands dug into Ifash's shoulders as he muttered into his ear.

'You have less than two hours or she might just rot in hell and I can bet that won't suit you. And again, have been wondering if you'll be able to cope with the rest of them, once she's taken in?' he asked smiling sardonically.

'Back in the days, selectivity is a headache for you, it has always been. Worse still, an order has just been passed; we may soon be rounding up those sleazy little bitches at 15th avenue. 7, 17, and 21 avenues are included as well. It's going to be a clean sweep, once and for all. The type you can only get in...."

"Just what exactly are we talking about here?' Ifash cut in furiously. 'You've not said a word about what really happened, it's all bla, bla, bla nonsense since I came in. Tell me where she is at the moment, give me something solid and shut the fuck up,' he fumed.

'Jesus', Adam said barely audible. 'You sure don't know how to address your superiors. I haven't details to discus with you and even if I do, this isn't the right time for them. You should be out there panting like a dog, looking for a real smart lawyer. The lawyer she needs must be really good at twisting facts,' Adam said returning to his seat and puffing at his cigar.

'Press time here is 8:45am, but I can extend it by an hour by the power bestowed on me by the King, John III. And yes, she's here with us in custody of murder section and you can't see her,' he said swiveling on his seat to face a file cabinet. 'A fucking good attorney is all she needs,' he stressed and inhaled the last nicotine from his tobacco.

He faced Ifash and puffed heavily into his face. Ifash flinched, watching as he stubbed the tobacco in a small ashtray. Then he stood up to leave.

'Extend my greetings to your sis, she might just be next,' Ifash said and darted out of the office slamming the door behind him. The frames on the wall rattled as a result of his action.

Outside the station, the rain had lightened to a drizzle. He checked his back pocket for a coin and found two. Quickly, he crossed the road and entered a phone booth.

* * *

Mary Lens and Ifash met outside the Sterling Island police station at 8:25am. Mrs. Lens was a pretty young lady in her early thirties. She was the wife of a biology teacher at Elton secondary. She dressed like a lawyer, wearing a blue suit and skirt with a brown briefcase in hand. It was only through a lawyer that Ifash could gain access to Jane and he had to settle for the inexperienced Mrs. Lens, being the only attorney in town willing to take up a murder case from a black client. Before her, he tried most of the experienced lawyers in the city, but none deemed him serious. Among those he called was Sir Williams Sean. He was a nutty racist attorney who threatened to sue him the next time he called his number, consciously or unconsciously. Sir Williams's unprofessional attitude made Ifash conclude that the United Kingdom was no country for blacks. He wondered depressingly on the fates of those blacks who were not privileged to be Gordon. As dejected as he was, he resolved to visit the ghettos and get first hand information about life in the black community. He thought about the blacks in North America, Spain, Germany, France and elsewhere. He thought of Africa and only then did he become convinced that Africa must be the only likely place where a black man could raise his head up on the street and rightfully experience a sense of belonging.

Mary Lens and Ifash were taken to the legal section of the station. It was a large hall with a long table at the center and several chairs. They waited for fifteen minutes before Jane finally emerged in-between two female officers. The officers left to wait for her at the door. Mary watched Jane carefully with disbelief as she walked towards them and settled for a chair opposite Ifash. Mary leaned sideways and whispered to Ifash.

'I don't like forming opinion about people. You're sure she's no druggie?'

'No, not at all,' Ifash said shaking his head and staring at Jane as he did so. He wondered at the extent of anger that would have made her want to commit murder. He had always thought her incapable of such things. He was wrong.

Jane rested her elbows on the table, then buried her face in her hands and began to weep. Mary kicked Ifash gently on the leg.

'What are you waiting for, say something to her,' she whispered. Ifash took a deep breath and deliberately let it out gently.

'I don't know what to say,' he responded quietly and kept his eyes fixed on Jane. A few seconds later, he offered her his handkerchief.

'If you don't stop weeping, you'll turn the room into a pool,' he said softly. Jane sobbed for a few more seconds and wiped her tears with her bare hands.

'I'm sorry,' she said, gasping for breath.

'We are most sorry,' Ifash replied brashly. 'This is Mary Lens, your Attorney,'

'Good morning Jane, we hope we will be able to assist you,' Mary said, smiling warmly at Jane's displaced mascara.

Instinctively, the lawyer became convinced that Jane was probably doing drugs without Ifash's knowledge.

'Down to business,' Mary said removing some sheets of paper from her briefcase and placing them on the table. 'Tell me what happened and why you stabbed him?' Jane took her time, drawing a worried expression from the lawyer.

'The bastard is a sonofabitch,' she blurted out. 'I warned him the first time he tried that on me. I told him I don't dig it, God knows, I warned the bastard!' She gritted her teeth and continued.

'The Sonofabitch, dope-head, mother-fucking bastard is a New York creep that takes London for some Pleasure County. The fucking asshole sold me some trash. He tried to shove it all at me, like hell I didn't let him. Pain-ass faggot got so furious at his mama. I shove the shit back at...'

'Wait a moment,' Mary interrupted her, astonished and un-impressed. 'Look Jane, I can understand how you feel about this guy; but I need something tangible, and I want to believe you can do better. Fine, he may be all the stuff you just called him but what I need from you is to give me something I can write down, do you understand my plight?'

'Got you, right,' Jane said and nodded in understanding. Her eyes darted to Ifash and she wondered sickly why he was looking at her that way, like it was finished for her in the world. She sighed deeply and turned to the lawyer.

'First, the bastard won't pay the right charges...,' she emphasized with a finger up. '...because, in New York he doesn't pay a cent for a blow-job. He said it comes naturally with the deal. Second, he tried poisoning me. The bastard creep dropped valium in my soda, can you beat that?' she looked from Ifash to Mary but both did not say a word.

'Third...,' she said raising three of her fingers to her guests' faces, '...he's completely insensitive, probably neurotic! I told him I was sore but he refused to listen. He kept his pace, moved astride, hit me and pinned me down, maintaining his dominance. I thought I was just going to black-out, it felt as if I was dying, it was horribly painful.

Four, at a point he rolled me over and tried venturing through my butt, the son of a bitch abused me and he was so cruel, he...' she broke off and covered her face with her hands.

'And what happened after?' Mary inquired softly trying not to flinch as she was now sure, that indeed, Jane is a druggie.

'Then I remembered I had this pen knife I kept long ago under my mattress. I managed to reach it and I...I stabbed him thrice at first, then again and again. I stabbed the asshole severally, until suddenly, I realized his eyes were rolling woozily in their sockets. I hurt his ass real bad, I didn't want to kill him though, but I wanted badly to inflict pain on his butt. I wanted to hurt him real bad, I was eager to see him cry. I wanted him to understand how I'm feeling about what he was doing to me. I was hoping he will carry some scars to his bitches in New York! He took me for a ride; he was rude, abused me and violated my rights!' She concluded breathing heavily.

'It's alright, Jane,' Ifash said leaping over the table. He settled beside her and stroked her back gently. 'It's alright now, we here for you,' he said and kissed her twice on the cheek. 'You did the right thing, I could have done worse. It's alright baby, easy. Let it go, come off it, I'm here now.' Ifash glanced in Mary's direction. She looked devastated and was not writing any longer. Her pen was tucked in her mouth.

'You've heard it all. What do we do? What do you make out from all she said?' he voiced with a shrug. Mary remained speechless and slowly, she bent and began to scribble fast on a sheet of paper. This was her second direct case in life and it appeared very challenging and tougher than the first. She hoped that through this case, she would be able to create an impression that will send some warning signals to those standing on her path of progress, especially her husband who kept referring to her as baby-lawyer.

'Well, Jane,' Mary raised her head allowing the pen to dangle between her fingers. 'Did they find any other thing with you that might be incriminating?'

'They found a joint, it belongs to him,' Jane said.

'Can you prove it?'

'It was found in a pocket in his shirt,' Jane said.

'Smart ass,' Mary voiced her thoughts to the accused. 'If I should be honest with you, I'll simply say that you're in a deep shit. I'm sorry I have to make it clear. I'm not one of those solicitors that try to put a round peg in a square hole.' She paused to see if her statement has any effect on her.

'It's as simple as that Jane. I believe you know the gravity of your action,' Mary completed bluntly.

'So what do we do?' Ifash queried.

'We can only hope to save her by trying to reduce her jail term; that is if she doesn't get the big bang,' the lawyer declared placidly.

'What do you mean by big bang?' Ifash asked with a frown. He hoped she would not say what he was thinking. He really hoped she would not say it. As if sensing the tension building within Ifash, Mary decided to lay it down more softly.

'In this country, England to be precise, if she's found guilty of first degree murder, she'll be on death row. What I mean by first degree murder is when someone intends to kill a fellow human being for whatever reason,' she said and smiled at Ifash before looking away and focusing on Jane.

There were tears in the Jane's eyes and she made no attempt to wipe them off. She was demoralized, shocked and disappointed that her own government could end her life because of a Yankee.

'Jane, how old are you?'

'Twenty-four,' she replied with a straight face. Her expression was unreadable.

'I understand from Mr. Gordon that you're a graduate, a linguist. You speak French fluently?'

'Voir Paris et mourir,' Jane stated in flawless French. Mary shook her head in obvious pity, 'what a waste', she mummured under her breath.

'You'll be tried as an adult of twenty-four, but you can be rest assured that the firm I represent will do its best for you.' Mary said and paused, flipping through some papers in her briefcase. 'I should let you know that the fellow you stabbed died 45minutes-ago of haemorrhage. So the case we have at hand is a murder case. It's now left to us to prove in the court of law that it wasn't deliberate,' she stated with a frown.

A grave silence followed in which time Ifash wished he had tried harder to get the most competent lawyer. Perhaps, he should have promised Sir Williams Sean heaven and earth. He should have given him the farm in Dublin. Who needs a farm anyway, he wondered. He should have pleaded further and even condone more insults. He should even have supported his notion and confirm to him that, yes indeed, niggers are maggots who should be wiped off the surface of the earth. But it was all too late. He could only hope Mary would be up to the task.

He drew Jane closer and held her in his arms. He tried to assure her it would be okay. Mary set the last pieces of paper into her briefcase.

'I thank you for your cooperation Miss Jane,' she said sounding business-like. 'There won't be time for us to meet again, except of course in the court. But please do note the following points. First and foremost, don't use obscene language in the court of law. Also, your first and third points are insignificant for the path I wish to trail, so ignore them in the court. Again, it's my duty as your attorney to bring to your understanding, without meaning to upset you, that flirting and prostituting are not things of pride in our society. It's against the constitution of this great nation. And lastly Miss Jane, do not speak to anyone about this matter. I don't mean the press alone. When I say anyone, it includes your inmates, the warders, your visitors, the police and detectives,' she concluded with a rueful smile and reached for her briefcase. She signaled Ifash that she was through with her client.

'You've got to hold on tight Jane,' Ifash said to encourage her. 'It's going to end soon. It's not the end of the world, so pull your self together. You've got a whole team on your side and we're all going to get over this pretty soon,' he assured and planted a wet kiss on her forehead.

* * *

A week later, they were in court. The prosecutor presented the state's case and tried to convince the Judge that Jane Wool had planned to kill Mr. Henry Stanley that fateful night, in order to steal his money and his 18-carat gold wristwatch. He went further and paraded three young men, probably close friends of Mr. Stanley, to the witness stand. The three men, like spin doctors, spoke well of Mr. Stanley and his decency in the society. The chief prosecutor whom Mary later found out was hired by the American Higher Commission, rounded off his statement by appealing to the Judge to make sure that Miss Jane Wool faces the ultimate penalty for first degree murder.

Later on, Mary Lens took the floor. She spoke convincingly about the attitudes of men who left their wives back at home and slept around with helpless young women. Such men she maintained should not be regarded as decent in the British society. A society that bred men like Mr. Stanley was a one with no self-respect, no common sense and no cultural background. She also mentioned that Mr. Stanley was an alcoholic and his moral behaviour at his place of work was said to be erratic and contrary to the British standard. She pleaded for young Miss Jane by emphasizing that she had no intention to kill Mr. Stanley, rather, her actions that fateful night was in self-defence against a stronger opposite sex who lured and compelled her into sodomy. It was a crime that God Almighty, the

Supreme Lord of the world, destroyed not just one man like Mr. Stanley, but an entire nation, she concluded.

She later called four witnesses to the stand. All were prostitutes. She asked them simple questions about Miss Jane Wool's integrity and academic background. The prosecutor also asked them questions. He asked them embarrassing questions that almost made Mary regret inviting them in the first place. But she knew she had no options, since Jane did not have any decent friend to stand in the witness box. She hoped the point she wanted to drive home that Jane was an intelligent balanced individual had been noted by the judge and would outweighed the prosecutor's strategy to discredit their evidence. With that fact in mind, her confidence was restored and she felt she had not slipped. She called her last witness and Ifash Gordon stepped into the witness stand.

The instant he took the oath, flashes from different cameras nearly blinded him. Members of the press were excited and they fought to take positions in front of him. The Judge was furious and dissatisfied with the conduct of the media. He banged his anvil thrice to restore order. The attempt failed and the police quickly got in the midst of the confusion and pushed the cameramen back to their seats. Ifash retook the oath and Mary asked him few questions about his friendship to Jane Wool.

When it was the turn of the prosecutor, he cross-examined the credibility of a person like Ifash on the witness stand but was careful not to make racist comments. Ifash knew what the prosecutor would have wished to say. He could guess that by the bewildered look on his face. If permitted he would have wanted to ask everyone present what a nigger was doing in a British court of law? He crossed-examined Ifash tediously, but Ifash remained steadfast. At times, he had to lie under oath about Jane's moral conduct which he knew very well was nothing to write home about. He knew she was temperamental and could act violently, but he did not know she was capable of murder.

After about two hours, the Judge permitted a break.

Mary Lens was convinced about her performance and was mostly delighted about the good show Ifash put up. She confidently assured Jane and Ifash of victory.

* * *

When they returned to the defendant table half an hour later, the Judge was already making his entrance. He handed a paper to the foreman and sat. The foreman rose and announced the verdict of the Judge.

'Miss Jane Wool, age twenty-four, from Leicester, you're hereby found guilty of involuntary murder of Mr. Henry Stanley in cold blood. You'll face five years in prison and another two years in probation, a total of seven years, c...o...u...r...t!' the foreman pronounced.

Mary Lens bent and whispered into Ifash's ear.

'The world is like a walking shadow; but in times like this, we can say its nothing but a broken crystal ball. As far as I am concerned, she's really lucky, very lucky.' she said.

CHAPTER NINE

UNITED KINGDOM, December 1878

On the last month of the year, as the days goes by and the familiar heavenly stars began to take their positions in the sky. Queen Abekeofin Tobiolah II was dressed in full aso-oke attire. She checked her wristwatch as she disembarked the Celine at exactly 20.00hrs G.M.T.

'Here at last,' she breathed in relief. Her visit, unlike previous ones, was not official. She was not expecting to see British government officials waiting at the lobby. With mixed feelings, she recalled her last visit to the U.K. Back then, she was slightly heavy with Ifashanu and her sea voyage was indeed a memorable one. She had with her then hundreds of slaves and other events that followed shortly after.

On arrival at Liverpool exactly twenty-eight years ago, she had received a red carpet treatment with gun salute, typical of the British. But this time around, she had traveled like a commoner after successfully convinced the elders and chancellors why she had to make the journey alone. Huge royal escorts always slowed her down; worse, they attract unnecessary attention everywhere she went.

After completing the customs checks, she put her hand inside her handbag and extracted a coin. She looked around and saw the section that indicated "Telephone." Walking briskly through the crowd, she wondered why the hall was excessively crowded with uniformed personnel in military jackets. Perhaps, they are returnees from battle grounds, she thought.

Having spotted an empty telephone booth, she entered and began to dial The Continental Hotel to confirm her reservation. The male speaker at the other end assured her that her first class reservation made in Ethiopia twenty-four hours before was intact. The speaker was quick to suggest sending down a chauffeured car to pick her up when she told him she was calling from Liverpool.

'How would the chauffeur recognize you, madam,' asked the speaker.

A cynical smile appeared on the queen's lips, because she seemed to find his question rather amusing.

'Your driver won't miss me,' she said simply. 'Just inform him to look around for a strong African woman, gorgeously dressed and standing a few feet from the dock,' she stated.

* * *

As soon as the chauffeur introduced himself, the queen paid an attendant to wheel her bags to the parking lot while she followed behind. The chauffeur was gesticulating here and there in an attempt to make her acquainted to her new environment. As she walked along, her uniqueness was greeted with inquisitive glances by passers-by. They drove silently all the way to London.

The Continental Hotel was situated at the center of London, over-looking London Bridge where William Wallace's head was hung centuries back. The hotel was a fabulous twelve-storey building, with interior decoration fashioned to meet the class of renowned politicians and royalties.

The moment she entered her suite, she pursed her lips in stern disapproval. Queen Abeke had never seen luxury blended in such style. The room was lavishly decorated far above her taste and imagination. She did not have to move an inch; every thing she might require was at her disposal. Like a luxury prison, there is a large bed, a reading table, a mini-sitting room, a bar-corner and a lot more than she required. She shook her head and hissed in disgust.

After a long shower, she changed into a light gown and then ordered for a meal to be served in half an hour. Meanwhile, she sat leg-crossed in bed, with pillows propped-up against the board. A dizzy feeling crept over her but she took it for fatigue from her long journey. She was confident that a nice meal would clear all her fears. Sickness was the last thing on her mind. Gazing at the ceiling, an idea struck her. She reached for the phone beside the bed and punched two buttons.

'Please is that the reception?'

'Yes madam, this is the reception; what can we do for you?' a smooth unruffled male voice responded.

"Please, I will appreciate if you can place an urgent call for me.'

'We will be delighted to do that for you, madam.'

'Good, help me to call the foreign secretary's office tomorrow morning.'

'It's easy madam, but who are we calling and what time exactly should we place the call.'

'I want to speak with the foreign secretary very early in the morning,' she said and glanced at the wall clock.

'Madam, may I ask, do you have a fixed appointment with him or something?' The queen felt irritated by the enquiries, but she decided to take them calmly.

'Not at all.'

'Well madam, should that be the case, I'm sorry I'll only be able to link you up with his personal assistant,' the voice said. 'I'm really sorry madam, but I'm sure this person will be willing to make necessary arrangements on your behalf. You needn't worry.' The queen was quiet, allowing some space of silence between them. She was thinking about the urgency required in her mission. She wanted to talk with the real people, not some under-dogs.

'Madam, madam, are you still there?' he drawled, sounding a bit startled.

'Oh yes, I am here,' she answered.

'We really are sorry madam, there is nothing we can do from this end than to go through his personal assistant. We do not have direct access to Mr. Lawson, the Foreign Secretary. We are sorry for any inconveniences this might cause you,' the voice apologized as if it was really the hotel's fault that they did not have direct access to the Foreign Secretary.

'It is alright, be at peace,' the queen said.

'Is there any other thing we may do for you apart from the early morning phone connection,' the receptionist asked dutifully.

'Nothing for now, thank you very much. You sound like a very good man.'

'It's our utmost pleasure. Once again madam, you're welcome to Great Britain,' he said and terminated the call. The queen replaced the phone on its cradle and reached for a soft pillow. For several seconds she admired the logic behind telephones. She wondered if it would ever be necessary to have such thing in Africa.

She was busy unpacking her bags when a soft knock diverted her.

'Come inside, the door is open,' she called out. A young man dressed in a white shirt, red trousers and a fitting bow-tie entered with a troller ladened with selected sea-foods, drinks, and a bowl of fruits. After a delicious meal, she got into bed and slept off at once.

* * *

The shrilling sound of telephone filled the suite at 6:45am, bringing an end to her much desired rest. The queen snuggled under the satin cover and managed to raise the phone off the hook.

'Hallo', she greeted with an African accent.

'Sorry to wake you up madam,' said a familiar voice. 'It's the reception calling to inform you that your request had been placed. The personal assistant to the Foreign Secretary is on the line to speak with you, if you don't mind.'

'Oya kee, let him talk now,' she said and sat up on the edge of the bed, now fully awake.

'Good morning,' a husky male voice greeted. The huskiness in his voice gave her a premature idea of him. It indicates that he must be a no-nonsense man. She rubbed her face with a hand.

'Good morning sir. I'm Queen Abekeofin Aina Tobiolah II of the Odua Kingdom.'

'What did you say?' the man asked in an oppressive tone and paused. 'Repeat yourself and could you please raise your voice a little louder?'

'Speaking with you is Abeke Aina Tobiolah of Odua Kingdom,' she repeated raising her voice.

'I see, I see, you sure speak some English,' he acknowledged in a mocking tone. 'So, what exactly can I do for you? Who did you say you are again, didn't get that part?'

'I already told you who I am. What I want is to meet the Foreign Secretary today, period. No more, no less, and who are you sef?'

The man coughed deliberately to clear his throat. The casual amusement in his eyes was gone and his grip on the phone tightened.

'Look, I don't know who you are and why you requested for this call. But not withstanding, I must let you know that we are bound by regulations in this department. It will not be possible ever, for you to meet the Foreign Secretary today, or in three weeks time, or probably ever. To my knowledge, his appointment sheets are filled for the next few weeks. However, out of consideration, should I suggest that you and one of our officials fix an appointment at your convenient time and place? You know, we can discuss whatever you intend to discuss with the Secretary. I can assure you that I will get your message across to him. Who did you say you are?' he asked for the third time.

'Queen Abekeofin of Odua Kingdom,' she repeated simply. The man scribbled it down as she pronounced it and hoped she was not who he thought she was.

'What I want to discuss with the Secretary is a highly personal matter,' she said.

'I am extremely sorry,' the man intoned. 'I'll like to apologise if I sound churlish. The clear cut point is that we don't handle personal matters in this office. This is a government establishment designed basically for official matters. We do serious business here, and we do hope you're not of the opinion that…'

'Look here Mr. Man, only you know the grammar you're blowing,' the queen shouted. 'Can't you be reasonable? Do you take me for some tourist? You think I probably came here for fun, to see bridges or see your lifestyle, or perhaps shake hands with the white man? What is the matter with you by the way?' she queried with annoyance.

'I beg your pardon madam,' his voice said.

'Which pardon are you begging for? Are you alright at all? We are talking to you and you're doing as if you're more than who you are?' she said and noted that it was past seven as shown by the Chinese wall clock. Suddenly she grew impatient and felt she was wasting her time talking when she could easily walk straight to Buckingham palace and knock at the door. But that was not part of the arrangement, she thought depressively. She must not go off the track she wished to trail because of a mere civil servant. With a little soul searching, she remembered the notion of her husband about the British colonists. In his assessment, they stood out as the most corrupt set of human species he ever dealt with.

Tactically, she murmured softly into the mouthpiece, 'It is okay; we know you people too well. Let me know what it will cost me in gold and ivory. I must see your boss today, unfailingly.'

He wanted to say: "Madam, are you nuts? Are you out of your fucking mind?" However, he controlled himself and decided to choose his words.

'Madam, it's not about cost. The Ministry is no trading place, we are not discussing about some items in a grocery shop. What we're talking about here is protocol. These are set-up rules that cannot be altered without several hours' notification to the person in question. What you should understand is...'

'Look Mr. Man,' she began in frustration, her African accent coming to the fore. 'Are you trying to emphasize your so called protocols that give no respect to people and urgent matters? What rubbish protocol is that? I believe it is listed in that same protocol of yours that you should invade other people's territories and cast away their valued antiques and their people for that matter. What are you telling me, you think...?'

'Madam, will you listen to me please?' he interrupted and loosened his tie as he scouted for the right words. Eventually, he came across much slower and calmer.

'What's your suite number, madam?' he enquired.

'Suite no. 003 is what is written on the door,' she hissed.

'Alright, let's say I'll reach you in an hour's time, if necessary,' he said.

'What do you mean by "if necessary",' she retorted. 'So you really take me for a tourist, abi?'

'Madam, on my part I'm trying hard not to sound insulting to you, I hope you'll accord me the same. I'd like you to understand that before this conversation of ours, I have got my own obligations in the office, a very busy schedule we operate. If I can't catch up with you, I'll endeavor sending someone over. It doesn't matter who sees you, the important thing is to get your message across to the Secretary,' he said with an emphatic tone.

* * *

Less than twenty minutes later, Mr. Roger hastily arrived at the reception, unsettled.

The queen had left a message that her guest be led to her suite. She had a soapy bath and was dressed in her native attire. She was munching crabs and carrot salad when a double tap on the door got her attention. She reached for the napkin, dabbed her mouth thrice and pushed away the table. As she held the knob, she guessed who was on the other side.

'Good morning, Your Majesty,' a slim man with spectacles on the tip of his nose bowed slightly in respect. 'I'm Roger Spencer, personal assistant to the Foreign Secretary, Sir Lawson. We spoke on the phone minutes ago,' he said politely with his hands behind him. The queen regarded him critically. She took in his green coat and thick mustache and found them amusing.

'You're welcome Mr. Spendicer,' she greeted. Her accent turned "Spencer" to "Spendicer." 'Have your seat,' she said and pointed to a black sofa before strolling to the bar. Mr. Spencer murmured his thanks, but remained standing and looking at the queen with unspoken curiosity. The queen returned with a small silver tray bearing two glasses of lemonades. She offered him a glass and was surprised to see he was still standing by the door where she had left him. She sipped her lemonade and pointed once again to the black sofa.

'Why don't you have a seat?' The response she got was a hush. He crossed his lips with a finger and beamed at the queen. She could not figure out his action immediately, and she thought it was absurd and childish. Mr. Spencer pointed to the veranda and she got a slight idea of what he meant. He walked briskly past her and unlocked the glass door leading to the veranda; then he beckoned to her. She put down her drink and joined him there looking flustered at the attitude of the Brit.

'Are you sure something is not doing you? You're alright? What is worrying you?' she asked severally. The man closed the door behind them and smiled knowingly, paying little attention to her curious expression. Then he removed his spectacles and replaced them with dark sunshades.

'I'm sorry Your Majesty, its cleaner we discuss out here. As you know we are in the era of cold war,' he explained and smiled with satisfaction.

'I don't understand what you mean at all. We are not at war where I'm coming from, abi what's wrong with this man?' she wondered aloud, baffled.

'It's okay your Majesty. All is well with me. I have checked you out with our agents in your locality. They confirmed that you are who you said you are,' he said, gesticulating and sounding more serious. 'We understood you left Casablanca a few days ago. But Your Majesty, it's highly unconstitutional for you to be lodging in a hotel abroad without informing the home office prior to your arrival. I also understand that you have no entourage, no escort, no security, I mean, this is incredible!' He stared at the woman and wished he could have added: "this is barbaric and awfully crazy!"

'I am not here on an official visit mind you,' she said, dismissing his notion.

'Your Majesty,' he said removing his sunshades and slipping them back to his side pocket. 'It doesn't matter whether it's official or personal. You're a very important personality, a leader of a great Kingdom. My government ought to know you're with us inside the empire, chiefly for your own security,' he declared.

'The gods of my ancestors will watch over me, I don't need your security. Security for what?' she demanded angrily. 'Look, can we continue this discussion inside? This Kingdom is too cold for my liking,' she said.

Mr. Spencer brought out a handkerchief from his breast pocket and wiped his sweaty face. He looked searchingly into the busy road far away. Making sure no one was watching them; he turned and faced the Queen.

'We can't converse inside, your suite is bugged,' he announced to the amazement of the queen.

'What do you mean? I didn't see any bug or mosquito since I arrived,' the queen protested.

'Well Your Majesty, I don't mean insects,' he said and cleared his throat rather deliberately. 'I should be very honest with you because the Ministry I represent will be held responsible and incompetent for any shady development that transpired during your impromptu visit. We normally protect our guests, and we have our own guest houses at our Ministry to prevent any form of scrutiny by the security intelligence bureau, the Scotland Yard precisely. Anything you do or say in that room is wired straight-down to the backyard of the Scotland Yard. So the next time you're going abroad, endeavor to inform your host government to protect you against developments of this nature. In addition…'

'Wait, the language you're speaking is that my room is under study somewhere else I don't know,' the queen cut in furiously. She could not comprehend the reason for such invasion of people's privacy. She could not understand why white men never cease to amuse her; why they like to do the odds. She shook her head disappointedly.

'I'll bring us chairs,' said Mr. Spencer, hurrying inside to fetch two chairs. He placed one behind her and another in front of her. He sat facing her.

'Your Majesty, may I ask what brought you to the United Kingdom? What we can do for you,' he asked and waited with concern for her response.

'Actually, I will like to talk with the Secretary, not you,' she replied firmly.

'Yes, I know you said it's personal, but you'll have to discuss it with me first as it won't be possible for you to meet the Secretary right away. I'm here to offer my full assistance to you, Your Majesty. Please feel free to discuss the matter with me,' he said glancing at his wrist-watch like someone in haste. 'Knowing your agenda is important to my Ministry. We only want to know if your visit has anything to do with trade development, bilateral relations or security arrangements and others.'

The Queen sat upright, wondering why Mr. Spencer looked so disoriented and impatient.

'Mr. Spendiser, I am here on a personal issue like I said before. My visit has nothing to do with internal security or anything you might consider of great value to your government. I am not here to sell you gold nor slaves, do you understand my

English or I should try to make myself clearer,' she said with raised eyebrows.

For a moment, Mr. Spencer was silent with his head bowed. He was gazing intensely at the floor. The Queen noticed the redness spread over his face as if he were on fire. She decided to avert a possible danger; perhaps it was high time she gave him a hint of her mission before the blood runs through his nose.

'Mr. Spendiser,' she called-out softly. 'I am here on behalf of my people. They sent me here to bring back the heir to the throne of the gods, that's all.' Mr. Spencer raised his head, bewildered.

'Did they say it's here in Great Britain?' he asked warily.

'The heir to the throne of the gods is human, not a thing, and we know he's here,' she corrected.

'Is that the only reason that brought you to the United Kingdom, you're not going to discuss trade in any form?' he asked and reached for his handkerchief to wipe his face.

'That's the sole reason I'm here, no more, no less,' she restated.

'Very well then,' he said and sat back relaxed, studying the composed look of the queen and her extravagant native dress. 'Your Majesty,' he continued. 'If it's the case of a missing person, we have a fact-finding department here in Great Britain which we call "Lost and Found." I have contacts over there and my niece works there, by the way. She'll be honoured to help us out. I'm quite optimistic we will get a fast result as to the whereabouts of...' he paused and scratched his head for a clue. He peered closely at the Queen.

'Did you say the heir to the throne of God?' She made no reply, but he understood what her silence signified; so he looked away down the busy road and waited patiently for her to say another word.

'Are you sure they can handle this matter fast?' she asked worriedly.

'Your Majesty, this is Great Britain, they can handle it in 24hrs,' he smiled brightly at her, watching as she heaved a sigh of relief.

'However, before making any contacts, it's important you give me some vital information, such as…' he paused and dug his hand into an inner pocket. He brought out a small paper pad with a pen. 'Such as the full name of this fellow, his height, and his complexion?' he said. Their eyes locked and he noticed with renewed concern when her chin came up that her calm expression had changed to that of a bereaved woman.

'We named him back then as Ifashanu Abedi-Deng Tobiolah,' she said and bit her lips in uncertainty. 'I don't know his height,' she added. Mr. Spencer scribbled down the names. When he heard a chuckle from her, he mistook it for over-excitement.

'What's his complexion like? Is he like me or like you or in between?' he asked using his pen to indicate each of them. The Queen frowned.

'What sort of question is that? Like me of course, black!'

'I am sorry,' he said.

'When did he come to Great Britain? His address, under whose custody, and his last contact address, social security number?' he enquired wearing a smile on his face.

'He arrived here twenty-three years ago,' she said and hesitated, trying to recollect the answer to the next question. Her eyes rolled upward and slowly settled on Mr. Spencer's sharp nose. 'If my memory is accurate, I think we sent him here in custody of one Mr. Frankane Garden, former British Coordinating Officer in West-Africa,' she said, nodding her head. Mr. Spencer leaned forward. He wondered if he had heard her correctly. Could he have heard her right? Yes, he did, he nodded to himself thoughtfully.

'Your majesty,' Spencer called, running his fingers through his hair. 'If it's Lord Franklin W. Gordon of the British Empire you meant, he died long ago in the year of our lord 1860. It was a sad day for all; I was still in the academy at that time,' he said. A pure agonising fury blazed the queen's eyes, and she moved closer to Mr. Spencer piercing him with an iron gaze.

'What did you say? Say it again, clearer.'

'He's dead. I'm sorry your majesty.'

'Who's dead?'

'Lord Franklin Gordon of the British Empire.'

'For how long has he been dead?' the queen asked in a calmer tone. Baffled by her show of concern, Mr. Spencer stared at her.

'That was some 18 years ago, I read about him when I was in the academy,' he announced. The queen closed her eyes in grief; she wondered why everyone that matters to her in life had passed away. Fear gripped her at the thought of Prince Ifashanu. She hoped he was alive, strong and hale.

'It's alright Your Majesty, I can understand how you feel,' Mr. Spencer consoled and passed her a facial expression of concern for her feelings. 'You know, death is a natural thing. It'll always take it course,' he said and shrugged. 'He was a good man, a conservative statesman whom we all had a great deal of respect for,' he concluded, clasping both hands between his thighs. He could not understand why an African was so touched by the death of a British Lord. He would not have been bothered the least if ten kings died at the same time in Africa.

'So Frankane is dead long ago,' she mumbled under her breath.

'Your Majesty,' he called out cheerfully. 'Let me inform you that we've arrived at a short-cut, we can now solve the problem in less than 24 hours! Our best bet for concrete solution is for you to request for the hotel chauffeur to take you down to the countryside, to Lord Franklin's home,' he announced and stood up. 'I'd like to inform you also that royal guards will be sent to man your door 24 hours throughout your stay. Please don't say no, Your Majesty, please don't,' he implored, watching the queen nod her approval calmly. 'Thank you Your Majesty. In addition, two cooks and three servicemen will arrive soon to specially cater for your needs in the hotel. This arrangement will go a long way to give my ministry some rest of mind and assurance that all will be well. May I beg to take my leave, Your Majesty,' he said, bowed and left.

* * *

Some hours after the departure of Mr. Spencer, the queen sat at the veranda enjoying the subtle breeze of London. She later resigned to bed in order to subdue a backache. As she lay in bed, her hatred grew increasingly for her suite. She was being watched. Meaning she could not undress again, take her bath, eat, or do anything in private. Whiteman, so they have witch-craft, she wondered. She would have to do something about it, she concluded.

Allowing herself a few moments of pleasurable deep trance, a thousand thoughts raced through her mind, especially that of a glorious re-union with her son, Ifashanu. She felt nervous by the reality of the possibility. She hoped the prince would have grown up to be a man of humor and understanding. Maybe she should not discuss the issue of his expulsion with him; she should just concentrate on his return home. Above all, she hoped all was well with him wherever he might be at the moment. But if at the end he declined to return home, she would not force him and would not invoke the gods to take control of his feelings. She would make sure she formed a solid image of him by taking a good look at him and memorize the shape of his face, his build, the sound of his voice and his manners. That would be all she would take home, enough to last her a life time. With her face creased with smiles and heart beating with joy, she rolled over in bed and dialed the recep-tion.

'Good afternoon,' she said in her African accent.

'Good afternoon, this is the reception. What can we do for Your Majesty?' a female voice replied.

'I will like you to arrange for a chofor to drive me to the home of Lord Frankane Garden,' she said.

'Yes Your Majesty, it's been arranged by Mr. Spencer and our chauffeur is ready anytime you are.'

'Thank you. There is one more thing…' she said and paused deliberately. 'I will like to speak with the hotel manager for a change of suite.'

'That's no problem at all, Your Majesty,' the voice said. 'That will be possible in about forty-five minutes. He's in a board meeting at the moment.'

'So I should wait here for forty-five minutes for you to be watching me as you like, even as I'm already dressed and ready for my engagement for the day? I want to talk with him right now; I have no time to waste and no time for your nonsense. I must talk to that man, whoever he is!' The queen shouted.

'Alright Your Majesty, I'll do my best. Please give me five minutes.'

'Thank you,' she said and replaced the phone.

* * *

Moments later, the manager tapped on the door.

'You may come in,' the queen called out. He was a short robust man dressed in black suit with a socialist expression on his face. He closed the door behind him and bowed slightly.

'Good afternoon, Your Majesty. It's a wonderful privilege meeting you on such a beautiful day. My name is Sir. Edwin Eastwood, a knight of the British Empire and the director of this prestigious hotel,' he said with a broad smile.

'Good afternoon manager, you must be a proud man. Please have a seat,' she gestured to the chair in front of her.

'It's wholesome to be a knight in the most prosperous Empire in Europe, Your Majesty,' he said.

'No, that is not it,' she waved. 'I mean to say you are an arrogant person.'

'That, well, surely I shall never be arrogant to Your Majesty whom I'll be serving. Long live the queen, long live your kingdom,' he gloated as he sat facing her. He eyed her attire and was fascinated by its rich texture.

'Your Majesty, I understood you've requested for a change of suite. I'm willing to be completely at your service. May I ask what your desire is, I mean in terms of class.'

'The class does not matter. All I ask of you is a private suite, not a public suite,' she said roughly. The manager shifted uncomfortably in his seat, took another quick assessment of her attire and grinned.

'Your Majesty, is this not private enough? This is our Royal suite; it's meant for your status, Your Majesty.'

'Be honest with yourself Mr. whatever your name is,' she said dryly.

'Sir Edwin Eastwood is the name, Your Majesty,' he answered hastily.

'Sir Yeastwood, I am aware some people are sharing the suite with me, your fellow collaborators,' she hinted raising a brow. Sir Eastwood stared, and then forced a smile. He sat on the edge of his seat so he could bring his face closer to hers.

'Who are those sharing the suite with you, Your Majesty?' he asked with a note of surprise. The queen smiled. She needed no other evidence because she could see the guilt in the manager's face. She decided to hammer home her point.

'The Scotland yard,' she said. Sir Eastwood eased back on his seat. How could she know that, he wondered. It was all hopeless, he thought. But he must protect the honour and the credibility of the Continental, so he sat upright and adjusted his tie.

'Yes, Your Majesty, you're absolutely right, and I am ashamed of the action of my government. Though, my government meant no harm, spying devices are installed in selected suites simply as a security measure. It's been like that since after the Nazi uprising and the Operation Black September. You'll admit we are in the era of cold-war. We regret the inconvenience. Please accept our apology based on our good intention to protect our Kingdom from terrorist attacks. We are extremely sorry,' he said and bowed politely.

'Your apology is accepted Mr. Yeastwood,' said the Queen. 'In fact, your hotel is very beautiful indeed, never seen any place like it,' she said and raised her hand airily.

'Please make sure my luggage is kept in a very private suite before my return. I hope my English is clear, Mr. Yeastwood.'

'Can't be clearer, Your Majesty,' he said and led her all the way to the reception, where the chauffeur was waiting.

CHAPTER TEN

The queen sat uncomfortably in the back seat of the Rolls Royce with dark tinted glasses. The sun glared down at 26 degrees which was quite natural for her, but definitely not for the driver who in spite of the air conditioning still had a white handkerchief in hand, wiping perspiration intermittently. The chauffeur was an old man, probably in his late sixties. He was dressed in black tailcoat, with a hat that matched perfectly. He was more or less like a man with one foot in the grave and the other on earth, judging by his gait. And scarcely did he have the energy to fully turn the wheel. The occasional eye contact he made through the mirror, left the queen with an impression of a hunting dog whose day had just been fulfilled.

Queen Abeke sat quietly at the owner's corner, bored. Though her worries and anxiety had increased, she did not want to decide right away what she would say or do when she set eyes on her son. The moment would decide her reaction; she had no definite plan in mind.

A blasting horn of a trailer behind them caught her attention, only then did she realize how slow they had been moving. The driver who introduced himself simply as George swerved the Rolls Royce, allowing the trailer to pass. Her interest shifted to the roadside. She noticed the empty frontiers, large expanses of primeval wilderness, just like Africa. It was a shiny day because the sun very bright like she was in Odua. The green hills along the road were hemmed with adorable silence, except for the howling of the timber wolfs and birds. They encountered a smooth pebbled road, and drove the entire length. Then came the bumpy road that made them stumble. They climbed over bumpy rocks, before being faced once again with a smoother tarred road which extended for a couple of miles before the sign that read: *Welcome to the Ranch of Late Lord Franklin W. Gordon.*

George switched off the engine in front of the lawn facing a small brick house. The queen brought out a long silver chain-watch from her hand-bag and gazed at it. By her calculation, they had spent three hours on the road. George came over to her side and opened the door. She stepped out gracefully and her eyes dashed to the figure seated on the porch with a pet dog. The queen thought she saw a man, but when she took a closer look, she realized it was an elderly-woman dressed in blue-jeans and a pink shirt. She had sparkling white hair. George led her slowly to the porch. Every situation came naturally for George, having had several experiences with royalties and renowned politicians for thirty years as a chauffeur. He knew exactly how great personalities liked to be treated. He was a professional when it came to pampering the rich and the most influential.

'Good afternoon ma'am,' George greeted, extending a hand to the woman. The queen did the same, with a lumpy feeling in her throat. She was almost trembling.

'If we are not mistaken, this is the residence of late lord Franklin W. Gordon of the British Empire,' George said, his hands tucked inside his pockets. The woman grinned delightfully.

'Yes, there is no mistake. Please step over here and have a seat,' she said and pointed to an area in the porch where four cane chairs formed a rectangle. The queen looked on with fascination at the woman who had raised her son, a widower she thought. Gradually, she began to experience some dizziness at the expectation that the prince would soon step out. She sat gently on one of the chairs beside George. They watched as the woman hurried inside and came back with a tray bearing mugs of water and a bottle of liquor. Romana picked a small table by the side of the chair and placed it before the queen. George filled a mug and offered it to the queen. She took it, murmured her thanks and sipped gently.

'Sorry for any inconvenience,' George said after a sip from his mug.

'It's all right and you're welcome', replied Romana with a reassuring smile. Her gaze went to the queen. The attire she wore, her sharp eyes and flat nose fascinated her. She could guess who she was. The queen put down her mug gently, wanting to break away from the inspective gaze of Romana. She introduced herself.

'I am Queen Abekeofin Aina Tobiolah II of the Odua kingdom,' she said authoritatively. Romana passed her a broad smile, still fascinated by her clothes.

'I knew who you are the moment you stepped out of the Rolls Royce,' Romana said. The queen glanced at George and the dizziness suddenly disappeared. It was as if the woman has restored her confidence in life, and she felt buoyant.

'If you know who I am, then you must have an idea why I'm here?' the queen said.

'I certainly do,' Romana said and smiled placidly. 'I know why you're here and who you're looking for.' She took a deep breath and her expression changed from one of delight to depression. She gazed at the ground in hopelessness and the queen became quite fearful.

'Is my son alright?' she asked nervously. 'Madam, is the Prince alright?'

'The name is Romana,' she said and went quiet as she began to feel her blood surging rapidly through her veins. She knew her greatest fear, what she had been daring for so long was about to come to pass. Her life was about to be looted clean of all she possessed. Her only companion was at the center of the debacle. The tears in her eyes were signs of her failures and her despaired. She wished she could crawl away and become extinct.

'I hope he's alright wherever he may be,' Romana muttered to herself and continued in a louder voice. 'Ifash left home some four months ago. He mentioned looking for a job in the city. He said he would visit home every forthnight. He never showed up till date and what is most depressing is that he won't even call to say where he is and if he's alright,' she said and paused to take a deep breath. She shifted her gaze to George.

'I know a close friend of his. He's the Sheriff at Sterling Island police station. I contacted him more than fifty times about Ifash's whereabouts, but no luck. He wasn't cooperative, you know those nutty city boys; they've got this lousy approach to life in general. The last time I called the sheriff, would you believe he banged the phone on me, after waving my calls for weeks? He's rude, one of those unfortunate kids brought up after the war. His father died in Berlin as a soldier, and he was raised by a Norwegian sailor. What good could come out of such?'

'What's the name of this Sheriff?' George asked.

'The sailor's name is McCarthy.'

'Does he have a phone number?' he enquired as he extracted a jotter and a pen from his chest pocket. Romana giggled.

'I've learnt to memorize his number despite the grays in my hair,' Romana said and called out the figures. He returned the jotter and pen back to its place and hastily poured himself some liquor which he guzzled. He attempted to serve the queen but she declined.

'We'll leave now for you to take your siesta,' said George.

'Won't you stay for lunch? You've been driving over a long distance,' Romana pleaded, turning to the Queen.

'We are sorry Mrs. Garden, I wish I could stay and enjoy more of your hospitality, but we must leave at once because time is not on our side,' the queen said with a disarming smile that appeased her host.

'The name is Romana Hawkins,' she corrected. 'I hope you'll re-visit me tomorrow or the next before going back to your home.' The queen flashed George a smile of amusement.

'I thought you're Mrs. Garden, Frankane's wife,' the queen said.

'No, I'm not,' Romana said with a smile. 'But I was with him all through the years. He never got married,' she informed, stretching out both arms for an embrace. The two women shared their emotion and affection in a few gloomy seconds that seemed to have lasted a lifetime.

* * *

The sun had already set by the time they returned to The Continental. The queen was led to her new suite, flagged by four attendants. Suite 012 was not as lavishly decorated like suite 003. It had a small reading table at the corner, a sitting room made up of three red couches with a central rug and a large bed. On her left was an obscure angle. There was a small bar section represented by a thick glass shelf on a mahogany with highly fashionable legs. She walked slowly around the room, inspecting it under the watchful eyes of the attendants, gazing at every object, as if she had a device to detect a bugged room. On their way out, one of the attendants asked if her supper be served. She declined with a wave of the hand. She had lunched with George on their way to Sterling Island. In fact, she had no appetite for food. The hunger in her was not that of the belly, it was of the spirit, the joy of re-uniting with her son.

In the night, she lay in bed far away in trance. Her mind was filled with the day's events. They were at the sheriff's office, just after lunch. In her opinion, the sheriff was the lousiest uniformed man she had ever met. He made no attempt to veil his disrespect for people, especially the prince, whom he referred to as *"my nigger."* Worse still, he puffed smoke indiscriminately into the air throughout their conversation. At a point she had lost her cool and shouted angrily at him.

'Sheri Macati or whatever they call you, you're a very vulgar and insensitive human being. Don't you have parents at home? You have no home training at all,' she accused the officer. The Sheriff placed a hand on his chest and cleared his throat uncomfortably. She and George had glanced at each other without a word, stunned by the policeman's lack of integrity. As she expected, the officer offered an incongruous response.

'Oh no, I didn't mean to upset you, I was only laying hardcore facts about all those damn niggers out there terrorizing the law enforcement agencies. Take it easy ma'am, I can understand how you feel about your boy, he's probably out there doing the wrong thing, and you here doing the mother thing. You'll find him, just take it easy, and take a deep breath, loaf madam, loaf,' he had said.

However, she was glad that at the end of their futile meeting, the officer gave them a reason to be hopeful. He gave them a good clue on a way to trace her son.

"Look here guys, that nigger was mine. Really, have never cared about where Ifash is at a particular point in time. I mean for Christ sake, we keep saying that everybody in this great kingdom should mind their own business. If there is any one person that cared about him apart from the witch you saw at the country side, that person will be the celebrity bitch, I mean Jane Wool. Yes, she's a celebrity slut; she got this huge press coverage during trial. Unfortunately she's in the cooler at the British max, good news for us and terrible for my nigger. You also have the option of running an advert, or you may hire a detective to fish him out. You've got lots of options and I don't know what you're doing here in the first place wasting me precious time,' the officer had said before dismissing them promptly.

* * *

The following day, the queen woke up sedated with hope and joy. She felt a reunion was imminent. She was not expecting it to happen in five hours or even twenty four hours, but the journey of a thousand miles begins with the very first step. She rolled over in bed and began to dial. Halfway she stopped and replaced the receiver. She remembered her spell coin, a gift from her grand mother. She walked briskly across the room to the reading table where her handbag was placed and searched for the coin. When she found it, she touched it with the tip of her tongue. Then she held it high in the air, an inch away from her mouth, and let off incantations in the dialect of the gods.

'*Itu ma tu won ka! Agba ko ma gbon won danu ko! Gbigbo aja kin pajanori! Enu gbo gbo kin pa agbigbo! Okiki amu pofo kogbolo poofo! RogerSpendiser, ounba wi funre ni koma gbo! Ounba wifunre ni ko ma gba! Nitori kosher kosher ni tilakoshe! Ajigini aringini aringinigini woja! Eyin iyami oshoronga, iba yio! Ema she jekioju koti omo yi no ilu oyinbo! Ashe!*'

After these, she mumbled some silent prayers and touched the coin with the tip of her tongue. Satisfied at last, she tucked the coin back inside her handbag. Again, she picked the phone confidently and dialed directly to the office of the P.A.

'Good morning Mr. Spendiser,' she greeted in a confident tone. Mr. Spencer's eyes narrowed at the other end when he recognized the caller.

'Good morning your majesty,' he greeted hesitantly. 'I believe there is progress, you found the god.'

'There is progress to some degree,' she replied soberly.

'Never mind, Your Majesty, this case is a very simple one. We'll soon find light at the end of the tunnel,' the P.A. said. There was a momentary silence over the line.

'Mr. Spendiser,' she called authoritatively. 'I will like to meet the Foreign Secretary.' Another moment of silence, and Mr. Spendiser flared in surprise rather than anger.

'But your majesty, I thought we've gotten over this. You don't need the Secretary about some missing god,' he said. Hanging the receiver between his neck and shoulder, he reached for a stick of cigar and lit it. The queen's mind flashed back to the spell. Mr. Spencer's reaction was contrary to expectation. All he was supposed to say was: *Yes Your Majesty, you can see the Secretary anytime you choose.* The queen was distraught and she let the man know that she was angry.

'Mr. Spendiser, I said I will like to meet the Foreign Secretary now,' she shouted.

'Madam…I mean Your Majesty, you should know that in as much as I do not have the right to question your wishes, it is my duty in this office to pass on messages of great importance across to the Secretary. In respect of this, I'll want us to work together on this issue and I don't think the Secretary need be bothered about a missing god,' he explained.

'Mr. Spendiser, we cannot work together because you're not up to the task,' she complained.

'There's no extraordinary task required in locating a missing person. This is Great Britain, Your Majesty,' the P.A. said.

'The key person that can locate the prince is currently in your jail, can you guarantee her release for this purpose? Are you up to the task, answer now?' the queen fired back.

Mr. Spencer swallowed loudly, crushing his cigar in an ash tray.

'I certainly cannot grant such an outrageous demand, not even the Prime Minister! This is a court decision you talking about, a judiciary system that dates back centuries.'

'Mr. Spendiser, I believe you're a very busy person, so am I and your Foreign Secretary. I don't want to waste any more time talking with you; In fact I'm fed up with talking to you. It either I meet your Foreign Secretary today or you forget about the relationship between Africa and your country. I hope my English is clearer,' she stressed.

'But you're not on official visit, Your Majesty,' the P.A. protested while he reached for the Secretary's itinerary on the other side of the table. 'O.K, I'll suggest we meet at Galaxy Foods at 1:00pm prompt. I will inform the hotel,' he said in a placating tone.

'*Alakora, o ma fi tie ko ba mii!*' The queen cursed as she replaced the receiver.

CHAPTER ELEVEN

The Queen ate her breakfast in haste, showered and then changed into a green and ash attire. She walked to the full-sized mirror, inspecting her elegant look. Pleased, she nodded approvingly. With luck, today might just be the day of re-union, she told herself. By 9:20am, she was at the reception. On her left she spotted George busy scrubbing the Rolls. When he saw her through the glass door, he quickened up and later came hurrying to announce his readiness. Within minutes, the Rolls Royce was slowly moving to their destination, the British maximum Prison.

It took them over thirty minutes to arrive at the giant gate of the prison. She no longer complained, and resisted boredom as she seemed accustomed to his slow drive. His occasional glances through the rear mirror were also less provocative. George silenced the engine in front of the gate and slipped out a piece of paper through the window to an officer in blue. The officer showed the paper to three other officers. The most senior officer took the paper and commented on it, then waved George inside the yard. The gate spread open before them without any visible aid. Amazing, the queen thought to herself.

The yard was a large one with various brick buildings and aluminium sheets. George halted the Rolls in front of a white building with the inscription, **B.M.P. Administrative Building.**

He got out at his usual slow pace and moved into the building. He did not come out until fifteen minutes later. He came to the side of the Rolls were the queen was seated, flanked by two officers. Cheerfully, he opened the door for her, doffing his hat slightly as she climbed out. George led her into the building, while the two officers trailed behind them.

Jane Wool sat quietly at the far end of a table. It was their favourite spot anytime Ifash visited her. As usual, there were handcuffs on her wrists and chains on her legs. She was anxious to see him after three long months of abandonment. She had thought seriously that, perhaps, he had fallen out of love and respect for her. Heaven knew she had felt totally neglected by his long absence. He was her only visitor. Although, he had advised her a couple of times to write home to her family in Wales and inform them of her predicament in London, but she had shoved away his advise on the grounds that they had never really been there for her all these years. What difference then would it make now that she was in jail. She did not want to attract their sympathy and gospel ideas.

Ifash agreed with her as he always did and never talked about it again. He had always respected the girl's views. To him, the girl was an intelligent, small town girl with big dreams but only lacking in the way she carried herself. That aside, she was everyman's dream, a lioness determined to break through the numerous obstacles of life, with or without anyone's assistance.

As Jane sat consumed in thought, a ticking sound from the wall clock snapped her back to reality. She became conscious of her surroundings again as if she had been deprived of her mind all along. Depressively, she perceived something strange in the prison's operations that day. The basic rule was that the prisoner never waited, it was the visitor that did the waiting.

It was also unusual to visit prisoners in the morning hours of Sundays when they should be preparing for the Church service. She glanced at the clock behind her; it was 9:30a.m. Suddenly, she felt a cold sensation and folded her arms tightly under her breasts. She noticed her breasts had grown smaller as she gazed down at them. Her bras no longer fit and the same weight shedding was taking place around her waist. Surely, her figure was fast shedding weight like trees shed off dry leaves. She cried softly. She had not completed a year and she was already a mess, she told herself. The thought of what she would look like in five years time forced the tears out of her eyes. Just then, the door at the far end opened.

She wiped off her tears at once and concentrated on the old man standing by the door. The man opened the door wider and a woman in wraps and flaps emerged. The man gestured politely to the woman to step inside and she did. When she got closer to where she was seated, Jane noticed her erect shadow. She raised her head and blinked rapidly hoping to gain a clearer vision.

The queen stood rooted to the spot and looking down disdainfully at Jane. 'Unbelievable,' she murmured. How could her son ever hang around with such, she pondered. Jane's blue uniform had faded with dirt and stench, and her short black hair looked brown and unkempt. She looked sick and deprived of essential nutrients. The queen took a deep breath; she was stung with a sense of guilt for having been unfair to the prince, for not having fought enough against the judgement of Ifa-Eledumare. She blamed herself for her negligence and believed she was solely responsible for the prince's association with the lowest class in the British society.

'Are you the person I'm meeting,' Jane broke the unpleasant silence between them. The woman standing like a tree trunk before her seemed to have a striking resemblance to someone she knew. The queen took a final look at her unkempt hair; then she drew up a seat and sat facing her.

'Yes,' replied the queen, her black eyes fixed upon Jane's. 'I am the one who wish to see you.'

George sat comfortably at the other end of the long table, playing with the car keys and pretending to show no concern in their conversation.

'O.K.,' Jane mumbled and sat back crossing her legs. 'So, who are you and what is your problem?' she demanded. The Queen hesitated, looking at her shrewdly.

'I am Queen Abekeofin Aina Tobiolah II of the Odua Kingdom. I was informed that you know the whereabouts of the Prince, the heir to the throne of the gods,' she said in a voice that carried authority.

'I dunno,' Jane said and shook her head. 'I don't know anyone like that, I don't know what you're talking about.'

'They said you see him more often than anyone else.'

'Well, I tell you what, you've been misled by whoever told you that.' Jane said and smiled cynically. 'I've never come in contact with a prince or an heir to the throne of God,' she stated staring into the queen's eyes. 'Did you say God or Angel, you mean Christ, right?' The elder woman's eyes were filled with unanswered questions but she remained silent.

'Okay,' Jane said raising her hands in the air. 'I think I now know why they sent you to me. Yes, it's true I've seen a couple of black Africans that wear dresses just like yours; but you see, none of them is an heir to the throne of God and none would ever be. It's not as if I am being unnecessarily pessimistic, inconsiderate or a racist, it's just that I'm pretty sure of what I'm saying. They can't make it to heavenly paradise.' Jane paused and took a quick look at the queen whose expression was unreadable. She decided immediately that she looked too serious for her liking. She wondered what was really bothering the woman. Did she think she was the answer to her problems in life? Did she really think she could help her out and she was just not cooperating?

'You know, majority of these guys are not spiritually inclined, they're full of filthy stinking habits that I personally feel are intolerable in the sight of God. Those habits alone cannot allow them a place in heaven not to mention sitting right on the throne of God. That sounds weird, I mean it's absurd, it just doesn't seem right,' she said and smiled at her own humour. She was hoping to steal more time and enjoy the fresh air in the hall not minding the unimpressive expression on her visitor's face.

'Have you checked out the joints in town? They've got their own joints. These joints could really get rough at times; you just need to see it yourself. Those guys are die-hard groovers, frustrated to the core. But the good news is that, they're all determined to make it at all cost. They adore marijuana and all kinds of toxic stuffs. I was told marijuana could really groove, but I'm yet to discover that myself, do you smoke? And, I must say they've got great African music and reggae calypsos that really touch the soul. In short, they're a very interesting bunch to hang around with, and fun to look at when happy and dancing. The cops don't dare think of trespassing their territories, they are like above the law. Because when it comes to brutality, they've got no match, and they are fierce with every dangerous weapon you can think of. So, I won't agree with anyone that says such lots will have access to the throne of God one day. I mean these are guys that possess every evil the mind could conjure, evils that lead straight to hell. And again…'

'Excuse me, young lady,' the queen interrupted frostily wondering if Jane was mentally stable. 'I did not come here to be lectured about the activities of black society in your country, do you hear me?'

'Yap,' Jane replied.

'Okay. You must also know that I am not in the habit of talking with prostitutes. My question to you is simple and direct, do you know the Prince or not?'

'Well, break time over,' Jane responded frowning. 'I guess it's the end of this conversation as I'm not really in the habit of talking with barbarian monsters.'

'What!' The queen shouted, stunned. 'You small girl, you call me a monster?' She stood abruptly and gave Jane a resounding slap on the face. Jane fell off her seat and landed on the floor.

'Who are you in the catalogue of humans to look into my eyes and address me like that,' she demanded. At that point, George rushed to the scene and tried to assist Jane to her feet, calming her down as he did so.

'Are you alright?' he asked.

'Yap, I guess I didn't expect that,' Jane said with her hands on her face.

'Please get me out of here before I do something you'll both regret,' Jane shouted.

'Take it easy and calm down, young lady. We are your friends, and not here to intimidate you,' George pleaded. 'You just spoke rudely to the queen and she was as upset as any other person would be. She just couldn't control her anger and the result was what you got. I'm sure she didn't mean it,' George said.

'What do you guys want from me? Are you also looking for a Princess?' Jane demanded with a hand still on her hurt cheek. George smiled into her face; his last daughter was probably her age. Gently, he sat on the chair Jane had previously occupied and asked leisurely.

'Miss Jane Wool, how are you today?'

'Terribly bad,' Jane replied sharply.

'This is Her Majesty, The Queen of Odua Kingdom, just as we have Queen of Wales, Queen of Edinburgh, Queen of York, and so on and so forth,' George stated. Jane nodded and passed a quick glance at the queen who sat stiffly away from them. Without another word from George, Jane stared at the queen and realized that there was really a striking thing about the woman before her. Though it seemed quite doubtful, she could now sensibly match the resemblance. Ifash was the only black person in her world and his mother died long ago during the war. The woman must be some next of kin, an elder sister, an aunt or a distant relative. But why come to the prison to look for someone walking freely on the streets; she hoped nothing was wrong with him.

'She's in Great Britain in search of her son, a Prince who's an heir to the throne of God. She needs your help to locate the Prince.'

A short silence followed.

'Now, do you know anyone by the name Lord Franklin Gordon?' he asked grimly rubbing his chin with a hand. Jane felt her pulse raised by the reality of her assumption.

Everything was coming together. She changed her expression to a frown before replying.

'Yes, he's dead. He died of heart attack many years back, so what?' she demanded.

'Good,' acknowledged George. 'You know every little detail. You know the woman and the Negro kid living at the ranch, don't you?'

'So?' Jane asked with a raised brow. 'Aunt Romana and Ifash,' she answered with a puzzled expression. Jane noticed that the queen took a deep breath when she mentioned the names. No doubt her knowledge of Ifash had brought the elderly woman some relief.

'Young lady, you know the Prince, Ifashanu Tobiolah II?' the queen asked eagerly. Jane shifted her gaze away from her and nodded at the wall clock. She could feel her temperature rising and she was shaking all over. She folded her arms under her breast and got hold of her system, not wanting to embarrass herself.

'Asshole,' she cursed under her breath. The bastard had been lying to her all along; he had lied about his mother, she told herself. She was depressed, fighting back a spasmodic shock that ran through her. Gradually, a thought struck her and her cold intensified. She came to the realization that there was really nothing between her and Ifash other than sex. Why should he care about things he told her, after all they were not lovers in the true sense of the word. He had the right to lie to her; he had every right to lie to a slut a thousand times.

'How old are you?' the queen interrupted her trance. Jane raised her head only to discover that she could no longer look at the woman straight in the eyes

'I'm twenty-five,' she replied flatly.

'What was the crime you committed, and they said you are a prostitute?'

'Murder was the crime that they charged me with.'

'Did you commit murder?' the queen asked, startled. The intensity of her voice made Jane stare at her curiously before replying.

'No, I'd never thought of killing anyone in my life. I stabbed a guy in self-defence and the Judge ruled that I committed involuntary murder.'

'What is your relationship with my son, the Prince?' the queen asked gently. Jane rattled for an answer, but her thinking cap let her down. She could not come up with an appropriate answer and she was numb. The queen's question had hit her like a tornado; she faked a frown, her eyes suddenly moist.

'Where can we find him?' the queen asked disregarding her mood.

'In his house in the country,' she said with fierceness and looking away.

'We checked, he's not been there for four months,' George offered.

'Then, I cannot tell you of a particular place,' Jane declared. 'You'll have to check him out in couple of joints in town, including the campuses.'

'You mean you can't direct us to a common joint?' George interjected.

'There is nothing like a common joint,' Jane stated matter-of-fact and shook her head. 'A joint is where they find themselves at a particular period, with the right stuffs,' she stressed. Through the corner of her eyes, Jane could see that permanent curl on the lips of the queen, a curl that expresses authority. Once again, she felt a shiver run through her body.

The queen stood, satisfied. She reached for her handbag and beckoned at George.

'I thank you for your cooperation young lady. I shall see you soon,' the queen mooted to Jane, as she walked briskly towards the door. George forced a polite smile and shook hands with Jane before scurrying after the queen. He got to the door before her and opened it ceremoniously.

* * *

They arrived at Galaxy restaurant at some minutes past twelve. An order was made for a light lunch of bacon with beans, and chilled French wine for George. While eating, the queen looked around the expensive parlor with adoration. In her opinion, Galaxy restaurant was another lavishly decorated British home for the rich and influential. She tried but failed to draw a comparison between the British way of life and that of Africans. The gap between the rich and the poor in Britain was as wide as the distance between Africa and Australia, she thought sadly.

Much later, after their table had been cleared, the queen spotted a figure entering through the rear door. It was Mr. Spencer in company of a man of average height in dark suit. Behind them was a lady in a Victorian outfit. They settled for a table at an obscure angle where foods and drinks were already served. As they took their lunch, the queen observed with irritation that they seemed more interested in the alcoholic drinks than the dishes. After a while, a waiter cleared their table, leaving the wines and fruits. Mr. Spencer guzzled his glass empty and leaned sideways, whispering to the man beside him. Mr. Spencer got to his feet and looked the restaurant over. George did not allow him to stray much; he raised a hand so that the P.A could see them. He noticed and came over to greet them warmly, before leading the queen to the Foreign Secretary's table.

The Secretary was a polite man. He stood to meet them halfway and shook hands with the queen, both exchanging pleasantries. As they walked back to his table he placed a friendly hand on her back, smiling. The Secretary introduced the lady with him as his new wife and offered the queen a seat.

'Please sit down, make yourself comfortable,' he said, adjusting the chair for her. At close range, the queen could see that the lady looked charming and she seemed fascinated by her aso oke attire. She made it obvious by her surreptitious glances at her. Mr. Spencer poured the queen a glass of wine, which she declined politely. The Secretary soon began to pass words of condolence to the queen on the loss of her late husband. He went further to compliment her attire and wondered how he would look in the same cloth. He praised the African culture and heritage and spoke well of his days on the African soil. Eventually, they drifted to the issue at hand.

The queen took the lead and began by carefully laying down her worries and interest. She laid emphasis on a temporary release of Miss Jane Wool to aid the search for the Prince, the heir to the throne of the gods. She concluded by expressing her confidence in the British royal family to solve her problems.

When it was the turn of the foreign secretary, he cleared his throat and began by recounting the huge benefits the British government and businessmen had derived over the years from late king Jajaha and how much his government and people cherished to continue the friendly relationship between the two kingdoms. He also stressed on law and order and respect to laid down constitution irrespective of ones stature in the society.

'I must let you know at this point that we hold with high regards our co-operative efforts and common interest for the good of the two kingdoms. In view of the fact that the subject concerned, Prince Ifash Jajaha Tobilah II, was raised and educated in Great Britain; and from all indications, he's about to step into his father's shoes. My government strongly believes this move will improve the chances for more open and direct trade between the two kingdoms. In that regards, my government is prepared in a very rare step, to revoke the sentence on Miss Jane Wool to allow perform a duty for her country in aid of locating the crown Prince of Odua Kingdom. It's however, our hope that this gesture will further cement the genuine interest and understanding between the two Kingdoms,' he concluded.

CHAPTER TWELVE

As Jane would recollect later on that fateful Monday in 1878, the inmates had woken up early as usual for the early morning roll call. The entire female prisoners gathered in the call room under the watchful eyes of the prison director, who stood with hands in his pockets between two smartly dressed men. The two men wore crisply starched shirt sleeves and trousers. They stood at a less illuminated area of the room near the director's office. The men did not make pretence of their malicious motive as they glued their eyes on her in a dreadful and mean manner. They stared at her as if they had received the final order for her immediate execution in the gas chamber.

Whenever Jane was under stress, she experienced cold shivers in her body and a feeling of uneasiness. In this situation, she tried desperately to hide away from her detractors, but she did not succeed. Their eyes followed her in every step she took.

After the final roll call had taken place without her, Jane became alerted. Her name had been skipped thrice in three different work distributions for the day. In a flash, she saw the director and the two men take their leave through the steel door. Only then did she feel less apprehensive. She ran to join her mates as they started to file back into the cells but a large hand drew her out of the line. Two warders towered over her and informed her that her papers had been processed for a transfer to the Liverpool prison.

'A transfer,' she cried, perplexed as she watched others marched inside. Her cellmate, Evelyn, looked back at the warders suspiciously; her expression filled with hatred. There had been reported cases of warders taking advantage of prisoners for sexual orgies.

The warders escorted Jane to the counter where she came face to face with the two men she had seen with the director and she was delivered to them. They flanked her on either side and ordered her to move, which she did. A red metallic Mercedes coupè was waiting for them. Jane was dazed with shock, seeing the shining sun glorying over the land. The hefty one with side burns got in behind the wheel, while the other with almost the same physic and clean shaven, ushered her into the back seat. He sat closely beside her and removed a black material from his pocket blindfolded her. Then she heard a match struck. They were going to set her ablaze, she thought fearfully.

'My Goodness!' she cried. 'Can you please tell me what's going on? Where are you taking me and why don't I have the right to see where we are going?' she demanded in terror. She held her breath for a few moments, trying to prevent the poisonous smell of custom-made tobacco from entering her lungs.

'Don't pull that garbage on us,' blasted the man beside her. 'And if you don't behave yourself and be a good girl, I'll be forced to smack your face with a backhand,' he threatened. His dreadful voice brought tears to her eyes and she stifled a cough, not wanting to test the temper of her captors. The smell of the customized tobacco overwhelmed her in spite of the fact that all her life she had been ever chilling, night clubbed, wild partied and did drugs; but somehow, she had remained allergic to this brand of nicotine. She pondered endlessly as to the motives of her captors. The warders said she was being transferred to Liverpool. Sitting in a luxury car did not seem the right way to transfer a murderer. She ought to be dangling in a rusty Black-Maria, she thought.

Unable to solve the puzzle, she remained calm all through the journey. After speeding for half an hour, the car stopped and they led her towards a building. As soon as they stepped inside, the one with the side-burns removed the blindfold. She was dazed; and glancing around the room she could not focus immediately. Her eyes had suffered greatly from the effect of the blindfold. She was in a large room with a wide staircase at the center. It was painted glossy white, with few interior décor here and there. The chairs were all covered with white sheets to keep away the dust. The floors were laid with marbles that shone so much that it could serve as a mirror. It looked too neat to be stepped on. Three covers were removed from the cushion and they sat on them. The guy with the side-burns cleared his throat unceremoniously.

'Do you know where you are?'

'How should I know when you blind folded me all the way? I don't know where I am and I don't know who you guys are? What do you want from me?' she demanded.

'Very well, we are glad you don't know a lot of things,' he said mildly, wiping his mouth with a hand. 'We are Secret Service,' he announced with a smile that was meant to be warm, but rather cold. Jane tried to ease the tension building up in her; she sat back attempting to read the expressions on the faces of the men who said they were secret agents.

'We are your friends,' affirmed the side burn agent. 'What is it that we have done that makes you feel so bitter and very unfriendly?' he asked factually. He slid a hand into the side of his suit and brought out an 1803 Niggetta pistol with a silencer. He motioned to the clean-shaven agent and he brought out his gun as well. They held their weapons in the air, aiming at her chest. Jane's blood overshot in seconds and she felt very dizzy. A cold sensation coursed through her spine and her throat turned dry. She wanted to curse God; instead she raised both hands and pleaded for her life.

'Please, I'll do anything you say! Please, don't kill me, I'll cooperate. I want to see my lawyer.'

The side burn agent gave her a broad smile.

'You didn't believe us when I said we are your friends. The rule is to disarm when an agent encounters a doubting Thomas like you,' he said feeling amused.

'We were simply trying to disarm and you took it as a threat,' his partner said. A grin split Jane's face as she saw the smile on their faces.

'You scared the living-shit out of me. I thought you guys are some kind of bandits with terrorist connections. Goodness! I almost…'

'We are pros,' the side burn interrupted her. 'Cool at rest and fierce in battle.' He looked at Jane proudly.

'Hmm, that's interesting,' she said, remembering her granny's warning never to trust guys that carried lethal weapons. She was desperate to discover what they wanted from her even as she decided to escape once she got the slightest chance.

'Listen carefully,' said the clean-shaved agent pointing upward. 'We've got people waiting upstairs for you. There are many rooms up there, the room labeled No.1 is your dressing room. Room 2 is designed for your medical check up. Room 3 is where you have a team of hair stylists waiting. Room 4 is for manicure and pedicure and body parts. Lastly, room 5 is where you'll find the day's costume. I must also let you know that you have no right to question me or anyone upstairs. You'll simply do as you're told. We don't want to get into battle. You have five hours at your disposal, and if I were you, I'll get moving,' he said with a mischievous grin.

Jane started slowly for the staircase. Her flustered mind melted into fear. She knew a transformation was about to take place and it certainly had little or nothing to do with the prison at Anfield. She climbed the steps stiffly, wondering if they were watching her. When she got upstairs, she discovered the truth. First, she took a long and cold shower. Afterwards, she put on a long brown robe and entered Room 2 where a robust female doctor examined every organ in her body. She stepped into the next room and she found three hair stylists wearing red linen uniforms. They retouched and prepared every fiber of her hair. In room 4, she was faced with a man who seemed to be suffering from thyrotoxicosis. He introduced himself as Cole, an expert in his field. Mr. Cole was a bore and he talked too much like a chatter box, but he was indeed an expert in his field. In the last room she found a costume designer, a woman in her early fifties. She presented Jane with a set of jewels, some lacy underwear and a black ankle-length silver stone dress that fit beautifully over her curves.

After dressing, she stood before a full-sized mirror. Marveled at her own reflection, she covered her mouth with both hands. She had been transformed to an epitome of beauty. She turned left and right to examine her sides. Delighted, she forgot everything about her current status as a state prisoner. So what's next, she thought with alarm. She reflected on all the events that has taken place in the past 48 hours. Perhaps, she was in a dream, a fairy tale. But then, if it were to be a dream, then it was certainly the dream of her life.

She checked her silver wrist watch, her time was up. As she hurried down the stairs, she hoped the dream would never end. Between the two agents, she preferred the one with the side burns. They could get rid of the burns much later. With him by her side, they would travel on a leisure trip to Hawaii and get married in Finland, the birth place of her mother. Then they would raise kids and live happily ever after.

* * *

The secret servicemen stood to meet her by the stairs. They hugged and shook hands with her in a new wave of respect.

'How do you feel now?' the agent with the side burns asked hoarsely.

'Never better,' she replied excitedly as they escorted her to the chair.

'You're no more in prison uniform,' said the clean shaven one.

'You're now a full civilian and your rights have been re-stored. You are free to ask any questions now. We will be obliged to answer. Have some sandwich,' said the side burns with a smile. He passed her the plate and a cup of iced-tea. Jane accepted it gladly and murmured her thanks. She bit hun-grily into the junk food and sipped her tea almost with the same intensity because she was starving.

'Goodness,' she mumbled, embarrassed by the way she ate. She could have eaten poison without wanting to know. Half-way through her meal, she summoned up courage to speak.

'You're sure you guys won't get upset if I ask any question, however silly it might sound.'

'We won't,' they replied, shaking their heads.

'Who are you guys and serious, serious, what do you want from me, no pranks?'

"We are who we said we are, S.S officials, Scotland Yard division. We've been instructed to restore you back to the sys-tem, freedom,' said the clean shaved. Jane froze at the word *freedom*. The sandwich stuck in her mouth and she reached for her tea and guzzled it. This could not be real, she thought dreadfully. She must be dead in some rubbish place. It must be her ghost negotiating freedom with dead secret agents, who in their days probably died of multiple bullet wounds in their brains.

'But with conditions,' the clean shaved said. She heard him from a distance and put down the tea.

'What condition?' she asked.

'That you'll fully cooperate with the queen and the prince respectively,' he said and studied her baffled expression. When she did not say a word he proceeded.

'And that you'll always put the British government in high consideration every step you take, at any moment and at any-where you are,' he said. Jane downed her tea.

'Is that all, is that the price?' she asked frostily.

'I believe that's all for now,' he said rubbing his chin with a hand.

'Delivering you safely at your next destination is where our duty ends,' chipped in the sideburn agent.

'Anfield?' Jane asked jokingly with her eyes popping out.

'No,' the agent said shaking his head in doubt.

'All we've been saying is nothing but the truth. It is a serious matter. We'll be delivering you at Hotel de Continental,' the clean shaven announced in flawless French.

'Her Majesty from the Odua kingdom is waiting to receive you,' sideburn said smiling.

* * *

Meanwhile, at the ballroom of the Continental Hotel, the queen dressed gorgeously in native attire was in a cheerful mood, honoring a lunch invitation effected by Sir Eastwood. When the Mercedes car got to the hotel, Jane was led to the reception by the agents. The female receptionist pointed out the queen's table. Earnestly, Jane shook hands with the agents. She was tempted to hug and kiss sideburn, but she managed to control herself. She took the direction pointed out by the receptionist, fighting her way against several stares, both seductive and innocent. Sir Eastwood was quick to notice her on reaching their table. In mid-discussion with the queen, the expression of the manager changed instantly. He wore an amazing expression on sighting Jane, and that made the queen to turn around. She barely recognized Jane.

'Good afternoon ma'am,' Jane greeted with a broad smile.

'It's you young lady. I almost couldn't recognize you again. Afternoon!' The queen responded and took in every detail of her person in one sweep. 'Now you look better. Have your seat and your share of the food,' she said with a nod of approval accompanied by a slight smile. Sir Eastwood drew a seat for Jane beside him, careful not to lose his sense of gentlemanliness.

'By the way,' said the queen, pushing away her beef soup with a feeling of satisfaction. 'This is Sir Yeastwood, the director of this luxury home.' Sir Eastwood nodded smiling at Jane.

'This is Jin Wull, an acquaintance of the Prince,' the queen announced and Jane extended a hand to shake him. Sir Eastwood filled a glass with French wine and shifted some fresh plates of foods to Jane's side.

'Eat,' the queen encouraged. Jane mumbled her thanks quietly and picked up a fork and a knife. She stared at the food and realized how much she had missed good food. Her appetite soon grew bigger. The aroma of the special dishes before her was not the type easily come across on the streets, let alone in prison. As she settled down to grub, her heart cried out, her whole being aroused. What she needed now than ever was to devour all the food on the table. She ate in silence and style.

The queen and Sir Eastwood were engrossed in discussions. By the time they were concluding their chat about black culture; Jane had cleared three plates clean, and was sipping the third glass of wine. Through the corner of her eyes, she noticed Sir Eastwood reach for his black suit and stepped aside with a slight bow.

'You will have to excuse me, Your Majesty,' he said.

'Thank you very much for the invitation,' the queen said.

'The pleasure is mine,' he responded. Sir Eastwood moved closer and shook hands with Jane before hustling ahead between clusters of chairs. Quickly, Jane put down her drink and stared at the queen for a while.

'Thanks for negotiating my release,' she said.

'Don't mention,' the queen said, brushing off her thanks with a wave of the hand.

'I hope you will help us locate the whereabouts of the Prince.'

'Yes ma'am, I'll do my best. I know some places of interest, his favourite spots.'

'Don't you think its better we start off on time?'

Jane took a final sip from her glass with her eyes still on the queen.

'If you're ready, I'm ready ma'am,' she said, deciding there was something she liked about the queen. It must be the royal stuff, she told herself. She had sparks in her eyes, in her speeches and her steps; and she looked totally in control of her world.

'Alright then,' the queen said and dabbed her mouth with a tissue paper as she reached for her handbag. 'I am ready, can we go?'

The two women walked out of the restaurant. At the reception they waited for George to bring the car. The queen sat in the back while Jane sat beside George; and the search began on a cheerfully good note.

CHAPTER THIRTEEN

At midnight when Londoners were fast asleep, an event was unfolding in the world of spirits. In their world, it was a sunny afternoon, yet the sky looked dark, misty and cloudy in readiness for a heavy downpour. Moments later, the earthling saw a shadow upon the misty cloud and gradually the shadow developed wings, a sort of human form. By the minutes, it became clearer as the shadow took the form of three angels displaying their flying prowess high above the earth. Their wings stretched a long infinite distance beyond the range of the eyes. The earthlings were stunned by their vision; they concentrated their gaze towards the sky. Some were amused, but a majority looked on in total dismay.

Those who heard the news and abided faithfully therein appeared distinguished, there was no fear, anguish, or sorrow in their eyes. The dubious of men were dashing about in absolute confusion, seeking shelter away from the shield of the angels' wings. Suddenly, like a flash of lightening, the angels took a sharp dive towards the earth and everyone ran for cover. In midair, they disappeared; gone, transformed into three flying saucers.

The fast revolving saucers were emitting rays of infra-red lights towards the beast in the forest. The light rays were shooting out like bombastic missiles. Anywhere they touched, they caused huge blasts. The animals in human forms, ranging from lions, zebras, chimpanzees, bulls, and snakes were hurrying in desperation into the thick forest.

Then again, all of a sudden, the saucers took a sharp dive like the angels. Half way, they were gone, transformed into three flying eagles. The three green eagles were flying stylishly above the sea with large wings and piercing eye-balls. In a flying moment, two of the eagles ascended while the one in the middle descended, increasing its pace steadily as it went down. With intent, her eagle eyes screened the fishes underneath the rippling sea. Target focused, she descended very sharply. And just when it looked very certain that she was going to crash into the water, she swerved using her claws to graze the sea surface. A fish swam into her claws; she held it firm and began to ascend squeezing the fish between her claws. She was probably aiming to crush the bones of the fish and devour it in the air, judging by her steady grip. She held firm and squeezed hard, and harder. But with every hard squeeze, a voice cried painfully in the world of the living.

'Noooo!' Ifash screamed out his heart, returning to reality in a flash. He held his neck like someone suffering from diphtheria meningitis. It was as if the eagle claws were physically curled around his neck. Quickly, he knelt, wiped the sweat on his face with the tail of his shirt and hurried out of his tent. He had no belongings except for a small bottle of gin which he plucked and dashed into the night aimlessly, looking behind him like a man pursued by ghosts.

* * *

The drive in and around town was tiring, far beyond the queen's expectations. George had to show more of his driving skills as he swerved the Rolls from side to side on narrow bumpy gravel roads that led into the black community residences. They had stopped over at six different places. Each place had its own name. The queen had memorized names like Black cat, Jazz 38, Dove and Redemption. Their next point of stoppage would be in Sussex, outskirt of London. The joint they would be visiting was tagged *Angolae.*

The peculiar thing about all the joints they had seen was that through it all, she had experienced a complete pathetic need as to the plight of blacks living in Britain. The so-called joints and the residential areas they had seen so far exposed the extent of poverty and social discrimination against black immigrants and slaves, whom out of frustration and hopelessness formed what she considered a joint of self-destruction by simply setting-out outlets where immorality had become the order of their everyday lives.

It was already sun-set when they drove into Angolae. As usual, she could hear loud musical instruments oozing from the back-ground. George halted the Rolls more than ten blocks away from the centre of action. When Jane saw how tired the queen was through the rear mirror, she offered to scout the arena alone. She stepped out gallantly into the luminous night. She was confident she would not stray much because she knew Ifash's favorite spots in every joint. With wariness, she thought of her gold bangles, the diamond necklace, and her style of dressing. This was not the kind of appearance expected at a jive. It was her lucky day, she told herself, but she must be extra careful not to push her luck too far. As it was a little chilly, she dragged herself along cautiously between dancing groups. She tried to be articulate and precise in her sense of direction. She did not want to start getting advances from the big drinkers.

Meanwhile, unknown to Jane, the Queen was walking right behind her a few paces away. The view around Angolae was stunning unlike other joints, thought the Queen. Looking beyond Jane, she could make-out the far lights at the end of the street, where young men and ladies gathered dancing almost naked. The ladies wore simple bras and bikinis, and the men danced bare-chested in short pants.

'Immorality of the first order,' she hissed. There were camp fires stationed in most corners, emitting black dangerous smoke that filled the night and the air with heat, rather than natural cool breeze. The queen stopped suddenly, realizing she had unconsciously drawn attention to herself. She looked around slowly assessing and trying to dismiss unfriendly eyes; so she coughed a couple of times as she progressed. The entire length of the street appeared highly polluted and she felt a cold sensation as the wind whipped aggressively against her face.

The big Conga drums, tambourines, and trumpets reverberated deep into her ears. She felt oppressed, intimidated and dishonoured as she walked into the smoky night. However, when Jane got to Ifash's favourite spot, he was not there. She immediately turned to her right, surging deep with urgency. She was getting closer to the end of the street when her eyes caught a figure not far from a lanky conga drummer. She had noticed the figure before turning right, but because she could not imagine Ifash in dingy baggy shorts, open sleeveless shirt, and a shaggy dark hair. She had simply allowed her eyes to pass over the figure. In what seemed a glimmer of hope, she looked sideways as she approached him. The closer she got, the more convinced she was.

Ifash was sitting on the roadside near a gutter, his back resting against an electric pole. He held a roll of marijuana in one hand and whiskey in the other. He did not notice her presence or anyone for that matter; he was in the world of his own. Jane stood towering over him with folded arms. She did not realize that the queen was steps behind her.

'Is that him?' the queen asked and Jane turned around in surprise.

'Ma'am,' she stuttered. 'I thought...'

'Is that him?' the queen repeated moving closer to Jane and holding her hand for support. For her, the sight was disheartening and catastrophic; she nearly fainted. Jane held her steady with a hand around her waist. She did not know what to do or what to say to comfort her. She wanted desperately to re-assure her, to say something soothing.

'That's Ifash,' she said.

Looking down at her son, the queen's heart raced as if it was going to burst out through the ribs. A long silence followed, the Conga drums had ceased, only the cracking of blazing drum fire could be heard. All eyes were on them. It was the sudden silence that probably made Ifash to raise his head. He needed to find out the reason why all was suddenly quiet. An erect structure stood in his view and he could not focus on anything. His eyes were burning from too much alcohol and he blinked intermittently, trying hard to fix them on the right image. He was unsure of the picture his eyes were bringing to his brain.

He tried looking more closely and then grinned. He cocked his head and spoke in calm tone.

'Who are you?' he asked and put the marijuana in his mouth. He took a long drag from it and savored it. Jane moved two steps closer, beaming.

'Forgotten me so fast?' she asked, looking bemused and raising a finger in mid-air. 'Remember the one that gives you unmatched pleasure.'

'Hmm,' Ifash sighed and opened his mouth comically. 'Whose daughter are you in this land and what can I do for you? My friends call me black hawk,' he said offering his hand to Jane. It hung in the air for a few seconds before it dropped. Jane had never placed Ifash as a heavy drinker and wondered how many more bad habits he must have added to his personality since she had been gone. He attempted standing on his feet but fell back half way, dropping the whiskey in the process. The bottle broke noisily, spilling its content on the ground. He smiled sourly and glared at the marijuana between his fingers as if blaming it for his fall. He threw it on the concrete ground and stamped on it with the sole of his feet.

Again he tried standing and succeeded this time with his back resting on the pole. He steadied his eyes intently on Jane, and his mouth dropped open as recognition dawned on his foggy mind. Jane smiled and held herself from laughing.

'Jane,' Ifash called in muted voice. 'Wasted,' he whispered and stretched his hands towards her. He felt her face with his fingers, feeling her eyes, nose and ear; then his hands moved slowly to her shoulders and he nudged her to shake off the ghost. Jane looked up at him and gave him a triumphant smile, one that could crack the Nuba Mountain or simply split the Nile into two halves. His attention shifted to her dress, the gold and the diamond; and he touched her everywhere he could lay his hands on. He knew he was not under the total control of marijuana. It was his second wrap of the day; the third and forth might knock you out and jingle your brain. For a final assurance, he drew her into his arms and kissed her.

Like a storm, he felt the wetness of her lips, her flesh, the passion, and the need to want to go all the way. The conga drums came alive the moment their lips touched. Jane felt her nerves rattled and her eyes heavy as their lips parted. Ifash's shirt reeked with sweat and he tasted of alcohol. She swallowed, moving a step away.

The queen looked on amazed at their public display of passion. She felt a sudden flush of embarrassment, but recovered quickly. Wondering what he would look like when he was not drunk, she saw a tall and very powerful looking man, very much like his father, neatly dressed and culturally conscious of his roots. She resisted the urge to reach out and embrace him.

Ifash gently pulled Jane aside. He had been staring at the woman behind her. He yawned and let out a stench of alcohol and rubbed his face with a hand. Again, he stared intently at the woman and found it strange that she did not flinch.

'Got them from Africa?' he asked huskily. The queen's face curled into a smile, she was on the verge of replying when Jane interceded.

'Ifash, that's the queen of Odua Kingdom in Africa; and your mum I assume,' she announced unceremoniously. Ifash passed a hand over his hair, trying to make some sense out of the whole event around him. He moved closer to the woman and nudged her with the index finger. The Queen was flustered in embarrassment and indignation, holding on to the belief that he was drunk and did not know what he was doing. But her inner mind told her something different though.

'You're from Africa?' Ifash asked without malice.

The Queen nodded.

'And Jane said you're, our mum, a Queen sort of? Is that right?' he asked and offered his hand to the queen while regarding Jane.

'Yes Ifashanu Abedi Deng,' the queen confirmed. 'I am your mother, the queen of Odua, like Jin said.' The tears were in her eyes, though she tried to hold them back. She waited for the earth to quake with her heart in her mouth. She imagined the cloud splitting asunder.

'I remember Pa Gordon told me I'm a Prince, from the Atlantic Ocean. Is that right, I am a Prince from the Atlantic?' The queen could only nod, looking downcast. She reached for her handkerchief in her hand bag and wiped her tears. She had a strong desire to hug him. Ifash was however a step ahead of her and opened his arms to her in a warm embrace.

'I knew you'll come back for me one day to say hi, and I've waited so long,' he whispered. 'And I know Pa Gordon was right, he's always right.' The Queen sobbed profusely in his arms. Everyone left them alone, including Jane.

* * *

The return ride to the hotel was done in grave silence and emotion. George maintained minimal speed and occasionally stole glances at mother and child. Ifash pivoted his jaw with a hand, so that he could view the road that had been beautified with glowing street lamps since the conservatives took over. Looking through the glass also enabled him to hide the painful look on his face.

The Queen on the other hand was consumed by guilt as she gazed ahead through the windscreen. Unlike Ifash, she saw nothing. Her thought went back twenty-eight years before when her child was handed over to the Ashanti horsemen, and the agony that followed afterwards. In no time, the tears rolled down her cheeks like a dam and she replaced soaked tissues one after another. Her feeling was a mixture of joy and regret.

For Jane, she sat with crossed legs, curled up as if wanting to melt through the glass of the window. A part of her hair fell over her shoulders on one side and the other side seemed well bound behind her. She could imagine the tension diffusing behind her. At a point, her mind drifted to the day she met Ifash at Cambridge. She felt glad for the turn that is about to take place in his life. She remembered their first night together in summer. They were at the ranch taking a rushed dinner courtesy of Aunt Romana. After dinner, he had reached across the table and kissed her.

At first, she had resisted the pressure of his lips on hers, but because he proved good in what he was doing with his lips, he succeeded in maneuvering his tongue to every part of her body, tickling her around the inner lining of her armpit. She responded eagerly to his exploration and they made love on the long cushion for the first time.

CHAPTER FOURTEEN

George halted the Rolls at the hotel lawn and hurried out of his seat to open the back door for the queen. He doffed his hat and bowed slightly as she stepped out. Ifash noticed the action of the elderly Brit and was taken aback. He felt a strange sensation of inexpressible shock at seeing a white man treat a black person with such degree of respect and adoration, like she was the Queen of England. Nevertheless, he had lived long enough to know that in spite of the respect or kindness a white man showed you, there was always that sense of apprehension in you.

Ifash stepped out of the car, placing a hand on the opened door. He was faced by a magnificent tower. His eyes quickly sized up the hotel he had always known but never got near. He heard as Jane slammed the door on her side, the queen was already advancing towards some countless sliding glasses, obviously the entrance. Ifash examined the building thoroughly and wondered what life would be like inside the Continental compared to Foray's Island, the ghetto where he had been living for the past four months.

They were met at the reception by Sir Eastwood, wearing a black tuxedo. He held out a hand to the queen.

'We are most glad you found the prince without much stress,' he said smiling while he shook hands with Jane and Ifash. He held Ifash's hand a little longer and looked directly into his eyes as if he knew him from somewhere in the past.

'You know, its one thing to have a mother, it's another thing to have a mother that cares, you've got both,' he husked into Ifash's hardened face. Satisfied, he turned to the queen.

'Your Majesty, we are having a special dinner arranged in your honour, and of course the Prince,' he said and glanced at Ifash who paid no attention to him. He engaged himself examining the large ballroom and its occupants. The people he saw belong to the elite class of the kingdom. The last time he was under the same roof with such persons was far back when Lord Franklin was around. He felt Jane's hand pressed against his, puncturing his trance.

'Will you pay some attention and stop looking vexed,' she whispered to him. Ifash leaned toward her so she could catch his response.

'Vex has been part of me ever since you went behind bars; just can't help it anymore,' he said. 'By the way, I've a question to ask you later; please, remind me of it,' he said turning around to face Sir Eastwood who seemed engrossed in conversation with the queen.

Stunned, Ifash had not realised how short Sir Eastwood was at first and how unfitting the black tuxedo looked on him. The only civilized thing about him was his expensive Rolex wristwatch and his black Giorgio Brutini. When Sir Eastwood caught Ifash staring at him, he flashed a smile at him without breaking his conversation with the queen. Out of sheer politeness, Ifash returned the smile.

'Prince of Odua,' the director called. 'You must be very tired, you've made that clear from the way you've been moping at everything and everyone around this complex. So Prince, we have prepared Room 009 for you. Everything you may need is in there, and the attendants are at your service anytime for anything. Miss Wool, your room is 006. Everything you may need is also there,' he concluded. On a signal, attendants materialized from nowhere and whisked Ifash and Jane away to their rooms leaving the director and the queen in the lobby.

With Ifash and Jane out of sight, Sir Edwin led the queen by the hand into the ball room.

'It will be irksome to dine without you on such a marvellous day of re-union. We have some special guest around tonight willing eager to meet you, Your Majesty,' he said.

'Who?' the queen asked, puzzled.

'Oh, they are friends of Africa; mostly politicians, successful captains of industries and business entrepreneurs, members of the royal family, great scientists of our time, the bishop and others like myself,' he said smiling lecherously at his last word.

The queen responded with a sigh. She had good reasons to be grateful to Sir Edwin Eastwood for all his care and goodwill. Still, this night of all nights, and this moment of all moments, she wants for herself, she told herself. She was not interested in any of his fancy arrangements. Her mind was fixed with the thought of her newly found child and indeed, the only person she wanted to be with at the moment. They needed to talk tonight. She had to strategise a way to explain to him the purpose of her visit to Britain. She had to impress upon him that if he was willing to return home with her, that they must leave early enough before the new yam festival in few months time. For now her greatest task remained unattended, that is, to find out if he would be willing to leave a kingdom with vulgar displays of wealth for a new life in a low profile environment.

* * *

Much later at the dinner table, the queen sat sipping her juice in the company of Sir Edwin. She swept her eyes over the ball room and decided it looked more beautiful that night, perhaps because of the special guest in attendance. There was a small podium at the centre and an all white band, *The Dearest* entertained the guest. Sir Edwin had prevailed and they had shaken hands with almost all the guests present before gracefully taking their seats. She was introduced to five members of the British House of Commons, two army Generals, and a Field Marshal. Also present were four members of the Royal family, a Physicist and a Biochemist.

Lastly, she met the bishop who discussed missionary interests in Odua Kingdom. He assured her that God would bless her for it should she welcome them into her territory. The queen was unable to give the holy man the green light he desperately needed as she was not in Britain for religious matters, and she knew absolutely nothing about the white man's God.

There were also a couple of interesting businessmen there. They jointly expressed their plans to create a channel for cocoa exportation from West Africa to Europe. There was no mention of the slave trade due to the recent civil unrest in America. At the end of one hour, she felt very exhausted. The table where she sat with Sir Edwin was a large one, too large for four or even six people. It was spherical in shape which enabled conversation without a speaker having to raise his voice. On the table were assorted dishes, vegetables, fruits and all sorts of drinks. No matter how much they consumed, she knew they would never be able to finish half of what was on the table. It was a table set for about twenty able-bodied men.

Sir Edwin busied himself with the service attendants who cut the roasted turkey and long meat into small pieces. Halfway through her drink, the queen caught a figure enter her field of vision. She then realized that other guests had noticed the approaching figure long before she did. Ifash dressed in a black tuxedo suit was heading towards them. His hair had been cut and the sideburns had disappeared. He was dressed in such a way that everything about him was black from head to toe. He looked much younger and handsome. The queen did not immediately notice Jane behind her son. She wore a red dress done up in stretch denim that reaches her ankles and showed off her curves. She looked gorgeous and very attractive to all who saw her.

The queen wondered if there was anything special between her and the prince other than sex. She hoped not, as it would be a taboo for a prince. Sir Eastwood met Ifash and Jane and led them to their seats.

'You both look highly refreshed,' he remarked taking the lead by serving himself. Two service attendants came over with more plates and bowls of fruits. They unloaded their trays and opened the stew bowl that was steaming. Everyone took turns to fill his plate. The queen took more shrimps and pork chop, while the prince concentrated on salmon with basil mayonnaise and vegetable tian. As much as they enjoyed their meal, Ifash and Jane only managed to speak with their eyes. They exchanged glances that left the queen without doubt that there was a bond between the duo.

However, she remained calm all through. She was confident that to destroy such unholy bond was an easy task for the *Osun*, the river goddess.

After a delicious meal, the foursome sat relaxed dabbing their mouths and hands with napkins; there was feeling of satisfaction on their faces. One of the service attendants delivered a bottle of champagne. As he placed it gently on the table, he bent and whispered to Sir Eastwood.

'From Lord Ferguson to Her Majesty,' he said and swiftly turned away. Sir Eastwood grinned at the champagne like a child presented with a Kalashnikov toy. More attendants appeared and cleared the table replacing the used napkins with fresh ones.

'Your Majesty, this is for you,' Sir Edwin announced and placed the champagne before the queen. 'It's from Lord Ferguson who you spoke with some minutes ago. That's him over there; at the extreme, the one with the white suit.' The director pointed out the man and the queen followed with her eyes the direction of his hand. She saw an elderly man in immaculate white attire who was laughing whole-heartedly with a lady probably a quarter of his age.

'Please thank him for me, I appreciate his kind gesture,' said the queen. Sir Edwin grinned, opened the bottle and filled everyone's glass with the chilled champagne. The queen took the first sip and did not like the taste. She pushed the glass aside and poured herself some lemon. Others sipped happily from their glasses. At that point the band, *Dearest* concluded a tune and was greeted with a big applause. Ifash joined subconsciously in the applause. He never understood what fascinated the white folks about the band. They had become the talk of the town and every recording company's favourites. However, they had no black fan base as far as he knew, because the blacks in the ghettos despised them with passion. They saw them as some fortunate kids with low musical talents.

The *Dearest* were still in sight when another musical group took the podium. This time it was led by a black guitarist whom Ifash recognised immediately as Jarvis Senior from Detroit America. The Americans call him the father of blues. He had arrived London four days before for a fund raising ceremony geared towards the eradication of sickle cell disease in the black community. Ifash took a quick glance at the queen. Her face was expressionless and she was wrapped in conversation with the manager. Definitely, the man on the podium meant nothing to her, he concluded. He took a quick sip of his champagne and turned to Jane. She looked lonely, toying with the rim of her glass. He had never seen her as gorgeous as she looked tonight. She probably had never seen him looking so bright as well. The overall effect was a balance mutual surprise, a surprise that has drawn them much closer in the past few hours, just like true lovers.

'Can I make a wish,' he whispered into her ear.

'It's your world,' she murmured and smiled sweetly at him.

'Alright then, like old time, would you mind stepping on the floor?' he asked softly.

'Not at all,' Jane responded.

'A moment please, mother,' he said, unable to read the expression on his mother's face. It seemed she wanted to say something but he turned away quickly towards the dance floor.

The legendary Jarvis Senior saw them as they approached and raised both hands in the air. When he brought down his hands, the melody changed from **Dancing in the Rain** to **Lovers Magic**. Ifash circled his arms around Jane's waist and she placed hers tenderly on his broad shoulders. They were locked together body and soul, swaying gently to the rhythm of love.

BASH BAKR

Many eyes followed them in their dancing, some in shock, and others in admiration. When the track finally came to an end, successive rounds of applause greeted them till they reached their seats.

CHAPTER FIFTEEN

Hours later, the ball room looked deserted; all the guests were virtually gone. It was approaching midnight and Ifash and the queen were finally alone. Sir Eastwood and Jane could be seen socializing with some of the remaining guests at the far end of the room. Ifash reached for a bottle of French wine, studied it warily and chuckled while he refilled his glass. The queen maintained an unlikely interest in her glass of grape juice. Her eyes were sparkling in anticipation of what to say and how to start.

'How's life in Britain?' she asked breaking the silence. Ifash licked his lips regrettably and the muscles around his jaw tightened.

'We're doing whatever it takes to make ends meet. The Brits are racist though; they are immoral and ruthless. I heard the Spaniards are worse, not to mention the Germans,' he said with a feeling of disgust. He looked up and noticed the bewildered face of the queen.

'Why are you looking like that, something I said?' he asked. The surprise was evident in his tone.

'How could you speak so harshly of these nice people? Isn't that tantamount to biting the fingers that fed you all these years?' she answered.

'They fed me with trash,' he said brusquely, putting down his drink. 'I'm going to be 28, born and bred here. What I just said is the bitter truth; I guess I can say I know them better than you do.'

'Ifashanu,' the queen called softly in a voice that seemed to come from afar. 'You have to know from now onward that you are not from Britain. Contrary to what you think, you have your own kingdom where you belong, the home of your ancestors.'

Ifash downed the remaining wine, poured another glass full and tore at the turkey. Then he sat back, relaxed in preparation for the conversation he had long awaited. He felt his heart pounding in his chest and the sweat on his face.

'Who am I?' he asked.

'You're my son, the crown prince of Odua. Sovereign by right of primogeniture and ancestral succession, of which no person, or group, or culture, may alter your right and authority; for you're not selected by men but by the gods of your ancestors,' the queen said.

Ifash felt the adrenaline in his veins as he listened to the queen. A defiant light flared in his eyes and he saw the signs of tension etched on the woman's face.

'Go on,' he said.

'We named you Ifashanu Deng-Abedi-Tobiolah II.'

'All these names?' he enquired with a smile.

'Your father, King Jajaha Kakah Tobiolah II, was a great man; a great King. His impetuous personality dominated the turbulent events that lifted the strength and integrity of our kingdom till date,' the queen said. 'Your father had five wives and nine legitimate children. I'm his first wife and I had two sons, yourself and your elder brother. The other wives gave him only daughters. Your elder brother Dada is deceased; he was married to Princess Ejide, the eldest daughter of Timi. They were blessed with two lovely children. We were all shocked by their sudden demise. They died along with many people on a voyage to the United States. Your father was a close associate of numerous slave dealers in Europe. In his dealings, he had a special preference for the British. Unlike you, he was fascinated by their simple lifestyle, innovation, strength and deep sense of humor. Your father had great respect for the whites and it has always been his wish that one of his children should have their type of education and understanding. So, it did not come as a surprise when the gods of our land chose you in response to your father's wish.' The queen paused and considered the lies she had rehearsed and fed to her prince; she decided it would serve for now.

'So, the gods are to blame for my miserable life. These gods hate me so much they had to throw me into a net for sharks. Why not someone else, why me,' he asked shaking his head in despair.

'Don't talk like that, the gods don't hate you. Far from it,' the queen said and reached out to touch his hand. 'In Africa, the home of your ancestors, we were brought up to respect the wishes of the gods, because their decisions are for the betterment of our community. The gods know the past and they can tell the future. We live happily today because of their favors to us, and also...'

'Mother, pardon me for interrupting you. There is something I'd like to understand before you go further. 'Which is which, I have heard about the God of the Jews, the Chinese, the Indians, and the Arabs. Is there anything like God of Africa?'

'Yes of course,' she replied promptly. 'You sound like a small boy. Indeed you're small. We do not follow the whites. We have our own ways of life which is deeply rooted in our historical heritage; that you will understand much later. We are the most cultured of all the creations of Eledumare,' the queen said.

'I see, that's cool,' Ifash said and nodded.

'In fact, you remind me of something. I met the bishop a few hours ago and he spoke about missionary works on our territories. My mind was so occupied I could not make him understand that our people have obdurate hearts against the white gods,' the queen said.

Ifash looked at the queen with a deep frown on his face.

'You met a bishop. Well, I don't think it's in your best interest to agree to any missionary work that will in the future bring a sort of confusion and disability to your kingdom. In this part of the world, I've seen quite a lot of bloody hypocrites that turned the gospel upside down. Be careful ma'am, don't be fed with grandiloquent tales of myth and legend,' he warned. The queen noticed the look of sheer vexation that crossed his face as he spoke.

'Your brother Prince Dada fought the imperialist all his life, not by violence though, by trade and regulations,' she said. Ifash looked on with interest and noticed the cynical smile on his mother's lips. He sipped his wine and smiled back at her. The queen was staring at him critically trying to visualize him as the king of kings he would soon become. She was convinced his reign would be very prosperous. To her, he looked like that type of king who would love initiatives because he was gentle by nature and principled in thoughts. He was kind and had a grand education in addition. It was clear in his actions that he hated injustice and hostility.

'If you're bored ma'am, why don't you take some rest, we'll talk tomorrow,' Ifash said.

'Not at all, my heart is filled with joy, inexpressible joy,' the queen said.

'The feeling's mutual,' he said and regarded her with a shy smile.

'How is trade in general in Britain, cocoa trade to be precise?' the queen enquired.

'Trade? To trade with a musungu? Are they honest, trading with shylock? Really, I know nothing about trading.'

'Who are these musungu?' the Queen asked curiously.

'It's nothing special; it's just a slang we use for the white brothers in the ghetto. They call us nigger, what do you call them back in Africa?'

'In your paternal tribe, they call them *eniyan fun-fun* and in my mother's tribe, we call them *Khawaja*. *Khawaja* is derived from the word trouble,' she affirmed.

'So those early men, your people, were quite wise to have known that white men are trouble makers. I'm surprised,' he stressed.

'Well, that is because they didn't understand them at that time and they didn't understand their mission to our continent. You know some still strongly believe that the white men are solely responsible for the chaos in Africa.'

'They must be, it's absolutely correct to think so. They are all over there as we speak now, setting-up colonies,' Ifash said angrily.

'It's not so,' the queen said. A man should take responsibility for his successes and failures in life. You don't blame it on others, it takes two to tangle.'

'Alright, I'll keep that in mind. Is it true that there is war all over Africa for self independence? We heard that people die every hour from wars, hunger and diseases. That you're uncivilized, living in forest and caves.'

'Ifashanu,' the queen called. 'War can break out anywhere around the world and at anytime. Africa is no exception. And a point of serious correction, we don't live in the forest. Civilization means different things to different people; our culture and tradition are our pride and civilization.'

Ifash nodded in understanding and took in the queen's elegant native attire. What he admired most about her was her short and intelligent answers to every question. He was glad the wine had made him more confident to look straight into her eyes and think clearly. He was not up to it some minutes ago because her eyes shone like the blazing sun.

'Can I smoke?' he asked and removed a fresh tobacco from the case lying on the table. He lit it and dragged deeply from it.

'Sir Yistwool told me yesterday that there are some terrorist groups operating in the North eastern part of this kingdom and that they are waging a destructive attack on the central authority. Tell me, how serious it is and how has it been affecting the people?' the queen asked with obvious concern, adjusting her head gear and feeling relaxed for the first time since their re-union. She was determined to make the best use of the night in knowing her son and assessing his intellect.

'These people are incredibly self-centered. You don't have to believe what a musungu wants you to believe. The stone that a builder refuses shall be the heck of stones. Guerilla warfare is one of the most deadly and destructive kinds of resistance known to man. Sir Eastwood didn't tell you the whole truth about what is happening in the North-Eastern part,' Ifash said and looked around as if about to unleash a coup plan no one should hear.

'There are different kinds of war. When an attacking group is headed by an individual who was once in a country's regular army, the persons are called mutineers. If again the head of an attacking group was once a politician who opted out and decided to attack the ruling party, such attack could be tagged a revolution. Another type is when a group is headed by a radical; such attack is termed a rebellion. Lastly, if an attacking group is headed by a renowned criminal, such group could be classified as terrorists. This brings us back to the group Sir Eastwood referred to as terrorist. The simple truth is that, this attacking group from the North-Eastern part falls under revolution. What is truly going on up in the North-East is an uprising, a revolutionary resistance demanding equal rights and freedom. They are not terrorists in any sense of the word. Whatever impacts their attacks have had on the government, the ordinary people for now are not aware of them,' he concluded, downing the remaining wine in a single gulp. The queen considered what she had just heard and smiled.

'The structure of life is mystified in the unknown. You're a pole of wisdom and you sound very much like your father. It's your father's attitude to lay down facts the way it should be. He despised referring to what is blue as red; he was a straight-forward man,' she said smiling proudly. For a moment, she gazed speculatively at her long lost child. For nearly twenty-eight years, he had filled her imagination with despair and grief.

'Your people sent me to you,' she said and immediately felt her utterance was a betrayal. Ifash flicked the ash from his tobacco with a finger and took a long drag from it. The queen coughed deeply. As the smoke diffused in the air, she reached for a glass of water. Ifash looked worried.

'Are you okay, ma'am?' he asked and hastily refilled another glass for her.

'Poisonous atmosphere,' she lamented.

'Are you referring to my tobacco?' Ifash asked, alarmed. The queen did not respond to his enquiry; instead, she continued the explanation of her mission.

'Your people need you back home. My mission here is to bring you back safe and sound,' she stated.

'Excuse me,' he said emphatically and brought his face close to the queen's. 'If I think of the hatred and irritation I feel, the injustice, bondage and negligence you and your husband subjected me to all these painful years, then I must surely render your mission impossible,' Ifash said and sat back with a hard expression on his face.

The queen felt embittered. She should have seen it coming, and she silently wished she had heard him incorrectly.

'I don't mean to sound ungrateful for the education and experience you gave me. What bothers me is if it was by accident or design that you came looking for me after all these years?' Ifash complained.

The queen's heartbeat accelerated when she heard these words. The truth was crystal clear. If Prince Dada had lived, she definitely would not have searched out Ifash. She felt she deserved worse humiliation than she was getting. Ifash looked away to the adjacent table where an old man was chatting childishly with his teenage son. He wondered idly how the boy could remain awake at that odd hour. Rubbing his face with a hand, he turned back to the queen. For a moment, they regarded each other eye calmly.

'The event of the past is gone with the past, I'm not the type who likes dredging up the past,' Ifash said expressionlessly. 'I should not give you the impression that I'm someone who is unfeeling and callous, who sees himself as very important. I must let you know that I find it absolutely difficult to deny you as my mother, because when I look into your eyes, I see myself. The resemblance is striking. And I know you've suffered enough as a mother in one life time, especially watching the people you love die one after the other, including your grand children. It won't make me happy to refuse you; no gain to make you sad the more and foster your grief. Your happiness is what I should desire at this stage, and of course mine too. I will do my best to make you happy always wherever I am, not necessarily in Africa. That seems the only way I can let you know that you're appreciated, despite all the odds of the past years,' he concluded.

'Do you have anything important you're doing here that will disturb you from returning home to your people?' the queen asked.

'I don't know which home and people you're referring to,' he said with a deceptive smile. 'I'm at home here in Great Britain. My people are British and I am now a British citizen. Lord Franklin told me this is my home, my country. My name is Ifash Gordon, have you forgotten?'

'That's total rubbish! This is not your root; every black man in the world is an African, says me,' she protested fiercely.

'What is the essence of a man? Is it not time and where he grew up?' he asked.

'You're just twenty-eight, Ifashanu. You've not fully grown.'

'But mother, why Africa? What am I going there to do?'

'To carry on the legacy of your ancestors; you shall be king,' she said flatly.

'King? Did I hear you say King? That's impossible, a far-fetch assumption,' he said quietly.

'Look Ifashanu, you may disagree with me, but please don't disobey the wish of the people and your ancestors.'

'I'm to be king in Africa of all places? No way. In fact, I haven't the qualification to rule a city as small as London; how can you imagine that I can rule a kingdom? I'm a socialist for

Christ-sake, not a politician. I don't know anything about making a constitution and passing legislation. I am blank. I wish you can see reasons with me. I know nothing about your culture and I can't even speak your local dialect. How on earth do you qualify a king who cannot communicate with his own people? My knowledge of your kingdom is completely hazy. It's damn too weird mother, damn too weird, unfounded.'

'Don't worry my son, greatness is nothing but a vision,' she consoled in a clear relaxed voice. 'We are aware of all your worries and defects. There are four chief virtues of a leader namely, wisdom, justice, fortitude and temperance. All these you possess and there'll be enough time to erase your fears and anxieties before you're crowned. The most essential part is your marriage. I am pleased to inform you that it has been arranged already. You cannot rule except you're married,' she said with a faint smile.

The muscles around Ifash's jaw tightened.

'Christ, your light smile commands assurance as always,' he mumbled. So she already thinks I will accept to be king and has gone ahead to arrange a marriage? That is the last thing on my mind. It has all been planned, he thought, closing his eyes feeling utterly disappointed. This could only mean one thing, if he returned with his mother to his ancestral home, his life would never be his again. The people had been conditioned to dictate the tone of his life, like a life in slavery, an anarchy. He shrugged his shoulders and glanced at his mother. He noticed she was searching the room with her eyes as if looking for someone. The eyes fell on Jane who was comfortably seated at the far end with Sir Eastwood and two other men. They were engaged in a lively discussion that made them laugh frequently.

'How's she to you?' the queen asked simply and directly. He did not want to beat around the bush for he knew who she was talking about.

'She's Jane Wool,' he replied casually, cupping a hand around his glass.

'I know her name,' the queen stated.

'She's my girlfriend since college. We go a long way,' he said.

'Isn't it amazing that you speak so badly of them, yet you go after their ladies, why is that?' she asked quizzically.

'My frustration is over their men. They control the affairs of this place, and they make the world a terrible place for brothers and sisters in the ghettos. They enslave us and make brothers live like animals. I have no malice against their women; I can tolerate them till eternity,' Ifash explained. The queen raised a brow at his explanation.

'Oh, I see, so you're in a tolerance affair with Jin, not love.'

'No mother, you got it all mixed up. People don't talk about love in this part of the world. We are friends,' he declared and glanced at where Jane was seated, but she was not there anymore. His eyes caught up with her heading toward the elevator.

'Intimate friends you mean?' the queen asked with a curious expression.

'Yes, very close friends,' he said and reached for the champagne bottle. He refilled his glass and sipped it slowly.

'I am asking you this because when I asked her about some of the things she knows about you, she mentioned that you talk in your sleep. I deducted you two must be pretty close for her to know that much.'

'I see', he said calmly.

'Ifashanu,' she called emphatically. 'I hope you're not too serious with her, or are you?' she asked with a heavy frown.

'Well, I like my woman trendy and contemporary; someone who understands the intricacies of the world and balance that with excellent knowledge of companionship. Race barrier can't be avoided. We are from two different worlds and any step we take further, her family will probably disown her on earth and in heaven, you can imagine that,' he said and smiled placidly.

'Never mind,' she said in a comforting tone. 'You will have the option to choose your wife, the one you desire among our numerous virgins. I am not trying to cajole you with promises of the best life, but it's indeed a fact that back home we have decent good looking ladies in abundance.'

Ifash laughed childishly at his mother's gesture. He wanted to tell her that virgins and looks meant nothing special to him. In fact, he preferred his wears ready-made, ironed and folded, and his food boiled and well-cooked. He took hold of the turkey part and tore the last bit of flesh from it; then he poured himself some wine and lit another tobacco. The queen waited till he lighted it and took a long drag from it.

'I observe that you like cigar as much as you enjoy alcohol. But it's such a silly habit to inhale and exhale smoke for no real purpose, unlike Sango, the god of fire and thunder,' she observed.

'Sorry mother can't help it. It's one of those habits I inherited from my environment, the place you sent me. What do you drink to combat depression in Africa?' he asked, tugging at his nose.

'We Africans are not depressed people; such drink and smoke have no place in our society. What is the pride of a man if he gains the whole world and has no good habit,' she queried. They were not aware that Sir Edwin had joined them. He bent slightly beside the queen and whispered to her.

'Your Majesty, I'll never be wise enough to advise your greatest glory on personal issues. But may I say it's 1:00a.m and my heart rejoices with you tonight for finding the prince, and that task itself gave you a hectic day. You will be busy again tomorrow at the Buckingham Palace. You deserve some rest right away. May I be privileged as a Knight of this great Empire, to escort your grace to her suite?' The Queen did not deprive Sir Eastwood of the privilege.

* * *

In suite 009, Ifash sat on the edge of the bed facing a full-size mirror. His black suit was flung across the room on a sofa rich in quality and size. He looked about with his thoughts far away from the present. I have to overcome the crushing apprehension that fills my life, he thought to himself while rubbing his chin and face with both hands. As he tried standing, he realized he was a little tipsy. He stood with hands akimbo in front of the mirror. The reflection of the marvelous interior décor of the room was all he could see. He imagined if any room in the world could be better furnished. Through the mirror, he could see the mini-sitting room, the cabinet corner, a reading angle and the master bed.

Spontaneously, his hatred for the government aggravated.

'They live so big and dump us in some slums,' he shouted. Strangely, he wished he were in a position to join forces with the eastern block and attack Britain. Slowly, it crossed his mind that, should the brothers in the ghettos see the luxury inside the Continental, they would probably return to their homes the next day and commit suicide.

Furiously, he smashed the mirror with his bare fist in solidarity with the poor and watched as the entire upper region of the glass shattered noisily on the floor.

A sharp pain ran through him and he examined his fist. It had slight bruises all over it, nothing deep. He hurried to the bathroom and opened the tap fully so that water could wash away the blood. After that, he wrapped a towel over his fist; he could feel spasms of pain coursing along his veins. He turned off the light in the bathroom and went into the room. He sat on the sofa and gently nursed his fist by pressing the area surrounding the wound with the tips of his fingers.

He considered the events of the day. He thought of his dream, the angel, the saucers and the eagles. He thought of how he had woken up in a street tent and how he was about to sleep in a luxury tower. When the thought of Jane crossed his mind, he froze.

'How did she escape from prison?' he shouted. He paced about the room trying to figure out what could have happened. He loosened his bow-tie and flung it across the bed. He wondered what Jane would be doing in her room. She was probably fast asleep, he thought and decided to find out. He went over to her room and tapped gently on the door, not wanting to disturb her sleep. His eyes raged indecisively. He heard a click and guessed she had just replaced the telephone receiver. Jane opened the door slightly to prevent the intruder from entering because she was half clothed. When she saw who it was she swung the door open.

'What are you doing here at this hour, it's past your bed time,' she said with a slight frown on her face.

'Just making sure you're comfortably asleep,' he replied hoarsely, closing the door and leaning against it.

She noticed his eyes roaming over her body. They rested on her short Caribbean silk towel that covers her lacy silk bra. She smiled brightly at his boyish face, looking cool and composed, a picture of a successful actor. She smoothed the thin brown hair falling over her shoulders to his fascination.

'Jane, you look beautiful today,' he commended huskily.

'And, how did I look to you before today?' she asked weakly.

'Before, you're beautiful, but tonight, you're twice as beautiful.'

'Thanks,' she said with a smile, turning away from him. 'Come and sit.'

He obliged, watching as she seductively walked across to the cabinet. She returned with a scotch bottle and a glass.

'What's all this jargon about being heir to the throne of God?' Jane asked as she sat on a rocking chair beside the bed and staring at him as he poured the scotch into his glass.

'How did you get out of jail?' he asked in a voice of steel. It reminded her of the secret service men, side-burns and clean-shaven.

'You sound weird and drunk,' she said. Ifash eyed her un-impressively. He had been more shocked seeing Jane walk the street than seeing his mother after twenty-eight years. He summed it up as double effect.

'You haven't answered my question,' he pressed.

'My goodness! You're already sounding like a dictatorial king. I guess perhaps you're better off the way you are, than ending up becoming a dictator king in some far off place.'

'Those born in the royal courtyard are never devoid of behaviors that are majestic,' he said with a smile. He guzzled his drink and gently massaged his fist where it hurt.

The expression on his face showed discomfort.

'Why are you clutching your fist like that?' she asked curiously. 'I don't think you want to break anything?' Casually, she got up, walked to the window and drew the drapes. The room became dark except for the light of the reading lamp. She went over and knelt close to him, passing him a suggestive look.

'It's alright baby, I didn't mean to upset you. It's still the same me, I'm one person, same person, your silly rude headache,' she whispered and brushed her lips gently over his, but she did not get the expected response. Her eyes went to his hands and she saw the bruises.

Jane held the injured hand in hers and rubbed it over the silk bra of her breast. At first, he felt some slight pains but as the friction persisted, the feeling changed. A soothing comfort replaced the spasms of pain along the line.

'Did you hurt yourself?' she asked in a tone laced with passionate concern.

'I had to, because very soon we will not be together again,' he lied but soon realized that it could be true. Jane closed her eyes in exasperation. She had refused to think about it since the queen mentioned it. It hurt her so much to imagine life without Ifash. He arched his eyebrow and looked at her amusingly before drawing her closer to his chest. She inhaled his thick masculine smell and gasped when his nose nuzzled her neckline. Her eyes began to moisten from the effect.

As the tension heightened in them, they started kissing passionately. She remained on her knees. Her hands went around his neck while he cupped her butt. Though this was not their first kiss or the hundredth, it was their first affectionate kiss of passion and love. The heat was gradually building up in him and hers was chasing behind. His hands moved up to her waist and found the knot of her towel. He flipped it off her body, exposing inviting white silk underwear. Deftly, he undid his trousers with a hand while she helped him unbutton his shirt, revealing a strong hairy chest.

'I love you Jane,' he whispered into her hair. God knows I love you too, probably more than you do, she thought. Ifash looked over her beautiful body, her shape and her gift. Idly, a funny thought crept into his mind; he thought she was beautiful enough to walk about nude.

'Marvellous shape,' he muttered as he carried her in his arms and deposited her on the king-sized bed. They sprawled side by side, before moving closer down to baptize her veiled breast with the saliva of his tongue. He drew her bra top below the ribs. Jane reached for the tip of his hardness through his shorts, sliding her hand beneath him. She ground his manhood into her palms and began gazing her finger nails on his testes. Ifash responded with a shuddering sound. He eyed the perfectly shaped glands on her chest and kissed the nipples, one after the other till they both stood erect. He explored further, listening to her as she sighed in contentment. He used is tongue to tickle her umbilicus, his sole intention was to treat her completely like a lady, with little interest in his own desire.

When his tongue traveled down touching the sex bud between her thighs, she arched against him as the pink satin-spread rumpled and tangled beneath them. His tongue skimmed expertly, loving every side of her mound. With great effort, she observed him beneath her eye lashes. His strong black head was between her thighs, devouring her.

'Goodness,' she breathed in pleasure. It was the most wonderfully branded gift a prince could give to a princess and a king to a queen. Ifash watched with an eye of accomplishment as she muttered her words of pleasure. She closed her eyes, spelling-out his name and clasping her thighs against his head. When she could no longer contain the feeling, she groaned, her long hair curtaining her frenzied face. She dug her fingers purposefully into the muscles of his shoulder to prevent herself from screaming.

's-l-o-w-l-y,' she cried softly, arching her waist toward his mouth, wriggling and clicking. She arched again and again, until at last a thundering climax sent her to a distant planet far away from the earth.

She was floating on the moon when Ifash moved over her body, peeled her bra over her head, and kissed her on the lips so she could taste the coconut scent of her mound. She clung to his neck, kissing him hungrily as if her return to earth depended on it.

He cupped a hand around her butt, he was ready, done. He aimed to slide inside her but she slipped away from his grasp. She lifted her head and looked at him.

'Love is an act, an act of sharing,' she said. She moved down to his waist till his manhood was beneath her eyelids. Gladly, she curled her hot wet lips around its crown-shaped head, tasting his pure male organ, completely. She felt the powerful muscle of his shaft pulse and quiver in ecstasy inside her mouth. It slowly convulsed to the rhythm she was dictating with her tongue. She placed a hand over his chest and felt the thunderous beats of his heart below. He was emitting strange words of pleasure, his eyelids fluttering in anticipation.

Timing, satisfied and drilled, he pulled himself gently out of her mouth and lowered himself over her, resting on both hands. He buried his face in the hollow of her shoulder, crushing her breast with his chest. He Shifted down a little to nuzzle her breast and inhaled the light fragrance of her womanliness with his nose. He felt her mound with a finger, in readiness for the drive.

Her hands were again around his neck with a cynical smile plastered on her face. For a moment, they engaged in an orgy of kissing. It was possessive and pretty cruel. He parted her thighs with his knees and she wrapped her legs around his hip, gently allowing him to slide all the way to the depth. He started with a steady thrust, rocking her forth and back with ecstatic groans. Only the base of his manhood was unsheathed in his drive. Their body had become one, melting together as a whole. He gasped as he arched his butt with Jane shaking him from beneath, in a move to maximize their pleasure. His organ soon began to convulse; he held back for a short while and later let go. His shot was heavy and deep as he cupped her breasts in a final grip. Passion overcame Jane once again, and this time she held him firmly as their pleasure stretched home like in a marathon.

Later, they sprawled motionless, tangled with unmatched fulfillment. Her nipples remained erect as she rested on his chest. They listened to the breathing of each other till their bodies returned to normalcy. Jane sat up slightly and cradled his head in her arms. Gently, she began to rock him with simple massages on the forehead, like a child being laid to sleep.

CHAPTER SIXTEEN

At the Continental where early morning tea was served at 6:30am, Ifash lay curled up in Jane's arms. Jane heard a knock and crawled out of bed to receive a large tray that had two mugs of milked tea, a roll of crackers and fruits. She put it down gently on the bedside table, careful not to wake Ifash. Soundlessly, she entered the bathroom and emerged later looking fresh and scented. Ifash had woken and was sitting up in bed, brandishing a radio antenna like a toy pistol. Jane glanced at the wall clock; it was 7:45am.

'Where am I,' Ifash asked, switching on the radio. Events at the large auditorium of the cathedral church sounded with background voices of some kids staging a morality play in remembrance of King David, Solomon's father.

'You're in wonderland,' she said with a smile as she walked to the wardrobe and began dressing. Among the many gorgeous dresses hung there, she selected a blue sheath dress done up in stretched lace that reached her ankle, hugging every curve of her body.

'Where to?' he enquired.

'Nowhere, just getting ready,' she replied and sat on the dressing table near the bed.

Ifash eyed her suspiciously. She noticed the curious expression on his face from the mirror.

'You're scheduled to be at the Buckingham by 10:00am. Sir Eastwood said I can come along. And we're expected downstairs for breakfast in thirty minutes. You don't look set to me,' she said with a broad smile.

Ifash rose and hurried into his trousers. He passed by the table and sipped twice from his mug of hot tea.

'Too hot,' he complained and walked briskly into the bathroom.

* * *

At 8.45pm, Ifash returned to his suite like others, exhausted and red-eyed. Never had he visited so many people and places in a single day. Their first call was at the Buckingham palace, where they had breakfast with selected members of the royal family and some government officials. They proceeded in the chilly winter to the country side, where Romana presented them with another tasty cuisine.

Romana was cheerful throughout their stay until they stood to leave. She knew what was about to happen when Ifash called her aside.

'I have to go Aunt, my people need me,' he said softly. To her, those words meant the end of her world, they were painful to digest. In a desperate move to win him over, she made futile attempts to remind him of Lord Franklin's statements. But the look Ifash gave her was a familiar look, she had seen it a couple of times. It meant no retreat. Later, they embraced each other, shedding endless emotional tears. Wholeheartedly, Ifash gave her in writing all that belonged to him, including the large farm in Dublin and the adorable Starlat piano. He left the ranch with a sports bag containing books, a radio communication set and a pair of binoculars.

Their next stop was at Sterling Police station. The queen declined to go inside, so he went in alone. Their conversation was brief and thorough, as if there was no time to waste on frivolities. Adam looked on disappointedly indifferent. He liked Ifash, but he disliked other niggers with a passion.

'I can't imagine you could be so fucking out of your mind to want to go to Africa, a dark doomed continent!' He spat at the departing Ifash.

On their way back to the hotel, the queen stopped over at the city's jewelry cave, an ancient store where pure gold and diamonds were sold to the extremely rich. After shopping, she sat with Jane at the backseat and gave her most of what she bought in appreciation. She presented her with two diamond bracelets and a set of gold bangles and necklace. Jane was silent when the queen offered her diamonds and gold as parting gifts.

She was short of words. Her face dimpled with a warm girlish smile as she showed the gifts to Ifash.

'Is it right if I take all these?' she asked. Ifash smiled, wondering what prompted such question.

'It's not every day you get diamond for free. So baby, don't look at a gift horse in the mouth, I think you deserve much more than stones, keep them for good,' he said.

Jane hugged the queen, her eyes filled with tears. Ifash knew the exact worth of the gift. He tasked his brain calculating and decided that if he were to spend another century in Britain working hard, he would never earn half the value. He noticed the tears of gratitude in Jane's eyes, they were not ordinary tears. They were tears tearing poverty away from her life indefinitely.

For a while, Ifash laid static in bed thinking, staring unseeingly at the ceiling. Sleep refused to come, although there was fatigue on his face. He would have wished to make love to Jane for the last time, but the pleasure of the previous day still lingered in his body. Now that he had fully agreed to return with his mother unconditionally, they were scheduled to set off for Africa the next day. He realized that his mother had grown pensive, nostalgic and nervous. Perhaps, they were signs of satisfaction for a mission accomplished.

THE FOLLOWING DAY

The black Mercedes limousine came to a halt in front of a large building with the inscription *Departure Hall.* The smartly dressed driver, a security agent, stepped out immediately to open the back door for the queen. She was alone in the back seat while Ifash and Jane occupied the middle seat. As the agent led them into the hall, their flamboyant dresses caught the attention of onlookers. The queen had insisted he wore native attire. To her it was the only decent way to dress in Africa. He could hardly believe the weight of the costume on his body, though it fitted well.

Jane looked elegant as ever wearing a tight short-sleeved shirt blended with linen fabric that stretched to the ankle with a slit on the side and a mid-calf. Her long brown hair was loose hiding her expensive ear-rings. She wore her gold and diamond bracelets; she cut the image of a celebrity.

They were taken to a quiet restaurant overlooking the shore. The queen was some distance away from where Ifash and Jane were having drinks on a ceramic table. Jane was doing most of the talking. Ifash sipped wine and drew deep draughts of smoke from his tobacco with his head hangling slightly like a doll displayed at a mini-mart. He was listening attentively to Jane and admiring the smooth velvet skin of her face, the face that would forever remain a part of him.

Suddenly, the sound of a noisy engine from a roving vessel invaded the serene environment, causing Jane to pause in her chatter. She sipped her drink briefly and looked down at the rippling sea. She watched as the master engine of the vessel came to life and began to slice along its path with speed until it became tiny and eventually invisible, piercing her heart. The disappearance of the ship brought out her fears. In her heart, she dreaded his leaving her for good. She loved him so much and was going to miss him in every way. To her, Ifash was a man to the core. It was true that one cannot have it all, but Ifash had it all. She believed this and would always believe so.

'What are you thinking about?' he asked. She smiled shyly, not knowing how to express the burden of loss that had been weighing her down.

'I'm thinking about us,' she said.

'What about us?'

'Ifash,' she called softly. 'You know, I think I'm indebted to you a great deal. And now it's like you're going away forever, how will I ever pay back?'

'Your indebtedness to me is nothing compared to the love and affection you've shown me from the very first day we met at Cambridge.' He expected a response but she kept quiet. He watched as her face was drained of colours.

She could perceive what was going on within him. Perhaps, he needed words of hope as much as she did. There were times in life one was forced to make decisions out of one's control, and he had just made one, she thought.

'Jane,' he called quietly. 'I don't belong here as much as you don't belong there. We're both caught up in a trap, a trap of destiny. I've got this high-tech radio set. It belonged to Pa Gordon, it's one of those powerful gadgets used during the war. I'm taking it along because of us, for time to time communication. Mother said there are no telephone facilities back there. Maybe one day we can arrange for a short visit, don't rule it out,' he said with a giggle.

Jane smiled back in despair, pushing away her pain to a remote part of her mind. She shifted her attention from her impending loss and looked over Ifash's head, and spotted the limo-driver approaching them. When he got to their table, he bent and whispered to Ifash.

'Thanks,' Ifash murmured and took a long drag of his tobacco with his eyes on Jane's.

'The Eagle has landed,' he announced. Jane nodded, forcing a smile. Through the corners of her eyes, she saw the queen shake hands with some officials and head towards them. Ifash eased himself upright and pulled Jane up. He drew her gently into his arms feeling the softness of her bosom and the sweet fragrance of her skin. They hugged warmly and he brought his face close to hers. She shivered and buried her face in his chest. Jane noticed the fascination and understanding on the queen's face while she was in her son's arms. Ifash felt the moisture in his eyes as her hair brushed his face.

'I love you,' he whispered to her and kissed her ears, neck and lips as passionately as he could. 'Remember that,' he said and disentangled from her gently and slowly.

She drew away from him partly shy and partly weakened from the effect of his affection. Jane felt unnatural, like an alien. She felt as if a hole had appeared in her heart, one she would never be able to fill again.

'Bye,' she managed to whisper with extraordinary effort.

CHAPTER SEVENTEEN

(Three Weeks Later)

The main road leading to Odua Kingdom was demarcated by a large giant rock, named Lumo-rock. The rock is surrounded by a forest and a swamp, important territories for the village hunters who specialize in hunting wild beasts.

On arrival, the queen and the crown prince, Ifashanu were met by royal guards at the base of the rock. They helped them climb the rock. At the top of the rock, Ifash stood perplexed watching as some of the guards blew their long trumpets to announce their arrival. The trumpets were so loud they could burst the eardrums if blown a little longer than necessary. He eyed the guards critically.

'Christ! What's this?' he murmured under his breath.

Some among the guards were in different regalia underneath some tattered leather covers and carrying short shoulder bags. They had no sophisticated weapons like their counterparts in the United Kingdom. Instead, each one held a long stick and different sizes of sheep and cow horns, looking like some bandits or some group of jesters preparing for a play at the Broadway theatre. He tried restraining his curiosity by focusing on the far distance ahead. For a few minutes, he held a hand to his forehead trying to shade off the scorching sun. From the position where he stood, he could see clearly the entire gulf of the kingdom. His eyes caught the magnificent ultra-modern palace his father built across the river. The space that separated the river from the palace had been decorated to look like an artificial forest.

'A crossover smash villa,' Ifash mumbled to one of the well-dressed guards. He admitted bluntly that the front and side views of the palace alone would charm the eyes of any observer. Hardly had he completed his survey when his ears picked huge delightful screams echoing from far below. He took some cautious step further from where he was standing and looked down at the huge mass of people running towards the base of the rock. His eyes swung back to his mother, and she made a gesture at him with a smile to move down through the smooth path of the rock where six guards were already trailing. He hesitated, assessing the rocky path. He could see the guards had no trouble finding their way through the path. He studied them and discovered it was quite an easy drag. With cautious steps, he followed them waving both hands in the air in salutation at the jubilant crowd. The countless sounds of powdered guns drew joyous unforgettable pictures on the desolate sky.

As he jogged down the rock, Ifash saw men with broad chests beating talking drums and other large drums, singing and somersaulting in joy at his return. When he finally touched the ground, he was covered the way bees cover honey. More people kept surging towards him, singing and shouting exultantly and extending their hands to have a feel of him. The Chief Priest and Chancellors were at an angle, jolting confidently on their lavishly decorated horses. They were gazing far ahead, all dressed in their ceremonial combat regalia, except for a large proportion of women and children rollicking in bright colors.

Ifashanu looked around and caught a glimpse of his mother whirling to the sounds of drums and beads. She was dancing between clusters of women all dressed in simple wrappers that was fastened above their breasts. Some wore tiny beads on their hands, waists and legs; and their slippers were made of cheap leather. The atmosphere was filled with melodious voices that blended perfectly with the drums and the young women swayed their flexible waists seductively. He nodded with approval and the crowd formed a circle around him. He watched bemused and completely overjoyed. The people danced in circles singing his praises in their native tongue.

It was the brightest moment of his life, a day he would always remember. It was a day every house in the Kingdom emptied its human inhabitants to welcome him. The Chancellors, the elders and the Chief Priest, all wore bright smiles that bore no malice, or rejection. It was a day of joy and reconciliation and everyone were determined to afford the Prince, their support and love. Everyone was singing his praises loud and clear:

'Ki ni e foba pe,
Oba ooo,
Oba lase Oba,
Oba to dade owo,
Oba oo,
Oba lase Oba...'

He was carried shoulder high to the Palace of his ancestors with the song chanted repeatedly all through the journey.

As he was carried along the forest paths, his senses gave in to the overwhelming richness of the African culture, the extravagant texture of their fabrics, and their melodramatic songs and dance steps. It was the most remarkable way to welcome a true son of the soil.

FOUR YEARS LATER 1882

In the four successive years that followed, the kingdom witnessed astonishing improvements in all sectors under the total control of Ifashanu, who added modern techniques to their traditional lifestyles. After much hard work and dedication, it did not come as a surprise to his people that the harvest increased and the store houses were filled up. The health sector did not report any outbreak of disease or difficulties in childbirth. The smooth progression of the years raised doubt in the minds of majority of the chancellors who had voted against his return in the first place. Most now believed that Ifashanu had truly been chosen by his ancestors to serve not only his kingdom, but the continent at large.

Amidst all the wonderful changes that were unfolding in the kingdom, Ifashanu was called aside and made to realize that he would not be crowned king until three years later, when he would be thirty five years of age. It was the age the people considered he would be mature enough to carry the burden of kingship. All the while he had been learning the language and history of his ancestors. He felt a lot of things were wrong in the way the people lived their daily lives. But then, he lacked the courage to say, *hey, you guys, the way you live your life stinks, because you're filled with rubbish stuffs in your heads. From now on, you must live my own way, because it's the right way, civilized, the best.*

He had resolved within himself that even if he could change them by virtue of the power that would soon be bestowed on him, he would not force them. He was going to leave it all for time to deal with. For now, he simply wanted to concentrate on improving the civilized aspects of their lives, such as making wrestling the kingdom's favorite sport. Thrice he had donated prizes and won them himself. Wrestling was one interesting sport he had mastered since childhood through his good friend, Adam McCarthy.

So far, the most striking experiences for him since his return to the kingdom were the rituals he had been subjected to partake in. The previous year alone, he had eaten the hearts of dragons cooked in a calabash on seven different occasions. In the present year, he had been told that hearts of lions and the liver of an elephant would be cooked for him.

As for drinks, he had lost count of the different concoctions he had swallowed. The encouragement of his mother had made everything look easy and normal. She said it was all for spiritual prowess and identification with the gods. The most disturbing of them were the several painful superficial cuts, lined vertically and horizontally all over his head. Some were lined fashionably on his chest, his back and arms, and below his lower lip. Ifashanu could not help but wonder frightfully how many more animal organs he would be required to eat, and how many more cuts he would endure before he was thirty five.

As destined, by the end of his forth year at home, he had become a rich and renowned prince on the African continent. His successes sent shivers down the spines of neighboring kingdoms who dreaded invasions of their territories by the powerful crown Prince of Odua. Ifashanu on the other hand was unlike his father who took advantage of situations like this to gain control of more territories and secure more tax payers. It never crossed his mind to wage wars of domination against weaker neighbors. He believed he lacked the white man's penchant for violating the rights of others by invading their homes. What really mattered to him in life were merriment, peace and laughter. These he considered were necessary to everyone in life.

His beautiful palace, extended family and his people gave him that merriment, peace and laughter; and he was contented. And of all the kingdom's possessions and assets, he loved the interior layout of the palace the most because it impressed him. Often, he would spend the better part of the day holed up inside the palace.

The exterior was also beautiful having a lush green carpet. On the right wing was a vault constructed with elephant tusks and fixed with silver linings. The vault was Ifashanu's favorite spot where he socialized with relatives and friends. It was customary that any time his servants spotted him seated on the centrally placed armchair in the vault; they organized a troop of female dancers and singers. Then they would stand before him awaiting his command. If at that moment he desired to listen to music and songs and to watch them dance, he would simply cast a look at the drummers. And whenever he wished to stop the merriment, he would make a gesture with his hand and it would end. It was a life he would not swap for anything else, not for war or for a return to Europe. He was more than ever determined to make his kingdom the wonder of all ages.

HIS FIFTH YEAR AT HOME, OCTOBER 1883

A year later, when Ifashanu became thirty-three, he fell in love with the most charming of the palace dancers named Idunu. She was a smooth-faced, pretty lady three years older than Ifashanu. When their secret romance leaked out from the palace to the outside world, the Chancellors and elders cried *taboo!* They were emphatic in saying that *never will their crown-prince be engaged to a dancer!* Their future king deserved nothing short of a virgin, an unsheathed lady with a good family background. The Chancellors and elders made no attempt to hide their disapproval and they spoke against it openly.

* * *

3 MONTHS AFTER

The fears of the Chancellors and elders became compounded when the dancer became pregnant and the kingdom buzzed with the news. The queen was most disturbed, she was almost very certain the dancer had seduced her son with spiritual powers. So for days she remained sad, depressed and confused, not knowing which step to take next. A week passed with no solution in sight. The queen soon took a more pragmatic approach with no sentiments. She weighed the advantages and disadvantages of the prince's action. She reached a decision on the tenth day with the feeling that the situation was bad and unfortunate, but that it could get worse if the dancer delivered safely. It would mean that a bastard would be bound for the throne of the gods.

In all her life, she had been a strict disciplinarian and a radical feminist against immorality. For the present situation however, she seemed to be caught in a tight corner, where discipline and strong-headedness would not do. So she summoned the prince on the tenth night and counseled him on the different characters of African women, the qualities of a good woman, and a woman who would make a worthy housewife.

'Women are like trees, you don't judge them from their glowing flowers, but by the fruits they produce,' she had concluded. In all she said, Ifash deduced one vital point which was that, his chosen love, Idunu was heavily out-favored. He made the point that Idunu was the only woman he had a crunch for in the entire kingdom. It was either her or no one else, he maintained.

The following week, a traditional marriage was hastily organized. In front of a large community gathering, the queen pronounced them husband and wife and every person that planned to thwart the union was disarmed. A horn of fanfare was blown around the kingdom. The flamboyant ceremony became the talk in the continent for days. Crown Prince Ifashanu and Princess Idunu received many gifts and messages of goodwill from within the kingdom and across the continent.

THE YEAR OF OUR LORD 1884 (His 6th year in Africa)

What brought about a turning point in the history of Odua Kingdom began one sunny afternoon on June 16th 1884. The Prince had just arrived at his palace from one of his usual goodwill visits to people in sorrow, the sick and the extremely poor. Entering his bedroom he found his cherished wife Idunu, who was seven months pregnant, looking consumed and devastated. She wiped away the tears on her face as he approached her.

Ifashanu took a careful look at her; it was clear to him that she was in an unpleasant mood. He sat gently beside her on the edge of the bed.

'What is going on, why are you weeping?' he asked innocently. Idunu burst into tears and her soft cries filled the room for a while. The first thing that came to his mind was a miscarriage. Impossible, he thought. He felt miserable watching her cry and he did not have the slightest clue as to what might be bothering her. Could it be that he had failed her completely as husband due to his busy schedules that left little room for care and romance? He wetted his lips in regret, a sign of guilt and marital failure.

'Idunu, will you tell me what the hell is wrong with you or you prefer to keep me waiting and keep having nonsense ideas?' he asked barely able to contain his annoyance. Idunu took her time making efforts to contain her hysteria. The insults were injurious to her heart and it was time she must spoke out.

'For how long will I continue to wait?' she demanded. 'For how long? When will I have a say and be respected?'

'Damn it!' Ifashanu exclaimed and snorted in disgust. He could not believe his ears. She had stood him up for nothing. He stretched out his long legs and folded his arms on his chest. With great effort, he took a deep breath trying to contain his anger, trying to relax; he knew too well that he must not react the way he felt about her silly statement. After all, she was only a woman, and he knew better how to deal with his women. Women were soft and fragile, physically and mentally.

'Perhaps I should remind you in case you have forgotten; as soon as I am thirty-five, you'll be Queen. Then you'll have all the authority, not just a say; you'll have power to move mountains,' he said trying to smile broadly.

She turned sharply towards him like a tigress about to unleash her fury.

'I see! Until you're thirty-five, so you support them to insult me before then.'

'What are you talking about, baby?' Ifashanu ventured.

'I am not a baby! I am not your age-mate at all, don't be calling me baby,' she snapped. 'So now, before you're thirty-five you approve that every imbecile in this kingdom should continue to call me a dancer instead of a Princess. So that is it, it's like that, I am the foolish one. It is said that every king deserves a fool in his palace. I am your fool, the foolish dancer of the Prince of Odua!' she shouted.

'Who among my people dare call you such an illicit name?'

She flared up in reply. 'Dancer is the name everyone calls me in this kingdom, if you don't know. And that includes your very own mother. I am tired and disgusted by you all. If you know you don't love me, or you feel you're too good for me, why then did you marry me? You should have allowed me to...'

'Cut the crap you saying!' he thundered. 'I don't want to hear any more of that trash.' With that he turned away with his eyes directed to a corner of the room. He was breathing fire, very upset. He wiped his face with both hands and stood up abruptly. He began to prowl around the room in order to calm himself. He was angry and could not understand why his people had refused to respect and accept his decision as a man, and their future king for that matter. Insulting his wife behind him, be her a prostitute, crazy, or dancer, was equal to insulting his sense of reasoning, his freedom and personality. There and then he felt completely pissed off; and he became wary of being over-dependent on the directives of his Chancellors and elders. He was weary of relying on them to keep his life rolling. What he needed was a rapid solution that will bring him peace of mind and absolute freedom. He hurried out without another word, his intent was crystal clear.

CHAPTER EIGHTEEN

The following morning, the Prince was the first to enter the queen's bedroom contrary to Palace routine. He knocked briefly and opened the giant double doors with both hands without waiting for a reply. The queen lay in bed like a child soundly asleep. He moved closer to the bed and noticed with shock the numerous grey hairs on her head.

Ifash froze at the discovery and took a closer look at her. Dizziness rocked him to his feet and he thought he was going to fall. She was only sixty-five, and had aged tremendously within the years.

Indeed, life had been very unfair to his mother, unleashing all the responsibilities of an entire Kingdom on her head.

'Mother,' he called and the queen woke up. 'I'm sorry if I disturbed your sleep, but I have to see you for a very urgent matter,' he said stiffly, sitting on the edge of the bed.

The queen wiped her face and sat up in bed staring at her son. The sleep and surprise were clear on her face. She looked introspectively at him and saw a forlorn expression on his face. She became apprehensive that something was wrong.

'What is the matter Ifashanu, are you alright?' she asked. Ifashanu turned his face away from her so she could not see the depression etched on it. He narrated all he heard from his wife and expressed his disappointment over the disrespect being meted out to his wife and his person. He further argued that the only way out was for him to be crowned king immediately. He wanted honor and respect restored to him once and for all, stressing that age was just a figure because he had been able to guide the Kingdom into prosperity irrespective of his age. He strongly believed now than ever that he possessed the wisdom and quality required by his ancestors to lead the Kingdom to greater heights.

'There cannot be a better time. I'm ripe mother, for goodness sake! Enough of these insults,' he concluded with firm finality.

The queen in a state of confusion had argued with her son, trying to make him see reasons with laid down traditions and ancestral regulations. At a point, she looked frustrated and saddened by Ifashanu insistence and disregard. It seems to her more or less a tragedy when she finally realised that the Prince was uncompromising in his stand. He had rejected all her advice. To drive home his point, he had threatened to return to Britain if his demands were not met. He did not want to stay in a Kingdom where people praised him in his presence but insulted him behind his back. He was no longer willing to lead a kingdom of hypocrites, he declared.

His arguments touched his mother's heart; she knew there was sense in all that he said. Eventually, she threw in the towel by assuring him of an immediate discussion with the Chief-Priest. Before Ifashanu could raise another point, she made him promise verbally that he would not do anything that would tarnish the image of the royal family. She could not imagine what would happen should she wake up one morning and discover he was gone. To avert the calamity, she resolved to use her influence and stretch her connections to the fullest.

Ifashanu stood ready to take his leave. He pecked his mother on the cheek and thanked her for her meritorious understanding. She managed a weak smile and gave a languishing look at her only child. The look she gave him was a combination of love and sympathy.

* * *

Later in the day, the Queen and Ifashanu summoned the Chief-Priest to the palace's garden. He was treated with fresh palm-wine, well-cooked bush-meat, and kola nuts. Ifashanu could count on his fingers the number of times he had set eyes on the Priest, maybe six. What fascinated him about the old man was not just his silent bad temper, but also, his archaic gait. He moved like someone stepping on ice and about to lose his balance anytime. And the expression on his face was always the same, like he had lost interest in life and death altogether. He wondered what could be his likely age.

The queen made known her intent with a brief history of the many positive developments that had happened since the return of Ifashanu, her son. Finally, she hit the nail on the head suggesting that the Prince be crowned the following month for things to return to normalcy in the shortest time. Just as it had been in the days of his father, King Jajaha, she argued. Her conclusion caused the Chief-Priest to shift in his seat.

'That Ifashanu, the son of Jajaha Tobiolah, be made king in a few weeks time, with few months to go to the d-day?' he asked in surprise. 'This child,' he pointed, 'after wasting more than half of his years in the white man's land, no way!' He declared wiping his face with a hand, as if trying to rub-off whatever effect the palm wine must have had on his sight and ears. Ifashanu regarded the Priest; there was this implacable expression on the old man's face, like he was going to pee in his pant.

'No,' cried the priest with a vigorous shake of the head. 'Despite the fact that Jajaha Tobiolah spent all his life in the land of his ancestors, he was never crowned at an age less than thirty-five. How do we explain our impatience and ingratitude to the gods of the land? I cannot understand why you young ones are always in haste nowadays!' He spat in disgust and allowed himself a sip of his palm wine.

'You can appeal to the gods, can't you?' the Queen inquired in a naïve voice. 'You can make them understand the advancement the Prince has facilitated in the kingdom.' She glanced at Ifashanu and added. 'Don't forget things are fast changing in our present world. You cannot compare the period of his father to today. Our children are wiser now than before,' she argued.

'*Shio!*' The old sage hissed at the duo. '*Oro rirun, oro idoti.* I can't believe you're saying this, Abeke, Queen of Odua. What are you saying? Are my ears deceiving me?' he asked touching his ears. He shivered at the mere thought of thwarting the ways of old allowing his eyes to wander across the garden like he was looking for an escape route.

The queen beckoned silently with a hand to Ifashanu. He got the message almost immediately and excused himself from the sitting. Alone, the queen and the Priest discussed at length about the affair. It went on for so long that their conversation must have lasted for an hour after Ifashanu's departure.

Later in the night, the queen called Ifashanu aside and informed him that she had reached a compromise with the Priest. The old-man had reluctantly agreed to make a long hard haul to appease the gods to accept a new king, the way they accepted his father, King Jajaha Tobiolah II.

* * *

Six days passed after the palace meeting. There was no word from the old man; everything was silent, peaceful and normal. However, the next day which was the seventh day, the Chief Priest rose very early in the morning to organise a suffrage, extending it to all the Chancellors and elders, for an important meeting in the evening at the palace hall.

The Consensus

At about 5:30pm in the evening, the Chancellors and elders gathered as scheduled. The discussion was elaborate and shocking. It lasted for hours. The priest, who by ancestral right was the spiritual leader, spoke emphatically on the essence of a king at the period.

'A body without a head is completely useless,' he stressed and went further to inform the gathering of the gods' willingness to grant their son, Ifashanu a trial. The gods acknowledged that so far he has lived up to expectation and there was no reason any more for further delay as the kingdom desperately craved for leadership and kingship. We are a strong people and will ever remain strong. The time has come because we do not want our neighbours, friends and enemies to continue to look down at us as a weak people, a body that lacks a head, direction and leadership.' The Priest concluded. His final words brought the meeting to climax.

When it was time for questions, majority of the chiefs asked curious and suspicious questions. Their questions were met and unraveled intelligently by the Priest and queen Abeke.

At last it was sealed and concluded that the Prince should be formally introduced to the gods and oracles of the kingdom. On acceptance thereafter, he would embark with the Priest to the thick forest of *Osau* where the god of wisdom dwells.

* * *

The following day, an announcement was made all over town that a new king would be crowned in seven days time. The moment the news went public, Ifashanu became the happiest man on earth. He thanked his mother and the priest endlessly for their understanding and faith in his capability. In the evening of the same day that the announcement was made, Ifashanu sent his servants to every house and places of gathering to proclaim his happiness at the turn of events. Throughout the day, he remained in the company of his wife Idunu, members of the royal family, and his friends. They had merriment that was characterized with excess food and drinks, like the kingdom had never witnessed before. When Ifashanu lay in bed that night, his heart raced, and the minutes chased the hours, and the hours leapt into the next day.

* * *

BASH BAKR

The Sojourn

Very early in the morning, Ifashanu sat quietly with the Priest in the palace. He could hear the cocks still crowing at that hour of the day and the sun was preparing to establish it dominance over the clouds. Ifashanu listened attentively to the instructions of the day. Their destination was the grand shrine where he was due to be introduced and initiated. As tradition demanded, he was made to dress in a sparkling white wrapper that reached his ankles and knotted into a small ball above his left shoulder. He had white and black beads hanging from his shaven head, and traditionally consecrated large beads on both wrists. He held a wand in his right hand.

The Priest on his part was in his usual sullen appearance. His fur wrapper was sparkling white, wrapped well above his breasts. An extra short fur lay across his shoulders. He was carrying a smoky pot in one hand and held firmly a long beaded rod in the other hand.

At the end of his short instructions, the Priest made a sniffing sound of uncertainty. He looked up at the Prince and gave him an assuring smile. Ifashanu suddenly felt like a lamb being led to the slaughter.

'May your ancestors be with you and grant you all that you require at this stage of your life,' the priest prayed, passing Ifashanu a satisfactory look.

'Yes Chief, I hope they'll grant me all my requirements,' Ifashanu replied with a smile.

'No, that's not what you're supposed to say. Say *Ase*, snapped the Priest.

'What?' Ifashanu shot him a withering glance. '*Ashi*,' he grunted.

'Better,' the Priest murmured and motioned him to follow. They left the palace filled with hope of success.

The journey to the grand shrine lasted more than an hour. They walked at snail speed. At times, Ifashanu would turn to inspect his surrounding in a suspicious manner. They were trailing a path he never knew existed in the kingdom. When the

Priest finally halted in front of a ramshackle hut made of straws and red mud amidst tall grasses and long Iroko trees, the Prince heaved a sigh of relief. He looked on without aspiration as the Priest laid down the smoky pot by the entrance of the hut. Instinctively, Ifashanu took three steps backward. The Priest was mumbling strange words as he shook the long beaded stick in the air, perhaps cursing the cloud to descend to earth. Ifashanu looked on in utmost amazement as the door of the hut opened on its own.

'Magic,' he murmured to himself and took three steps backward, fully alert. The Priest turned around and was surprised to see Ifashanu away from him. He gestured to him to move closer inside. Ifashanu's eyes bulged in fear moving from the wonder door to the Priest. He braced up and passed the Priest a gentle reassuring smile that says he was up to the task. They walked in backwards.

Ifashanu stood frozen when he turned and saw what was placed at the centre. A fixed scowl etched across his face.

'Holy-shit!' He cried and tore his eyes away from it, disgusted. The shrine was dimly lit with the early morning sun piercing through the bamboo walls. Its roof was thatched with networks of cobwebs and straw sticks. Ifashanu's eyes moved to the edge of the hut.

There, he saw the most shocking and demeaning sight he had ever seen in his life. At the four edges of the hut, there were four staked naked young looking ladies on their knees, exposing firm virgin black breasts. Each one was carrying a red smoky pot on her head and they appeared dazed. What was probably the chief idol was majestically placed on a blood-stained stool at the centre.

A thousand reasons crept into his mind. He could not understand why the great god of the land, the god that was supposed to shower bounties and blessings unto the people, could be so carelessly kept and subjected to a stinking and demeaning environment that did not befit a pig. Also, what were those four ladies doing there? This is cruel, he thought and turned to the Priest. He watched the old man kneel respectfully before the chief idol with both hands raised in the air. He was reciting some incantations in a dialect different from the common Odua dialect. Ifashanu stood and gaped hopelessly at the Chief Priest. At a point, he snorted and cleared his throat to draw the old man's attention, but instead, his incantations gained momentum. The old man was shaking the stick in his hand vigorously in worship at the chief idol.

Curiously, Ifashanu felt ignored. He decided to interrupt the priest to re-establish his presence. He nudged the old man slightly on the shoulder.

'Are you sure you're alright, you don't need help?' The Priest waved him away without a word and continued his devotion. Ifashanu took another look around the four corners of the room. The four ladies were dark, pretty and young. He fixed his eyes on their firm breasts for a moment; they seemed unaware of his gaze for they must be immersed in a deep trance. He wetted his lips and a tremor of sexual desire and nervousness ran through his loins.

Then all of a sudden, he felt an irritating sensation building up in him as a result of the stench, like a toxic chemical, emitting from the corners of the shrine. There were remains of germinating fruits, cooked and uncooked food, ducks and doves, palm-oil, palm wine, and all sort of liquids splashed all over the floor. Ifashanu fixed his eyes on the old man as he went towards him. Thoroughly fed up with his devotion, he nudged him again.

'Look Chief, I can't stay here for another minute. I'm running out of gas,' he interrupted the Priest's smooth flow of ancestral recitation. 'You ought to have at least informed me before hand,' he said. 'You should have told me you're bringing me to a shit hole filled with all manners of human bondage and stinking mahoganies,' he shouted tightening his jaw.

'*Gbaga! Oro kabiti, oro-rirun!*' The Priest exploded, whipping his head around to glare at Ifashanu.

'How dare you refer to the gods of your ancestors as stinking mahogany? Do you know where you are?' roared the Priest. Ifashanu watched as the old man's nostrils inflated and deflated with tension revealing grey hairs that aligned perfectly with the grey strands on his head.

'Of course, I know where I am,' said Ifashanu. 'I'm in a stinking bedlam!'

'*Gbaga!*' The priest bellowed holding his chest as if to prevent it from falling from his body. 'I am undone!' He repeated sorrowfully, his body shaking feverishly while still on his knees. The old man drifted into a true state of shock and disbelief. Ifashanu watched without care as the Priest's eyes crinkled at the corners in astonishment. His wrinkled chin came up and down changing his expression and his red eyes glared dangerously around the room and then settled on him.

At that moment, something inside Ifashanu told him to run for his dear life. The Priest was possessed, he thought. He looked left and right, and like a spark of thunder, he sped out.

* * *

When the sun reached it zenith the following day, the queen was the first visitor to be received by the Chief Priest. When he spotted her, he greeted her cheerfully from the distance.

'*Akinri egungun losan kabo,* Aina aya Jajaha, kabo, welcome,' he greeted. It was a long stretch from the palace to the Priest's home. It was her eleventh visit to his enclave in 25years.

'The reason why I made the surprise visit was to apologise for the unruly behaviour of your son at the grand shrine.' She knelt before the Priest with eyes surfing with tears. She implored him to overlook the misdeeds of the Prince and appease the gods to forgive his ignorance, as the young man clearly did not understand the gravity of his uncultured action.

Responding to the queen, the Priest spoke at length to explain the extent of shock and disappointment he had felt the previous day. And how he had thought he would not be able to return to his house because of his crippled limbs. 'Abeke, I was crippled by the attitude of your son,' he sighed heavily.

He further affirmed there and then that his mind had been telling him something was wrong somewhere. So, he strongly advised the queen to put a stop to the planned coronation. 'Ifashanu's attitude is a bad omen as far as we are concerned,' he stressed.

The queen quickly countered, emphasizing that the Prince's attitude at the shrine may have been influenced by his long stay in an uncultured environment. She pleaded until the Priest became sympathetic to her plight.

'The agony of a king's mother,' he whispered, shaking his head. 'Alright, Abeke talk to your child. 'Abeke, Queen of Odua, for this shall be the last.'

'It's well, leave that to me, Priest of Odua.' She assured him.

'Tomorrow is another day, I shall spend the rest of today seeking the sympathy of the gods,' his heart softened as he said it. He took a deep breath. 'Inform him to be prepared tomorrow before cock-crow. Our journey to the forest of *Osau* is most important and will determine his readiness to step into the shoes of his father, Jajaha Tobiolah II. If he fails this time around, let me assure you now, there shall never be any re-appeal,' he concluded frostily, inclining his head in an angle that indicated his mind was made up.

The Chief Priest arrived at the palace the following morning before the crow of the cock. He was dressed in the same outfit except that this time, he had a smudge on his forehead. His smoky pot and long beaded rod were in his hands. He helped Ifashanu to fix and suspend a sword scabbard around his waist and across his chest.

'Why carry a weapon, Chief?' he asked warily careful not to offend the old man.

'Tradition.' The Priest replied simply and short. The Priest took the lead and he followed behind. At the palace's green garden, they were met by four servants who handed over two strong black horses. Together, they rode silently out of town into *Osau*, the forest of everlasting wisdom and power.

CHAPTER NINETEEN

The forest of **Osau** was thick and full of nature's bounties. As they rode slowly, deep into the rain forest, they could hear bluffly sounds of wind brushing against leaves, branches and trees. Ifashanu's desire for some answers intensified by the minutes, but he was determined to enjoy the ride, and be calm. It was highly required that he remained calm when dealing with a man like the Priest, his mother had warned candidly. A short while later, the Priest pulled up bringing the horse to a halt. He concentrated his attention on a part of the bush. Ifashanu saw nothing other than the rustling of the bushes. He wondered stiffly if there was anything abnormal about a bush. It could be as a result of the wind or some lost animal seeking its way out, he thought.

Strangely, the old man instinct proved to be right. A middle aged man walked out confidently from that part. He was dressed in red tatters with a pair of horns on his head like a human bull. The Priest climbed down from his horse with an agility Ifashanu never thought he possessed. He reached for the scabbard fastened to his horse and removed the shinning silver sword. Ifashanu cleared his throat theatrically, he began to feel apprehensive. He dismounted impulsively, holding his horse by the bridle. He watched with concern as the other man approached the priest with a mischievous smile, his eyes poking out of their sockets like a vampire's and firmly grasping a long clothed horn on his right hand.

Ifashanu's impression of the man was that of an unarmed clown whose paramount duty was to thrill the audience and make them want to come again and watch him perform some other day. The Priest and the man spoke to each other softly, perhaps in a kind of introduction. The two laughed most time, but their amicable conversation soon grew intense and aggressive. Suddenly, they engaged in combative incantations that mysteriously took control of their physical movements, sometimes restraining and sometimes compelling. It was a battleground of magic, and of spirits, and of non-terrestrial elements. At intervals, each man staggered around like a drunkard in reaction to the effect of their incantations.

Ifashanu was not certain about the nature of the drama unfolding around him. Completely at a loss, he decided to find out by moving closer to the centre of action. The priest saw him through the corners of his eyes and warned him to stay off. Ifashanu obliged and remained outside the combat. To him, there was actually no sign that both men posed any danger to each other; there was no violence, just some staggering here and there. But before he knew what was going on, Ifashanu saw the other man suddenly freeze like a statue and thick black smoke poured out from his mouth while his hands jerked about like somebody under an attack of epilepsy.

'Can somebody tell me what's going on here?' Ifashanu asked aloud taking a bold step towards the priest. 'You're sure you don't need my help, you look very upset,' he addressed the priest who turned deaf ears to his enquiries.

The priest circled the man like a wild cat preparing for the kill but made sure he never took his eyes off him. He stopped unexpectedly still focused on the stricken man. In a flash, he thrust the entire length of the sword through the man's belly. The poor hapless fellow cried in agonizing pain, a cry that could easily have roused forest beasts. He slumped heavily on the ground shrieking and stretching. Gradually, his breathing ceased.

Ifashanu's mouth went agape, he was dumbfounded. The Priest extracted a rag from his leather bag and wiped off the bloodstains on the sword. He slid the sword back into its scabbard and remounted his horse. He found the bridle and was about to start off his horse when Ifashanu confronted him with an accusing finger directed at his chest.

'Hell No! Hell! Why did you have to do that, what for? You've just killed a man in cold blood, for no tangible reason and you think that was macho!' He took a deep breath. 'You've just committed first degree murder! That is what it is called and you ought to be tried somehow!' He shouted.

'Young man,' called the Priest, pulling back the bridle and making his horse to growl uncomfortably. 'I have warned you against unbearable questions in the forest of the gods, the forest of wisdom. I remember telling you in the palace that it was too much questions that made *Eledumare* to curse the *Gahuda* tribe. Please be patient; do not let our tribe be cursed by your nagging questions.'

'Be patient, that's it? That's your defence line, be patient?' he queried. At that moment he remembered the advice of his mother and he calmed down. 'Alright,' he said allowing the Priest to have his way. 'I'm cool,' he said and mounted his horse. The two men rode silently along the west side of the forest.

* * *

They stopped by a river, the largest of the many tributaries of *Osau*. Ever before they arrived at the shore, Ifashanu's eyes had spotted some shiny objects by the banks of the river. On getting closer, his eyes glistened at the thought of raw gold, he dismounted and walked nearer. What he saw was what he thought. Along the river bank, stretching a quarter of a mile were rows of precious stones, gold and silver ornaments, ivories, different designs of antiques and well woven traditional wrappers. He looked left and right and removed his sword in earnest ensuring that no one was watching or setting a dummy trap. He touched the fortunes with the tip of his sword. Gladly, his face melted into smiles, and then laughter. He looked back smiling at the Priest, there was no expression on the old man's face, strange, he thought, but was not too surprised.

Ifashanu knelt facing the riches. He started by touching them with his bare hands as if his hands would tell him if they were fake or real. Happiness shadowed his face, he had it made. Additional wealth, more money and more power, he thought silently. He scooped some of the precious stones into the air with happiness and fulfillment.

'What a splendid outing,' he declared joyfully.

'Young man,' called the Priest partly surprised and partly shocked. 'What do you think you are doing? Are you out of your mind?'

Ifashanu grinned. "Our ancestors have blessed us, as you can see. They've placed more wealth by the river bank for the betterment of our kingdom and I can assure you right here that it'll be judiciously utilized." He said.

The priest was not impressed. He regarded the prince critically like a father who had just discovered that his 13 years old daughter had conceived for a rogue on the run.

Unknown to the duo, a man and his wife with their little baby materialized behind them. They looked uncared for and deprived of life's daily necessities. Their clothes were made of animal skin fastened to their waist in an unfashionable manner. Ifashanu was still grinning with joy when he surveyed the area and caught sight of them. He nearly jumped out of his skin and he frantically searched for where they surfaced from. There was a sad expression on the woman's face and she seemed to be in pain. Her baby was howling in her arms and she was rattling some words of imploration in vernacular. Her ragged husband moved forward avoiding the priest. He knelt submissively before Ifashanu and began to explain how they had been enduring poverty in the forest. He requested for Ifashanu's kindness from the riches bestowed on him by his ancestors.

Ifashanu smiled at the enthusiasm of the poor man. Initially he had thought they were enemies, but he now realized they were only looking for what to eat.

'That's no problem,' he said, placing a friendly hand on the man's shoulder. 'You know I was like you, very poor, very poor indeed. That was way back in Europe.' He grinned. 'Unlike you,' he put another hand on the man's shoulder. 'My life over there was just like living in a civilized jungle, a place without culture or any sense of universality of man. You know, it's worse over there than this jungle you're living in, because as human, you're king in the jungle, you're not ruled by other people's mentality.' Ifashanu explained with a placid smile. He ran two fingers across the man's wet cheek, wiping off his tears. Briskly, he turned around. 'Tell your wife to stop weeping.' His voice carried effect. 'Now that we happened to have met in this strange circumstance, consider yourself made.'

'Thank you very much sir.' The man bowed excitedly, gesturing to his wife.

'Don't mention,' Ifashanu murmured softly. 'It's alright, just be cool, no tension. If you'd live in the city you would have known me better. I'm actually a guy with charitable quality. I'm going to give you something you'll never forget. It'll be enough for your wife and the child as well.' He smiled into the man's joyful face.

'Young man,' the voice of the priest pierced the atmosphere like a knife through silk. The old man dismounted and rushed towards the prince. 'What are you talking about and what are you giving out? Do you give out what does not belong to you?' he queried, pressing his wrinkled face against the Prince's.

'Ifashanu son of Jajaha Tobiolah II,' he called grinding his teeth irritatingly. 'Have you asked yourself how those bounties arrived at the river bank?'

Ifashanu felt the anger rising within him and looked away into the rippling water. The priest shifted his attention to the man in rags.

'And you shameless thing, is it in the forest that people who need help lives? Given gold and diamonds, to whom will you sell them to? Is it to the monkeys and squirrels? Get lost!' He ordered the man away, and removing a powder-like substance from his leather bag, he blew it gently to the direction of the man. 'Off you go, all of you. Your going shall be eternal, go now, go, go I say!' He screamed at the man and his family. As if that was not outrageous enough, Ifashanu watched as the Priest hurried towards the fortunes and began pushing them with all his energy into the shallow water.

'Damn it!' Ifashanu yelled. The thought of what he had planned and envisaged to do with the riches crept into his mind. He charged towards the Priest like a wounded lion, to restrain him. Their hands tangled and struggled in the air rebelliously, each fighting to take control.

'How could you be so heartless and wasteful at the same time? You need some reality check, you're a sadist!' Ifashanu barked angrily. 'These are ancestral gifts worth millions in the world market. You don't waste precious gifts dumping them in some river like worthless pebbles. What the hell is wrong with you old man!' Ifashanu sparked in obvious frustration, holding down the old man. Suddenly, he felt a pang of conscience and allowed the old man to rattle free from his firm grip. 'You're out of your mind, Priest,' he said pointing at him and backing off. 'You're completely out of your mind,' he raved repeatedly as he watched the Priest push the rest of the fortune into the river.

Ifashanu took a deep breath and wiped away the sweat on his face with a hand. He remembered his mother's warnings and he shook his head deciding to remain calm.

'I believe you have great spiritual powers,' he said as he headed for his stranded horse. 'But really, you lack the most important thing in life. You lack humanity and sympathy because even a mad man will not throw diamond and gold inside the river.' He lamented his loss quietly.

He could not understand why each time he was together with the priest, the old man drove him crazy the way no one did. He was the cruelest man he had ever met. He was crueler than any living slave master.

* * *

They rode ahead in uncomfortable silence and it must have taken them half an hour to get a path across the river. With the air soaked with tension, there was no further conversation between them except occasionally like: *Help me, move it, be careful*...No one spoke about the diamonds and gold as they rode southwards heading down the hills. They had not got to the hillside when Ifashanu spotted water gushing out from a cluster of rocks. It turned out to be a spring emptying into a nearby pond. Ifashanu's desire for drinking water was rekindled by the pureness of the water.

'I need to drink water,' he informed the priest, directing his horse in the direction of the pond. Ifashanu and his horse drank thirstily. The priest also joined washing his face and arms. After Ifashanu poured water on his head; as he straightened up he saw a shadow on the surface of the water and he turned around sharply with a hand on his sword.

'*Kabiyesi o, Igabakeji Orisa!*' The three sisters greeted together, kneeling in front of him respectfully. Ifashanu stared at them with astonishment and then smiled politely. He turned to the priest as if to say, *look what I've found*. He returned to the ladies and regarded them critically. Each carried a small pot of water on her head. They were dressed alike in exotic white silk garment that was fastened in style above their bosom, but exposing the delicate shallow cleft of their mammary glands. They looked amazing beyond the description of beauty.

Ifashanu remained interestingly attentive watching in fascination as the ladies put down their pots of water on the grass. The eldest of them spoke in the most beautiful voice he had ever heard.

'Please your highness; take me as your queen, the mother of Princes and Princesses. I'm the eldest among all and the most experienced in the various demands of kingship. Take a closer look at my adornment.' She turned around. 'You'll be pleased with mother nature's creativity in me. Take me, have me,' she said stretching out both hands to the prince. Ifashanu smiled, took one of her hands and shook it warmly.

'Don't mind her, your highness,' interjected the second lady. 'Take a very good look at this.' She swayed her butt displaying her curves in a most provocative manner. 'I'm the prettiest of all. You deserve nothing but the best, the choice is yours.' She concluded with a sexy smile on her face and running her manicured fingers down her cheek. Ifashanu's smile grew broader. 'This is absolutely terrific!' He said delightedly.

'My king, give me your affection and you shall not regret,' the third lady said in a sleek voice that could have woken the dead. 'I'm the youngest and the most pretty.' She rose to her feet and moved closer to Ifashanu. 'Take a look at me from hair to toe,' she pointed, brushing her breasts slightly against his chest. She traced a long delicate finger across Ifashanu's lower jaw, sending a flame of desire down his spine. 'From the look in your eyes, you do know I'm the prettiest, I can read your mind,' she declared and proceeded without resistance, circling an arm around his shoulders while she placed her other hand on his chest.

In response, Ifashanu kissed her lips softly, yet passionately. He cradled her head with a hand and kissed her scented hair showing some love. The prince ventured going further in his free exploit until the Priest cried from behind like a wild animal in deadly bondage.

'Abomination! A sacrilegious act before the gods!' The priest shouted bearing down upon them like a rattle snake. 'May my eyes bear no witness to forbidden acts!' He eyed Ifashanu wickedly and continued to shout. 'Ifashanu, son of Jajaha Tobiolah II, what is this you're doing in the forest of the gods, the forest of supreme purification, the shrine of your ancestors!'

Ifashanu was speechless. He held on to the youngest of the ladies in his arms and watched as the priest turned swiftly to the other two who were still on their knees. The burning eyes of the priest frightened them. Their heartbeats accelerated as they watched the priest remove his sword from it scabbard. He raised the sharp metal to the sky, baptized by the sunrays, and in two quick swampy successions he beheaded the two in cold blood. The third sister held by the Prince was about slipping down to the ground in a faint, but he held her up. Her eyes nearly popped in their sockets as she struggled out of his grip and raced into the bushes. The priest rained curses on her as she dashed into the forest.

Ifashanu stared at the old man in total dismay. Fury churned deep inside him and there was no mistaking his anger for a bear fighter. The priest had no idea about the passion building up inside him.

'You're the cruelest person I have ever come across in this life,' Ifashanu spat with a tough cold stare. 'You're worse than any white man that ever existed. I don't want someone like you in my kingdom. Death is what you deserve!' He shouted with much venom as he could muster. The prince of Odua removed his sword swiftly like a pro and swung the sharp shiny silver metal fiercely across the Priest's neck. It cut through the jugular forcing a strangled cry of despair from the priest. The old man stared speechlessly into space. The sword he held dropped to the grass and with the last effort he could summon, he managed to raise his hand to his bleeding neck. He felt the cut and looked at his blood helplessly. He clenched his fists in utmost pain and fell on his knees. He knew at that point that it was over. The journey of a thousand miles must have a beginning and an end. His had been brought to an abrupt end by a callous and ignorant Prince.

The king's sword, held by Ifashanu, is heavily charmed and divine. It had neither boundary nor respect for any flesh. It pierced through whatever and whoever it was aimed at, brushing aside spiritual powers. The priest took a forced deep breath and muttered in a husky voice that did not seem to belong to him

'You have destroyed your destiny and your kingdom, and Peace shan't be yours any more,' swore the old man. 'You shall eat what you see and not what you want all the days of your life. Success and progress will be yours no more. You shall wander in desperation all the days of your life.'

'That's bull-shit,' Ifashanu shot-back. You're talking craps. You're going to rust in hell, surely.'

The priest struggled in death throes that choked him like a fish that has just swallowed a hook. Then in his final moments he took a final breath.

'Ifashanu son of Tobiolah, the fruits of your labour shall not prosper, nor shall it be beneficial now and forever...' He ventured to take another breath as thick blood poured down his nose and his mouth. Then he stiffened and slumped face down. Ifashanu stared at the lifeless body for a while and turned away sliding the sword into its scabbard, spitting in disgust.

* * *

Indecisive of his next action, he looked desperately into the sky as if expecting salvation from above. He looked down at the dead Priest again and the thought crossed his mind to give the old man a decent burial. He shook his head instead.

'Let the vultures feast on him,' he spat and headed in the direction of the waiting horses. Instantly, thunder struck loudly splitting the cloud into two halves. He tried getting hold of his horse but both fled in fear, perhaps in condemnation of his action. There was no point running after them, he thought. A few steps ahead, he heard another rumbling of thunder and looked up at the sky in total confusion; it struck again, louder than the first and second. He felt uncomfortable and endangered.

Amidst the danger posed by the thunder and his loneliness in the jungle, the fear of the unknown gripped him. He began a rat race, growling in desperation as he tore through the forest, bumping into trees and flipping away obstructive branches and wild grasses. His eyes were streaming with tears.

In Odua, after the thunder it began to drizzle. Pearls of thunder punctuated the shower intermittently as if to reclaim its dominance. For Ifashanu in the forest, the thought that he had a river to cross and many miles to run made him shiver and his eyes red and saddened. Without hesitation, he raised his white garb to his kneels, and entered the shallow river. He splashed in the water and swam the entire length of the river without a rest. Getting to the shore, he knelt to squeeze out the water from the tail of his garb. Frightfully, his eyes slanted sideway and confirmed his suspicion. The creature that stood beside him was somewhat like a man, but an ape in every sense. He was brandishing a short axe in the air.

He grinned invitingly, but Ifashanu knew too well that those grins were far from friendly. It was not as straight as an Iroko tree, so Ifashanu rose slowly and carefully with his eyes glued to the ape-man. He made a final judgement by surveying him thoroughly, accepting the fact that he was a homo-sapiens with every human feature, though it had eyes that were steel-like in their sockets. His mouth, his zygomatic bone and nose, all seemed to be jammed to the upper part of his face like an orangutan.

An idea struck Ifashanu, an idea to win some sympathy and friendship. He flashed a reckless smile at the ape and extended his hand for a handshake. The ape got it wrong as anticipated.

'Son of man!' He barked in a deep voice that carried un-spoken terror. He wasn't used to command and threat. Ifashanu cowered, taking three steps backward. His heart cringed with each loud breath of the ape. Without warning, the ape charged towards him with murderous fury blazing in his eyes. Ifashanu thought fast, he knew he had to do away with fear, for fear causes hesitation and hesitation would probably make his greatest fear to come true. He would be dead and forgotten in minutes if he did not fight back, so he psyched himself.

The ape grated through clenched teeth as he noticed Ifashanu reaching for his sword. Skillfully, he threw his axe at him and the axe hit its target only slightly. Ifashanu saw it coming. His reflexes were as fast as the rolling axe. Swiftly he dived and the axe succeeded in brushing off some flesh on his deltoid, causing him to drop his sword involuntarily. He held the wounded arm for a brief second and leapt at the ape with a killer intent. He had a good grip of its neck and he tightened his arms around it to break it. But it was the ape that got the upper hand. He lifted Ifashanu up in the air and threw him down heavily on the ground. His princely body landed roughly on crispy dry leaves and he thought the ape had wrecked his spine. He moaned in pain and rained curses at it.

Promptly, the ape jumped over him seeking its axe. Ifashanu quickly realised the danger and leapt once again at the ape, seizing it more tightly by the neck. This time, the two fell rolling on the grass, locked and punching each other in the face till they reached the bank of the river.

When Ifashanu became convinced that his survival would not depend on holding the ape tightly around the neck, he decided to give it up. Its head was too hard to crack and it seemed a skilful wrestler with tough bones. As he released his neck, the ape rammed a powerful dent below Ifashanu's ribs who gave a choking cry. Another combination hit him in several places and a head butt followed. Ifashanu's vision blurred instantly. He saw stars dropping over him and the flaming sun bobbing and popping in the cloud, like it was going to fall and the world was going to end. He had one last energy, a feeble energy that he was determined to make the best use of in his bid to remain alive. With what was left, he crawled, grabbed and rolled the ape over, away from his bleeding head. Swiftly, he knelt over the ape in haste and began to bash its face with his fists and elbows. He delivered an upper-cut to the jaw, followed by countless slaps and beatings on the face and on the nose. The ape rattled painfully beneath him and made futile efforts to set itself free from torment. For once, it cried under intense torture, a cry that echoed through the forest, like the cry of a wolf.

Ifashanu searched for his sword and the axe, anything he could lay his hands on to nail the beast. His eyes picked out the axe first because it was nearest. He reached for it and raised it in the air so that the ape could see how it was going to die. He brought it down decisively across its neck and thick blood shot upward splashing on his face.

'Shit!' He cursed in disgust. The ape made a deep death cry as its bleeding neck twitched convulsively in a final twitch for a permanent rest. Ifashanu stood looking down proudly at his prey, a job well done. He crossed over the still body, got hold of his sword and drove it into the lifeless body of the lifeless ape. Just making sure, he told himself. He then cut a part of his white garb to stop the bleeding on his arm, tightening it into a band around the wound. He wiped his blood stained sword on the grass and surged ahead not bothering to tuck the sword back into its scabbard. He simply scurried through the bush with an energy he never imagined he possessed. Running toward no specific direction, he used the sword to scare away vultures that hovered above and around him.

* * *

After running for about a long distance, he decided to rest under a big *Aghari* tree that had wide branches like an aeroplane wing. His untreated arm bled, dripping red blood and turning the green grass into red-brown. He sat and heaved a deep sigh of relief as he tightened his wounded arm. He pulled the final knot with a hand and his teeth, absorbing deep spasm of pain as he did so. Exhausted and sick, Ifashanu placed his head against the tree, using one arm to cradle his bandaged arm. His gaze was fixed and piercing. The image of the Priest's last moments crept into his mind and he could visualise the way the old man lowered his head in death. How those glazed eyes stared at him blankly in disbelief, and in an unfriendly shock.

"Damn it!" How could he have gotten so crazy to do such a thing, to kill an old harmless man?" He knew at that moment that it will be one event in his life; he'll live to regret and be ashamed of.

'Shit! Those ladies, the three sisters.' He recalled, they must have cast a spell on him. A remarkable spell it must have been, a spell that has caused him to interfere in the issue of life and death. Halfway through his thoughts, he felt a strange softness at the back of his head and he turned very slowly to discover it was the tail end of a snake. The head was a little distance away, preparing for the strike.

'Snake!' He gasped fearfully and dived on the grass just as the snake launched its attack. It missed its target slightly and immediately tried to re-launch, but Ifashanu grabbed it by the tail and eased himself up like an antenna. The snake sniffed, as

Ifashanu flipped and tossed the reptile over his head in random motion. He released it suddenly in the air deep into the farthest end of the forest. He rubbed his hands clean and got hold of his sword lying on the ground. Well rested, he could no longer remember the path through which they rode. However, his sense of direction told him to move west-ward.

Having covered a short distance, the drizzling rain turned into a heavy downpour. Droplets of rain water ran obliquely across his face to splash aggressively at him like a shower turned to the fullest. So heavy was the rain it pressed down the leaves and pulled branches of trees from trunks. Ifashanu struggled ahead tirelessly, racing the steep ascent on the west-side of the forest. His heart was pounding to the extent that he could almost hear it. His mood starchy and pathetic, he cautiously stepped into a dirty pond. Aware of crocodiles, he hurried and successfully crossed it to the other side. He bent and took a deep breath. His leather sandals had become heavy with mud and were holding him back in the process. He unbuckled the pair, hitting them together to force out the sticky mud. Cleared of mud, he bent to re-buckle them.

Suddenly, he heard a roar from somewhere, from nowhere. The roar came alive more aggressively and became unpleasantly familiar as Ifashanu raised his head in anticipation of another unfriendly beast. Disrupted, he eyed a distant area where the sound seemed most likely. Apparently, what he saw was an uncomfortable reality.

'Holy-shit! Not again.' He cried under his breath and alert and on his knees. At first he thought it was a Lion, but closer look showed some spots on its body. It looked like a tiger. Ifashanu eyed the teeth, its whiskers were not long enough and he concluded it must be a Leopard. 'Shit,' he swore as his skin crawled at the thought of a wild leopard tearing him to pieces. He felt the adrenaline course through his system. Looking up into the gathering cloud, he felt like the sun was melting his body as quickly as a cheese and this was going to be the most pragmatic violence test in his life.

Earnestly, he strategically abandoned his left sandal, stepping backward. The leopard marched confidently towards him, roaring in such a way that made him to be almost too certain that his run of luck in life was over. All ideas and sense of direction departed him as he sighted the perfectly shaped tooth of the cat. It started at him more purposefully, sure it was going to have a human for lunch. Ifashanu spotted a big tree by his right, a little stretch from where he stood trembling. Two things struck his mind. First, he thought of hiding behind the tree and play hide and seek with the cat. Second, he thought of climbing the tree to seek shelter till the beast went away.

Unconsciously, his instincts took over. He picked his sword and sped to his right, catching a branch. From it, he flipped over to the bough and steadied himself on the tree. He squatted and held one of the branches for support. Vividly, he starred down at the leopard through the leaves. He could see the wild cat looking angrier by his action. What Ifashanu did not understand was that large trees were its home and cats knew how best to enter their houses. Cleverly, it raised her head, eyeing Ifashanu from below. It roared and took few calculative steps backward in preparation for a possible flight. Ifashanu could read it mind and he decided to make things easier for the beast. He shifted craftily to the edge of the branch, making himself obvious and vulnerable to attack. With one hand, he brandished his sword to the rays of the sun, as if to get some inspiration from it. The leopard did not notice the sword because it was partly hidden by the large leaves. And without much ado, it gave a final roar and sped. It climbed the tree majestically with its sharp claws and leapt all the way towards Ifashanu. At the count of three, Ifashanu swung the sword across the face of the cat right in the air. The metal sliced towards its head, capturing the face but not without her long sharp nails finding their bearings on Ifashanu's shoulder.

The damage done by the cat caused him to lose his grip on the sword. It fell along with the cat on the wet grass. Ifashanu stared at the bleeding leopard as it attempted to stand on its feet and probably recharge. Perplexed, he sat on the branch watching the cat collapse weakly on the ground. Victorious once again, he made a huge sigh of relief and wondered how long his luck would last. Standing straight up on the bough and breathless, he looked around to far distances and his eyes caught sight of the Palace, standing out magnificently on the East.

'There you are,' he muttered delightfully forgetting his pains and regrets. He realized he had been wandering about in the wrong direction all the while. Athletically, he jumped down from the tree and landed beside the leopard. He peered dimly at the Leopard as white dribble oozed from the corner of its mouth. Its eyes were wide open. Ifashanu smacked his lips satisfactorily, though his face was hazy with pain. He picked his sword and displayed it once again to the sun. With clenched teeth, he drove the metal deep into the leopard, pinning it to the earth. Irresistibly, he watched as it drawled, shrieked, and ceased all movements.

CHAPTER TWENTY

Tired and waned, Ifashanu jogged through the kingdom's gate and made it to the Palace in record time and heaved a deep sigh of relief. Strangely, everywhere look deserted. Perhaps, everyone must be resting after a hectic day on the farm, he thought incorrectly. A curfew had been declared for 10 hours by the elders of the land instead. He braved entering through the Palace backyard where the only emergency door was located. Gazing momentarily around the premises, he opened the backyard gate. Turning the knob, he noticed two strange looking women, each carrying a basketful of yam and cassava. He did not want to be seen in such condition, so he hid behind the small iron rod, standing straight and thin like a javelin.

However, the person the two women saw in a flash appeared unattractive and battered. He would have been easily ignored had it not been the way he tried to hide himself like a fugitive. Once they were out of sight, Ifashanu dashed into the Palace kicking the doors open with single swap. He removed the sword from it scabbard and hurried down the passage.

'Mother! Mother! Mother!' He shouted along the corridor. The queen heard him, rose and quickly rushed out of her bedroom to meet him in the hall. At first, she regarded him sceptically, then slowly her eyes opened wide like a dash-board. She spotted his bruised shoulder, the bandaged arm and her eyes settled finally on the blood-stained sword and she erupted.

'*Iye-moja o*! Didn't they say the beasts in the jungle manifest loyalty?' she exclaimed with her hands on her head and mouth aghast. 'You used the sword? *Ogun o!'* She shouted and got hold of her loose head gear which she fastened around her waist.

Ifashanu nodded his head in guilt looking downcast.

'I used it mother. I used it in self-defence,' he declared.

'What of the Chief Priest, is he alright? Who attacked you?' she asked, moving closer to feel his forehead with her hand. Rather than hot, it was stone cold.

'We got into a row, a misunderstanding sort of, and I killed him for his unkindness to the people we encountered in the forest.'

'What!' The queen cried mouth agape. Slowly she began to retreat from him as if he had become something unclean and forbidden. 'Ifashanu, you murdered the Priest? By so doing, don't you know that you have destroyed your destiny and that of your kingdom, and you have brought calamity unto the land, do you know that?' she queried, looking at him incredulously, like he's a duplicate of *Shaitan*, the god of disaster.

The look on his mother's face frightened him beyond measure. He knew that the battles he had been fighting all along was as good as over and lost if his mother, who had been his life-wire and ardent defender, should turn her back against him.

'Ifashanu,' she cried tearfully. 'You must hurry up, pack your belongings and flee far away, southward to the land of the Zulu or better still, return to the United Kingdom and seek asylum from her Majesty until the dust settles. You must not stay here and give the Chancellors and elders the time to assess and respond to the catastrophe you have brought upon the land.' She nervously tied, loosened and retied her wrapper. In response Ifashanu fixed a determined gaze.

'Mother, running away will solve nothing, and for how long will I be on the run? Have you forgotten that a man who fights and runs will return to fight another day? I'm staying mother. This is my prerogative and it's not my fault that all these are happening. Perhaps it's my fate, my war, and I'm of the opinion that it's better to die here and now, than run like a coward,' he declared. 'I'm not afraid of death. I won't run mother and I'm not trying to decide the type of death I want, but I can decide how I wish to meet my end. I'd rather die here.' He pushed the sword back into it scabbard. 'You don't have an idea of how I got here alive in the first place. And I'm sure my father wasn't a coward?' With that he stormed out of his mother's presence.

The Priest's Enclave

Ejire, the only daughter of the Chief Priest, noticed with shock that the flaming pot of life placed at an angle in her father's bedroom had gone off when she entered his room. It went off some hours after his departure. Ejire, having been initiated into witchcraft long enough by her deceased mother knew better when she saw the flameless pot. It could only mean one thing, a bad omen. Without much ado, she started for the village square in defiance of the curfew and cried out her sorrow for all to hear. In grief, she hurried to the compound of Chief Balogun and informed him of what her eyes had seen. The defence chief listened to her attentively because he had to reach a fast decision. He was now in charge if truly the Priest was dead.

* * *

Later that evening, the furious Chancellors and elders stormed the palace seeking enquiries about what transpired inside the thick forest of *Osau*. The queen was however a step ahead of them in thought. She had passed a firm instruction to the gate keepers and alerted the royal guards that no one should be allowed access into the Palace until further instructions. Because of the order of her majesty, the Chancellors and elders were barred from gaining access into the Palace. This action indeed confirmed their suspicions, indicating guilt on the part of the royal family. The two women who reported seeing the Prince with a blood-stained sword were no more to be doubted. No more hypotheses. Ifashanu was a murderer, they resolved.

At midnight, a meeting of elders was held at the residence of chief Balogun. Their discussions were elaborate, laced with agreements as well as disagreements. The general consensus was to select seven men from different households. They would be fortified to comb the forest and bring back the body of the Priest by noon of the next day in preparation for his re-incarnation. Their meeting was however adjourned.

* * *

Early in the morning the next day, Chief Balogun rose from sleep and sat in bed after the gruelling meeting of the previous day. He felt agile and full of life, swirling as he sat in bed. His bedroom was dimly lit and contained a single wooden bed, a small table and nothing more. Looking through his window he could see the firm structure of the magnificent Palace towering over his enclave. Reluctantly, he got out of bed, reached for his wrapper and a chewing stick on the small table. Shuffling to the door, he stood with his arms folded, gazing at the Palace with mixed feelings. His chewing stick dangled at a corner of his mouth.

Chief Balogun's stomach knotted with disgust as his thought shifted to Prince Ifashanu. Being a status conscious man, he cherished his position as Defence Chief more than any other thing in life. He'd never imagined a moment like this would ever arise, he thought while pacing around the room. This was a moment that had suddenly placed him in charge of the Kingdom's overall affairs. The situation at hand made him strongly believe that his happy days were just by the corner.

'*Ogun!* god of iron,' he called appraisingly. 'Another man's misfortune is certainly another man's blessing,' he said, with all sense of fulfilment. He knew gladly that in some hour's time, deep in the middle of the night, the cult members would converge to ensure that the bastard Prince was sent on a forced visit to the home of their ancestors. He stepped into his compound and addressed the sky raising both hands.

'Ile o fura ile joo.
Aja o fura aja jaa.
Para o fura para ree.
Ifura ni ogun agba.'

He laughed with his eyes fixed to the sky, watching as the cloud obscured the sun for a long moment.

'The black-hearted bastard has the guts to murder our Priest and he thinks he can get away with it, over my dead body!' He swore and then quickly added, 'He who takes our gods and tradition for mockery deserves nothing but death. A sin wickedly committed does not deserve any forgiveness.'

Chief Balogun continued to pace around his large compound. For a reflecting moment, he allowed his mind to drift slowly to the past and present. Along his line of thought, he remembered something and briskly walked to the lemon tree. He plucked three lemonades and washed his mouth with water from the pot buried beside the tree. He bit and squeezed the lemonades in his mouth and a sense of gratification adorned his face as he ate the sour fruit.

Excitedly, something crossed his mind. When he, Balogun, the defence chief of Odua, finally becomes King after the ultimate death of the crazy Prince, he'll send away all the King's former wives residing in the Palace with the exception of Queen Abeke, the indomitable diminutive fore-woman, a pretty goddess in her own right. Her wealth of experience will be useful in serious decision-making in the future. She must be maintained, he thought to himself. But will Abeke be able to live as his wife under the same roof with the mother of his children, his nagging Morenike, he wondered with a finger to the side of his head. By all standards, Morenike was an aggressive woman, he thought with concern. Perhaps, he should discuss his plans with her before taking such step. There was the likelihood that she would understand the fact that a King must have at least five women in the Palace taking good care of him. It was a right that shall be bestowed on him by their ancestors, he told himself.

Infact, if all went well, he might even use the opportunity to request for the hand of the young and beautiful Nubian slave at his mother-in-law's courtyard. He would take the young Nubian as his third wife. She would be referred to as *Olori Kekere*, he thought smilingly.

The Chief threw away the squeezed lemonades under the mango tree and returned inside the house. He went straight to his bedroom, loosened his wrapper and lay in bed hoping to catch some sleep so that he could wake up refreshed and ready for the day's activities. As he lay silently in bed, the image of the infant Prince when he was a baby came into his mind. He still remembered clearly the day they banished the child from their great land. He also recalled the ceremony that greeted his return.

'Bastard,' he spat. 'The gods are always precious, they know best.' He smiled mischievously. '*Enu ti igbin fibu orisa, yio figbole gbehin ni.*' He mumbled and then laughed excitedly at the turn of fate.

A moment later, he heard faintly his front door opened. It was followed by footsteps. For an instant he was sure of who was at the door.

'Morenike,' he called out, but there was no reply. It quickly occurred to him that she ought to be on the farm with the children at that period of the day. Maybe it was one of the children, he thought and relaxed. No cause for alarm. He waited in darkness as his bedroom door opened a crack and he saw a feminine figure slip inside. He could not make out the face immediately. He sat up in bed, and looked closely. When he recognised the person, his fear precipitated. The woman standing midway to his bed was the very last person he expected to see. It was Abeke, queen of Odua, wrapped fashionably in Aso-Oke and head gear. She put on lovely beads on both hands and looked unbelievably attractive in the darkness.

'Good morning Chief Balogun,' she greeted with a passionate smile. The chief grunted and re-adjusted in bed. His mind twisted silently asking himself many questions at the same time. What could Abeke be doing in his home? Why did she not even bother to knock to attract the owner of the house? Why did she just walk in straight into his bedroom? He cleared his throat to speak and then thought otherwise. Perhaps, she'd seen the light at the end of the tunnel. She had come to profess her loyalty to him as it was now obvious that he was the King in waiting. Smart Abeke, together they shall beat the odds, he thought confidently.

Their eyes locked briefly in the dark but they spoke no word. With extra touch to her beauty and like a professional, she swayed towards the bed.

'How's your wife?' she whispered and dutifully began to undo the tie of her wrapper. Chief Balogun watched in complete astonishment as her wrapper fell to the floor and the head gear followed suit. In an instant, she was completely naked. Stunned, he gazed at her breasts as they undulated provocatively. The Chief's mind raced a thousand miles. He must be dreaming, he told himself firmly. With arms folded on his chest, he blinked successively till he could no longer differentiate between reality and dream. Chief Balogun's mind was entwined and nothing seemed to matter anymore. The gods must have been listening to his whispers; perhaps it was a sign that his wishes had been granted. The support of a woman of Abeke's class is highly significant. He would need her in his kingdom to accomplish smooth governance. And with luck, she might bear him another Prince. A responsible Prince though, not a Prince with a mental case, not a Prince that will speak and think like a white man.

The Chief suddenly felt young as his face began to fold with acknowledgement, smiles and desire. A queen must pay a higher price to be pleasured by the strongest hands like his, he thought proudly. Abeke joined him in bed. She was astride so that her breasts could dangle excitedly over his face.

'Abeke is this really you?' he managed to speak at last. Grimly and anxiously, he crammed an obedient nipple into his mouth. He bit and sucked while she fiddled with his crotch through his wrapper. Confused as he was, Chief Balogun acknowledged the reality of his feelings. The way his body was responding to the touches of Abeke was electrifying. He closed his eyes in a rare moment of unmatched pleasure.

Oba ta llaho..., he invoked whole heartedly as intense pleasure moved through him in surges. He had never experienced anything like this, the touches of a world class queen. He held on to the other breast with one hand, grazing it, fumbling with it, and sighing as he felt himself rising under his wrapper.

Too soon he was ready, energized and ready to move all the way. There was no doubt anymore about the reality of what he was feeling. It was real and exotic, coming from a woman he'd long admired from afar. He was busy with her breasts, devouring them with his mouth when suddenly he felt a sharp pain, followed by a strange flow that emptied into his body. He managed to look up and spotted a dagger. Queen Abeke had succeeded easily beyond her fears and imagination. Sh'd just silently and accurately pierced a dagger through the belly of the strongest man in the kingdom. She held him down by the neck as tightly as she could. With all her might she jerked him against the head plate of the bed. Chief Balogun struggled to no avail. His eyes remained opened and dazed with shock. What a thin line between life and death, he thought helplessly and shocked in its entirety. In the chilly moment that followed, he became still.

CHAPTER TWENTY-ONE

At 6:45am, Ifashanu was still asleep when his mother returned to the palace, unnoticed. She headed straight to his room with a feeling of someone chopped in the head with a chisel. His door was wide open; she stepped in and sat nervously at an angle watching as he tossed and turned in bed. She had this nagging feeling, every mother's feeling; she wanted to protect him from impending calamity. She had determined to pay the price for his ignorance, and to that effect she has made up her mind to do anything that would keep him alive. Already, she had killed for him and was willing to fight the more and probably kill again. Her thoughts were cut short the moment Ifashanu stretched, and incoherently moaned in his sleep. She was gripped with fear.

'Ifashanu,' she called out, her voice shaky.

He heard her call from far, he stretched lazily and propped a pillow behind his head, facing the agonising expression of his mother. She looked terrified.

'Are you alright mother?' he asked on sighting the tears in her eyes as she approached the bed. She sat on the edge and looked down at her son.

'Ifashanu my son, you're the only child I have left, the only hope of the royal family. I want to help you to escape. I know our people better than you do, they could be impossible when it comes to issues of culture and tradition. They are going to harm you, one way or another, that is for sure. I implore you to take my advice and start thinking of a way to leave, go anywhere, till the mist settles,' she pleaded.

'And what about you mother, what about you?' he asked breathlessly. She wiped away the tears in her eyes.

'I am near my grave my son, whichever way you look at it. I've seen a lot, quite a lot, any harm they do to me is insignificant at this moment. You're still young and full of life and you deserve more years, more opportunities and more…'

'No mother, no,' Ifashanu retorted. 'If I must leave, I shan't leave without you, that's final.' The queen's countenance changed.

'Ifashanu don't sound impossible, what does it matters if I follow you? Was I there with you all your days in the United Kingdom? I want you to make the journey alone. Go alone, our ancestors will be with you all through.'

Ifashanu shifted a bit, trembling. 'I can't believe we are discussing this, mother. What exactly are you afraid of?' he snorted. 'Is it death? That they will kill me?' he asked with a faint smile on his face, shaking his head. 'Mother, I am not afraid of death, especially in this circumstance. And if you must know, I've met death ninety-nine times in that beast-filled forest. What difference will the hundredth encounter mean to me?'

'The hundred might just kill you,' she chipped in.

'Mother, I am staying and that is final!' He emphasized with a finger dug into the mattress.

'But you do not have what it takes to fight them. Why stay? Do you want to die when you know you can avoid it? This is suicide!'

'Mother, I'll not prevail if I'm destined to fail and I'll not fail if I am destined to prevail. I am asking you to please let me stay here with you.'

'I'm not sending you away, Ifashanu,' she frowned. 'I am only trying to avert another sorrow in my life,' she gave a deep sigh. 'You may be an elephant, strong. So also are the people you are facing and if you'd been born far back when *Sango*, god of fire, fought with *Obakoso*, perhaps you will understand what spiritual battle is all about.'

'I wonder what it is about this guy, *Sango* that makes everyone mellow once his name is mentioned. Was he that brutal? Damn it.'

'What do you expect from a man who spat fire?' she said, making a face as she stood looking around the room. 'If you insist on staying to weather the storm, then you mustn't sit-back and relax. You must think and come-up with a solid plan. Your enemies are blood-thirsty and they are right by our door,' she informed candidly.

'But mother, what am I supposed to think about? What am I supposed to do? I should extract my sword from its scabbard and start beheading everyone?'

'I wish it's that easy.' She forced a smile and shook her head. Anyhow, you still have to think up something and let me know.' She paused and then continued firmly. 'Henceforth, you must try to remain conscious at all times, no more deep sleep. I'll be in your room most times at night, just to ensure you're not deeply asleep. And as a precaution, avoid lying on your back fully when sleeping. You may lie on your sides.'

'Why all these?' he queried.

'Because it takes evil to combat evil, witch to witch, wizard to wizard, and man to man. This has always been the phenomenon of battle on our continent.' She extracted a coin from the hollow of her breasts. 'Take this,' she said, placing the coin in his palm. 'There is a tiny hole at the top, put a black thread through it and wear it around your neck.' Ifashanu looked curiously at the coin. He saw the hole and knew it was a good luck charm.

'Thanks mother.' He stood up and gave her a peck on the hand and the head.

* * *

Later in the afternoon, when the sun had reached its highest point, Ifashanu rose nervously in bed with pains in both hands.

He'd been lying in bed awake for six-hours, thinking about his next line of action. He put on his white T-shirt and jeans and went to a section of his wardrobe. He unloaded the radio-machine he inherited from Lord Franklin Gordon. He had never seriously thought about the machine until today. Also today, he remembered Jane, Aunt Romana and Adam. He wondered what they were doing now, and if they would have changed much. His own life was taking a down toll and he hoped theirs were steady. He might be lucky to have escaped death, he thought with a shrug, but the feeling of becoming a persona non grata seemed worse. There in bed, he resolved to talk with his friends abroad. He needed to hear their voices, perhaps for the last time. He would like to apologise for not having called all the while. He could also use the chance to in-form them of the impending danger surrounding him. He would ask that they wish him luck.

Ifashanu rushed out of his room with a briefcase in hand. The case was designed to contain all the apparatus for long dis-tance transmission. He went as far as the roof of the Palace. When he got there, he discovered it was breezy at the top and hoped it would not interfere with transmission. Gently, he placed the case on a cracked block. He bent on his knees, opened it expertly and started to press buttons. He turned the frequency modulator at intervals, until a rough voice sounded through the small speaker. It was not the voice he wanted to hear, it was the voice of an operator in Zanzibar-Africa inform-ing him that there was no direct line to the United Kingdom. The Operator advised him to try a connection through the Gold-Coast Satellite Network or the Cairo line.

The Gold-coast was nearest; so he gladly wiped off the sweat rolling down his face and pressed the numbers given by the Operator. He turned the frequency modulator a couple of times and waited a few seconds for the network to come alive. There wasn't much luck either way. The operator there com-plained of heavy rainfall that had recently disrupted smooth transmissions from his station to the U.K. In the end, he gave Ifashanu key codes to Sudan. With frantic effort, Ifashanu pressed the buttons randomly turning the frequency modulator till it finally gave him the desired voice.

'This is Major Martin Andrews in Khartoum, over,' a husky voice with a British accent announced. Ifashanu did not waste time or allow the officer to say any other word.

'Please officer, I've been trying to get through to U.K; please can you be of assistance to me?'

'Who are you and what's the purpose of your call?' The Major sounded as if he was going to explode. The officer knew the caller must be very important to have gained access to a powerful machine capable of by passing restricted military frequencies.

'Ifash is the name, the Crown Prince of Odua Kingdom. I'll like to speak with the Bishop, John Mathew of West Bromwich England. It's highly urgent.'

The officer hesitated. He lowered his head and checked through a list on his table. His bushy moustache stiffened as he realised who the caller was. The officer kept the prince on the line for twenty minutes trying desperately to fix a connection between Odua and Europe. He succeeded at last. Ifashanu could hear the final clicks as the Major switched over and informed him that the line was cleared and that the Bishop was on the line.

'May the Lord Jesus Christ be with you and your people. May he strengthen and guide you aright in the name of the Father, the Son and the Holy Ghost.' The Bishop's voice flowed over the line. Ifashanu beamed at what he just heard. Truly, the Bishop was the last person he wanted to speak with, but he needed him somehow. He could use him to accomplish his mission, he thought cleverly. For a few seconds, he did not know what to say to the clergyman. Should he just go straight to the point or beat around the bush for a while, he wondered. He coughed slightly, determined not to sound like someone on the death row and then began to speak in a near-perfect voice.

They spoke briefly about the benefits of missionary works across the African continent and about the multi-million pounds Christian crusade and aids project that would commence at the end of the year. The Bishop was highly delighted about the idea of getting an invitation to visit the seven black coasts under the firm control of Odua Kingdom. At the end of their conversation, Ifashanu made his move.

'By the way Bishop, I'll greatly appreciate it if you'll be generous to link me via your switchboard to my good friend, Sheriff Adam McCarthy, D.P.O. of Sterling Island Police Station.'

'I'm willing to assist you. Please hold on while I check the radio directory for Sterling Island,' answered the Bishop. Clearly, Ifashanu could hear the Bishop flipping through the papers. The line dimmed for a while and then came alive after some minutes later.

'Sorry for the delay, it is well. You may now press the button tagged *local* on your set. Please be informed that Adam McCarthy is the name of the Police Commissioner at the City Hall, Leeds. He's no more on the island, over.' The Bishop went off the line. Ifashanu pressed the button marked *local*.

'Odua calling Leeds, over; Odua calling Leeds, over,' he called loudly. Like a blast, Adam's voice boomed over unbelievably.

'Is it really you? Where the hell are you calling from and how's the weather over there nigger? Heir to the Kingdom of god shit,' he chuckled. 'God damn it, Ifash! Is the Bishop in his right frame of mind?'

'Speaking with you is Crown Prince Ifashanu Jajaha Tobiolah II of Odua Kingdom.'

'Hey, come on nigger, don't give me that jaj-jaj-tomb shit,' Adam barked across, crossing his legs under his table. 'You aren't different from those crookies downtown. If you must know, things have changed for them pretty well since you've been gone. Many are still in jail though and many are still out there making my life hell in this department. How you doing? Are you cool and how's your slut, is she cool too?' Ifash flushed, suppressing a choke at the mere thought of Jane.

'It's nice hearing your voice, buddy,' said Ifash.

'Its nice hearing yours too pearl.'

'Sorry I dint call for so long?'

'It's no problem, who's expecting your call anyway,' Adam wheezed.

'You know Adam, I have got a serious problem at hand and I need your sound advice,' he announced pathetically.

'Wuooo!' Adam burst. 'The king Chancellor! Good, at least you have a reason for calling. You calling me after many fucking years just to tell me how fucked up your life is in that dead end you call a Kingdom? You should have known better!' He twisted in his seat, reached for a dusty file and opened it at the middle. 'For Christ sake Ifash! You fucking graduated from a prestigious college and you ought to know better than allow yourself to be optioned by some woman in flaps and taken away to hell,' he shouted over the line, accompanied by a banging of his fist on his table.

'Look Adam, I am not calling you to listen to some of your craps and I don't want you to preach to me about hell and paradise because you don't know the difference. You've got eyes but you cannot see, and you've got a brain but you can't think…'

'Alright, alright, save your humour! Save the hell, what's your problem and why should I be interested, now talk.' Adam encouraged having detected the determination in Ifash's voice. Once again, he crossed and re-crossed his legs under the table and lit a tobacco. Ifashanu started slowly while Adam dragged on his smoke listening attentively. He did not interrupt but allowed him to talk while he smoked. His expression never changed all through. At the end, he could not understand what Ifash expected him to say or do after hearing his baziac story.

'How many weeks or months do you have left before they kick your butt,' Adam asked casually, releasing a huge smoke into the ceiling.

'My mother feels it could be less than forty-eight hours,' he replied breathlessly at the realisation that death was indeed near. Suddenly, he did not want to die. He was afraid of death. Life was more promising and fulfilling than to just waste it at thirty-something.

'Sorry nigger, you want us to assume now that you're about being relegated to the past tense, is that it? A dead man,' Adam said hoarsely. 'I can't help you, can't advise you, deeply sorry.'

'Adam, I have always maintained this, you've got no brain. You don't just put it very blank, no word of consolation or simple advise, nothing. Is that the way...'

'Did you say consolation?' Adam interjected. Look here, cut the bullshit! You're embarrassing your kingdom,' he stated, twisting in his chair. He put a leg up on the table and stubbed out his tobacco. 'You're calling because you need some words of consolation, Fine. You'll have it; in fact you've got it. May your soul rest in peace! Call me back in thirty hours time. Being a commissioner is vastly different from being a D.P.O., you understand what I mean. I'm a very busy officer, not like the old days.' He declared expressionlessly.

'I do know that, but before you switch off, kindly connect me with Jane. I'd like to speak with her one last time.'

'I thought the bitch is in your custody. That's good,' said Adam, lighting another tobacco. 'Those are the kind of people you should be telling fairy tales. You may also want to at least confess your everlasting love to her before moving ahead the rest of us. I will check the radio directory and see if she's listed and that'll mean you have to be patient,' he said after a lengthy puff. 'You were such a bright innocent child when you were a kid. How I wished you didn't grow up. You grew up and got too wise, too negative and now your life is about to be fucking over. I wish there's a way out for you but in this circumstance, I very much doubt your survival based on your story. As your mother was there for you at the beginning, so will I be there for you at the end, Adieu! Call back in 72 hours, if you're still alive.'

Ifashanu bit his lips and watched the red light on the machine dim a little. He regretted speaking with Adam and he regretted knowing him. This would be their last conversation on earth. He was through with him for life. Nervously, he wiped the sweat on his face and sat on the cemented floor. He knew it would take some time before Jane could be reached in London.

CHAPTER TWENTY-TWO

It took more than half an hour before Adam could give him go ahead. It was the voice of a child that came on.

'Halloo, hallow, hi, o.k. now, what do you want? Right, you can call the store for delivery, because, mom is in the shower, she just entered and she won't come out until night, so call the store and ask for Whitney, do you hear? Can you hear me? Can't you talk? Mom...'

Ifashanu restrained a scream. So Jane got married at last, he thought excitedly.

'Hi, I'm Ifash calling from Africa. I don't need deliveries. I've got to speak with Jane, it's urgent.' The boy scrunched and grinned.

'Afrocat, I never heard of a name like that before. Are you kidding me? Okay Afrocat, it's your lucky day. Mom is coming out now, stay there. Mum!' The boy hesitated. 'And don't you move, 'cause captain Stiga will be back. Telephone Afrocat,' he said aloud.

Jane jumped out of the bath-tub and hurried into the sitting room with nothing but a towel wrapped to cover her breasts down to mid thigh. She heard Jimmy muffling the word Afrocat. Then as she listened more attentively, her body tensed.

'Who the hell…' She sky dived through the door, snatching the receiver from him. Ifash leaned back to take a deep disappointing breath. Caught by surprise, he heard a different voice and his blood rushed to his head causing his heart to skip a beat.

'Ifash whoop! Can't believe it's you. After six solid years, you're such a sneaky, naughty bastard, heartless. Can't believe you won't keep your promise. You men are such lying idiots, global bastards.' She accused.

'How are you Jane?' he asked softly.

'It's really you.' She confirmed with a chuckle, sealing her mouth with a hand.

'Yes, it's me. It's me.'

'I'm fine, can't be better,' she answered excitedly. 'What about you and how's the queen? How's the Kingdom, your people and…have you become a god? You must have got everyone worshipping you. You've got all the women scurrying to take care of you. It's quite understandable if you forget the rest of the world, too bad, damn too bad, damn you!'

'Opposite is the case,' Ifashanu said in a clear shaky voice. 'Things just didn't level out fine the way I expected it. Kingship is a huge responsibility.'

'Did you miss me? I doubt that very much. If you do, you would have called long before now.'

'Of course I do Jane, you think it's just easy letting go like that, it…'

'I've got good news for you, had been hoping you'll call one day,' she said and paused swallowing audibly.

'Well, I hope I'll consider it good, what is it?' She was quiet for a while and thought sincerely about what he just said. Indeed, what is good news for her might not necessarily be good news to him. He had a point.

'I'd a baby, years back, a baby boy,' she said.

'Wahoo, that's nice, congratulations. That's cool, very natural, I'm glad for you, a big congratulation once again. Is he of Irish, Welsh, is he French, Italian, Dutch or German?'

'Who?' she asked, puzzled. 'Are you crazy?'

'Come on, you know what I mean. He's Irish, right?'

'I thought you know me very well Ifash. I'm an independent career lady, I can't commit my life and happiness into a man's hands.' She chuckled. 'Years back, I took a course in assets management and later opened an antiques and perfumes store at Brisborne Avenue. How does that sound?'

'Great, it sounds great. So you live alone with your kid, is that it?'

'Yeah, we live alone and he reminds me a lot of his father. He's the reason I didn't come down to Africa searching for you all these years. I wanted it and I got it. I got you sort of duplicated,' she giggled.

'How could you do that? I don't understand and why are you giggling like that?'

'You can't understand all I'm saying?' she smiled secretly. 'He's your child, nutty!'

There was silence for an instant; Ifash murmured soundlessly, and then he heard Jane call the name *Jimmy*. She passed the receiver to him, 'Speak to your dad in Africa.' Jimmy grinned at his mom.

'Africat, you're my daddy, Gush!' He smiled exposing chocolate teeth. 'Don't you ever come home? When are you coming home?' Jimmy laughed, amused and dropping the receiver carelessly. Jane caught it mid-air.

'Are you still there?' she called desperately. Meanwhile, Ifash had frozen. The sweat from his face dripped on his chest and the one from his armpits flowed down his pants.

'Jane, are you sure? You sure no one also was…'

'Sure of what?' she asked innocently.

'Are you sure he's my child?'

'What do you mean, am I sure he's your child,' she snapped. 'Do I look insane? Like I don't know what I am saying? You saying I can't differentiate between the men I sleep with? What garbage are you throwing at me? Do you think I…'

'Look Jane, I'm sorry if I took it the wrong way. I'm just a bit flustered. I mean, we haven't been in contact since then, how could it have happened?'

'Ask your mother the queen how did yours happen?'

'Come off it Jane, don't talk like that, that's insultive.'

'Alright macho king, you can suit yourself. He's not your child, do you hear me? He's mine.' She declared. 'How does that make you feel, does that make you feel better and uninsulted?' Jane sparked. Dizziness assailed her, and she became too upset to speak further.

'Jane,' Ifashanu called softly. 'I called you today not to quarrel with you, but to greet you. See how you're doing, and also to inform you about my predicament. I want you to know before hand that I'm on the death row. I don't want you to hear the sad news from any other source.' He propped his head in his hands for an agonizing moment. 'I made a very big mistake out here, a mistake that cannot be amended. Some people are trying to kill me for it.' He paused. 'I took some steps contrary to tradition and the penalty is death by whichever means, I don't know...'

'Wait a moment, did you say death?' Jane fumed. 'I can't hear you clearly. Take a deep breath and cool down. I can't hear you if your voice keeps cracking like that. Be relaxed and tell me all about it from the beginning.'

Ifashanu could not relax, no matter how hard he tried. He felt like someone at an advanced stage of fever. He knew he did not have all the time in the world. Anyhow, he started calmly, swallowing a lot of saliva. He narrated the events in the forest up to his present state of isolation. At the end of his story, Jane could understand how deeply troubled he was; and judging by his cracking tone, he needed comfort. She hoped whoever his wife was, she would be up to the task of reassuring him, sharing a portion of his pain and telling him everything was going to be alright.

'You sound terribly distraught, what are we going to do?'

'I dun no.'

'God!' Jane sighed, refastened her towel and sat back with legs folded. She tried not to think about Ifash's story. His story sounded weird, but she believed him. Only that she could not comprehend what must have led to battling with wild beasts and spirits in order to be crowned king. Suddenly, Jane went on her knees and her eyes narrowed in contemplation.

'Why don't you fly over, you'll be safe here.'

'No Jane.' Ifashanu shook his head. 'They can hit at me anywhere.'

'Are they some mafia with connections everywhere?' she asked perplexed.

'No, not that kind of hit and run stuff. They have their own ways much sophisticated in evil; you can't understand. It works like magic. You can't see it but you'll feel it. It's real.'

'Who are they?'

'They are elders and chancellors.'

'Then that no big deal Ifash,' she said earnestly. 'It's not as if you're against a massive revolt. You can solve it easily by sacking them or jail this group, period.'

'Period!' Ifashanu exclaimed comically. 'What are you talking about? That's not possible. You don't seem to understand.'

'I don't understand what? Are you speaking your dialect?' she asked with irritation. 'Alright, if that won't work, do you have the support of the military and in control?'

'Military!' He gasped. 'We don't have such thing like military.'

'But you have got body guards that have access to ammunitions, don't you?'

'Yeah, we got that. They carry powder guns.'

'Then that solves it,' she cried, taking a lungful of air.

'How?' Ifash asked anxiously.

'It's simple and straight,' she cracked. 'Round them up and let them face the bullet! Secret extermination, you know what I mean. Move a step ahead of them. You don't take chances with enemies whose sole aim is to destabilize you. Take action before they do. Take their lives to sustain yours.' She stated balefully. Ifashanu shook his head in disagreement.

'That's crazy, you suggesting I kill?' he asked nervously.

'How can I possibly do such and don't have nightmares the rest of my life. They are our elders and advisers. They are numerous, and you can't silent more than sixty people with bullets at once.'

'You bet your black royal ass you should and you know if I'm in your miserable situation, I won't think twice. There's nothing much we live for in this world. I just realize that this world is nothing but dust and air. We will all die someday anyway.'

'Moreover, these guys are fortified. They've got spiritual powers, and they are not easy to crack. It can't work, I tell you baby, it can't. That's cruel.'

'Ifash,' she called emphatically. 'You're a leader, remember, a king. You're like a General in the army, a commander-in-chief. Like king James, like Caesar, Robinwood, like William. If you're afraid to spill blood regardless of the nature of their crime and their numbers, then you must be prepared. Unlike you, they'll not hesitate to get rid of you by any means possible. Be prepared to swim in your own blood sooner than you envisage.'

'No!' Ifashanu shook his head at himself. 'They are our elders; they've been there for long, long before me.'

'I understand they are elders and your advisers, but they want to kill you. That makes them your enemies as we speak. We daren't wait any longer, let's move in on them.' Jane gave a resigned sigh and continued slowly. 'Look Ifash, I know how attached you are to these people. I must remind you that life is a process. The young will soon become elders, it's a time factor. Boys and girls, like we used to be, are now men and women like we are now. You can see the human race can never be short of elders and ideas. So don't be sympathetic with blood-thirsty mother fuckers! You've got to flush them out real fast, and I believe you can, yes you can.' She completed with a soundless giggle.

'Jane, I can't believe you've got such guts. You can never cease to amaze me!' He grumbled. 'I can't believe you're talking mass assassination! This is not Ireland or Scotland...'

'Christ!' She cut in sharply. 'Ifash, you're such a chicken shit, do you wanna die?' she raised her voice higher, furious.

'Baby, you can't understand.'

'Can't understand what?' she snapped. 'You keep saying I can't understand. Are you dealing with a situation out of this world? Stop saying I can't understand. The problem with you is that you think anyone who didn't pass through Cambridge with distinction is block headed. You think I'm a moron, right? You think I'm stupid and can't understand a thing. If you wanna die, then die. Be what you are! Be chicken! It's your damn coffin, have said all I can...'

'Reason with me Jane. Take it easy, I'm under stress. What do you expect?'

'Yeah, that's right! You're under unnecessary stress manufactured by no one but you,' she spat her disgust and pursed her lips pensively. 'Ifash,' she called a little cheerfully. She did not want to make it worse for him. 'If bullets won't silent them, what about putting them in a close vacuum and gas them dry, or you may go for the less expensive one. Get explosives and blow them up in one big bang! Don't you go telling me they are fortified!'

For a chilly hot moment, Ifash was quiet resting his back to the wall and wiping off the sweat on his face with the tail of his shirt. He looked cautiously around. Hot tears slipped down his eyes. The word explosive had hit him like a killer punch. He knew no one could survive the devastating effect of explosives. If after the use of explosives they all came out alive, he would gladly surrender and ask them to crucify him right at the market square. Rejuvenated, Ifash thought nervously how on earth he could get explosives. The reality of the impossible saddened him. Simultaneously, as sadness seared deep into him an idea crept into his mind.

'Jane. Are you there, can you hear me?' he called eagerly.

'I can hear you loud and clear. I can also hear you sobbing in the background. Why are you crying like a kid? What the hell are you doing to yourself there? You talk to me. I can't believe you're crying!'

'I'm cool,' Ifash cleared the tears in his eyes. 'I'm cool, just thinking.'

'No you're not! You're crying! I heard you weeping like a child,' she insisted.

'Jane, I've got to go. Switch me over to McCarthy, City Hall, Leeds.'

'My goodness, you are still in contact with that idiot!' She raised a brow. 'Alright, no hassles; make sure you call me back soon. Have got to know how you are getting along, and you are sure you don't want to come over?'

'No, maybe sometime later after the dust, I'll call back. Switch me to Leeds,' he said hastily. Jane made the switch as quickly as possible, leaving a firm instruction to the operator while she sat still reminiscing the good old days. She concluded she'd to take the most unusual step, she might just be lucky, she thought. She picked the phone off the hook and pressed.

'Please can I be on to the Duchess of York? It's of the highest priority. I need to speak with her right away.'

'You must be aware of procedures, please identify?' answered a personal aide who was seated three rows behind the duchess inside the main bowl of Wembley arena, listening to a written speech by the Archbishop of Canterbury.

'My name is Jane, no Ifash. Ifash Gordon, just say Gordon.'

'I got you. I'll be back only if she's willing to speak with you, over.' The aide stood smartly, walked to an open side and motioned a sign to Kemberly who was elegantly dressed and sitting with her legs crossed in front of her. She took note and beckoned at him. He went to her side.

'What is it Nicholas?' she asked with an obvious frown.

'Ifash Gordon is on line 8, she'll like to speak with your highness. She said it's urgent.' Kimberly grabbed the phone and turned away quickly, hoping he did not see the shock in her eyes.

'Duchess of York,' she said simply into the mouthpiece.

'Yes ma'am, I'm sorry I don't want to disturb your...'

'Who are you? And straight to the point.'

'Yes ma'am, I'm Jane, girlfriend to Ifash Gordon, son of Lord Franklin Gordon. The black boy that lived with him in the country side, whose mother…'

'I know, skip the details and go straight to the point,' Kimberly snapped. Jane took a deep breath and hastily informed.

'O.K ma'am, Ifash is in a serious situation in Africa and it is life-threatening. I don't know if what I was told years back by the Scotland Yard still holds, because i…'

'How would you know that, I mean the situation?' the duchess asked gently. She stopped listening to the archbishop with no anguish in her face as she stepped gracefully to meet Nicholas.

'He radioed me ma'am, we just finished speaking from Africa,' Jane reported.

Kimberly gave a sigh recognizing turmoil when she saw one. She moved closer to Nicholas.

'Thank you,' she said flatly to Jane. 'I'll take it from here.' The phone clicked as she placed it back, tilting her hat to one side for Nicholas to see the alertness in her eyes. Nicholas left Wembley in pursuit of her instruction.

CHAPTER TWENTY-THREE

Ifash looked on gladly as the green light dimmed, an indication that connection to Leeds was in progress. He gazed at his white T-shirt; it was as if he had just emerged from a pool. He felt sticky and miserable. Unimpressed by his resolution, he sat back on a pile of bricks with legs spread out like someone struck by a steam roller. He tried thinking; he needed to focus but his head was blank and arching. He glanced at his wrist watch, twenty minutes gone, no signal. Impulsively, he touched and fiddled with the coin suspended firmly around his neck. His eyes soon diverted to the machine when the dim green light had grown fully. With two previous experiences, he knew the air was jammed and a voice could sneak in at the slightest opening. He crawled closer and waited patiently for another ten minutes before he heard a voice crackling through the speaker.

'Hello, hello!' He shouted into the microphone.

'Fuck the shit!' Adam bellowed. 'It's you again. I told you to give me sometime to think. I said 72 hours, not two hours!' Adam paused to accept a file from his secretary. 'Pearl, I didn't hear you correctly the first time, I'd like to ask you one last question,' he licked his lips and rested the pen in his hand. 'Do you really mean it when you said you downed a spirit and a leopard? Are you really serious or you're trying to sound heroic. How did you do that?'

'I'm calling back for a more serious matter, Adam,' Ifashanu said with a frown.

'No, answer my question first. You could land yourself a good pay here if really you know how to chase spirits. The niggers here are like ghosts; they're fast and sharp like a razor, always out-running the force.' The anxious look on Ifashanu's face made him speak more stiffly.

'Listen to me Adam. Listen to me for once in your life. My life, my soul, is at stake.'

'Who gives a shit? I thought we've gotten over that,' Adam queried. 'Am I responsible for the wrong decision you made in your life? Do I look like your father or mother or anyone that loves you?'

'Listen,' Ifash interrupted. 'You're my friend, way back from kindergarten. There should be a great deal more between us than just the rubbish you say all the time. We're supposed to look out for each other. What good will it do you if you wake up tomorrow and read in some newsprint that I'm dead. Will it make you jump up and be very happy?'

Adam stared down at the bundle of files on the floor. He reached for the one atop and opened it and closed it almost immediately. A nigger file, niggers and Indians make his work hell, he thought with some bitterness.

'Why should I? I don't have to jump over another man's misfortune, but I'll understand it's your luck. Everyone has his, that's life, buddy. You're never assured of tomorrow. Niggers die here in custody everyday. It's not their wish, it's the system, and it's the...'

'Cut the crap Adam, I haven't much time at hand. I need your help and I'm ready to compensate you at any cost you may desire.' Ifash said with firm finality. He fixed his eyes on the machine and his fingers held tightly to the microphone as sweat dripped down his body like a fountain. He was tensed, desperate and pathetic.

'Ummmh,' chuckled Adam. For real, he had read of some rich African kings. The continent buries abundant minerals, known and unknown. He was also aware of his government's activities in the region, though classified. After a long silence, he responded.

'Pearl, you know what? If you'll compensate your man, your person might just be able to scrounge up a deal for you. Something straight and cool for everyone and you could sleep with both eyes closed. Your personal person will be at your service on that condition only.' He raised a finger. 'Let's hear you all over again and this time, don't tell me fictions. I don't wanna hear no spirits, don't wanna hear Leopards. I want it served raw and real. What's up nigger?'

'I don't want to go into anymore details with you,' Ifashanu said mildly. 'What I told you before was no fiction, it's the real deal and I only need one thing from you?'

'What?' Adam asked lighting a cigar.

'I need explosives at my end and I need them delivered fast.'

'What?' Adam jerked, grounding the cigar with his bare hand. He held up the microphone tighter and in panic lighted another fresh cigar.

'Did you mention explosives?'

'Exactly.'

'Tell me,' he breathed heavily. 'Do you wanna blow up your kingdom and run here seeking asylum. Have you thought of how devastating explosives could be in a jungle, which could accidentally start off bush fires for Christ sake? What has gotten into you Ifash? Do you now do drugs or something worse than that for…?'

'Adam!' Ifashanu roared across the line. 'Why don't you listen to me? Let me finish, listen.'

'Listen to what?' he barked. 'You want to commit some genocide and you wanna drag me into your obsession. No buddy, I'm way smarter than that. You're making a big mistake. You are talking to the wrong person. I don't ever want to go down in history as one of the collaborators of a world war.

You can stick your plan at the back of your head, I'm out. I thought you needed my help to make some arrests. You know the Interpol stuff, the police maneuver…'

'Adam!' Ifashanu shouted at him. 'I know how much they sell a stick and I can afford to pay ten times the amount. Does that not sound impressive to you? Think about it, this is a business with fabulous offers.'

Adam inhaled deeply and let out thick smoke simultaneously through his mouth and nostrils. He stood for a while; then he sat on the table and poured himself a glassful of whiskey. He sipped twice and sighed deeply. His index finger found the red button on the machine and pressed it.

'Really, that sounds like some fortune that could really make my head spin and turn shit around,' he whispered into the machine. 'You have that kind of money or are you just bluffing?' he enquired and blew out a heavy cloud of smoke. 'If you buy six sticks of candles at your price, that's my income for a year. If you buy ninety sticks, that's my basic salary for a decade, that sounds fanciful,' he grimaced. "So pearl, what are we blasting and how do you want it; then, when do you want it?' Ifash didn't say a word at first. He took his time before he made his announcement for effect.

'We are blasting a complex,' he said quietly.

'How huge is the complex?'

'It's almost the size of Buckingham Palace and the Piccadilly area in length.'

'Christ!' Adam erupted and struggled to his seat. 'You're full of shit, nigger,' he scuffed twisting in his seat a couple of times. 'Well, I'm not specialist on explosives, but I know very well that for good result on a building the size of Buckingham and environs, you'll need nothing less than 2000 grade A candles. Can you afford that?'

'I can afford anything; any amount. I'm worth more than you can ever imagine.' Ifashanu informed. Adam braced up and breathed some fresh air.

'Alright, I want you to press down the red button on your machine. Leave the green intact. What's the model of the set you're using?'

'Russian X.49 1867,' replied Ifashanu.

'Good. Look up on its left side and you'll see three slot pins. Remove the one in the middle and fill the slot with a tiny piece of paper or anything at all, just block it,' Adam instructed. There was silence except for the wheezy sound of the window on the decking.

'Yes, it's done,' Ifash said afterwards.

'Good, like this, it's just me and you on the same frequency. No watchdog, no Scotland Yard, and no C.I.A. The K.G.B will be off for a while. I hope we both won't regret this later.'

'We won't,' Ifashanu assured. Adam exhaled audibly and sat once again on the table. Hurriedly he rose again to lock the door.

'O.k, I'm going to give you some killer facts, killer strategies and killer execution. Don't talk, just listen and listen well.' He cleared his throat and allowed the cigar to burn freely between his fingers.

'It's like this, have got this contact in the north, full time American soldiers. They have this inner group that makes itself available in the black market for the highest bidders, like you. You can call them mercenaries. I think they are twelve in number, all specialists. These are rare gems that know the world by heart and they possess a religious doctrine for precision. Their track record around Latin America, India, China and the Middle East is breath-taking. Precisely, they have 17 international missions with no flaws. It's amazing. No other group that I know has that kind of impressive record in the world. I will advise that if you really have the dough, they are your best bet. Go for the best the world has to offer.' He completed candidly.

'Are you very sure they are good?' Ifashanu asked indignantly.

'Your Majesty, are you crazy? They are the best flawless pros.'

'Can I trust you on this Adam? Can I trust you with my life and that of my people?'

'Damn it! Basic rule, trust yourself first, before trusting anyone,' he fumed. 'I got a good job and a good life. Don't you ever think I'll forget! Don't think that because of some blood dough I'll put my head on the block for some amateurs. These guys are exceptionally good with extra ordinary courage and perfection. If you listen to me, you'll live and all those spirits chasing you will cease; will be wasted permanently, no doubt.'

Ifash allowed a momentary silence. He was sure Adam had more to say.

'Are you still there?'

'Right here, Adam.'

'Now, let's talk price.'

'Do you have three hundred thousand to cover the overall cost? Do you have it or you're just some bluff?'

'But that's ridiculous! It's too much.'

'Nothing is too much for the best. Nothing is too much for your life. You're buying back your fucking life, your majesty. Fuck you.'

'It's still too much,' Ifash insisted. 'That's worth more than the whole of Ireland and Middlesbrough.'

'Pal, perfection is expensive,' Adam argued. 'This is a cross-continental operation; they come expensive. You're lucky really, lucky to have me and to be talking to the right person. You'll be glad in the end.'

'But I don't have such cash,' Ifashanu said hesitantly.

'You don't have what!' Adam yelled. 'Have I been wasting my time talking with a nonentity?'

'What I mean is, I may be able to pay in gold and diamonds, what about that?' Adam breathed easy in relief allowing a momentary silence.

'Gold and diamond,' he repeated and flicked off the ash on his cigar. 'How do they get it?'

'On delivery,' Ifashanu answered.

'You're a very wise kid,' Adam said and stifled a giggle. 'So, what's the nature of their mission? Do you want them to cleanse your kingdom free of humans? What exactly is your problem? How do you want it blown?'

'Cleansing? No way, how could you think of that? I just want them to plant the candles around the palace. The effect should be on the building and its occupants only,' Ifashanu said.

'What's the timing?'

'Let say before 2:30a.m tomorrow morning, can they make it?' Ifashanu asked.

'They will if we set everything rolling right away. That period of the day matched the nature of their operation. They will surface for the price involved.'

'How do we get things rolling?' Ifash inquired anxiously.

'I'll have to catch the 2:00pm flight to America. It's just 12:30 in Leeds.' Adam confirmed, licking his lips.

'What of location, they may need advice?' Ifashanu asked gruffly.

'They don't need your advice. I told you they know the world by heart, I mean it,' Adam said, stabbing his cigar in the ashtray. 'It's why I said they're the best, they have their own connection and the only thing I think you can do for them is to slacken your security in and around the building. It must be slackened to its lowest to avert too much casualties on your part, and maybe leakages too.' He paused cautiously. 'And finally, you should also get the hell out of that vicinity once it starts to breath, you got it?'

'Yeah.' Ifashanu nodded.

'Good, I am going to lose you now. If I take the military jet, I should be back from Texas around 8:00pm. What's your time over there?'

'It's 1:30pm.'

'Good,' said Adam counting eight with his fingers. 'Expect my call at around 11:30pm your local time. By the time I call you tonight, they'll probably be on their way or perhaps mission turned down. So I wish you good luck.' Adam pressed the black button and the line went of at both ends.

U.S.S.R – Kremlin

The Head of Security Service, Colonel Luskovich, was in the large transmission room laying out firm instructions for the day espionage activities to junior officers. The lieutenant turned abruptly to the large screen transmitter which had been beeping for hours. It was not just the strange language but it was quite unthinkable on a chilly Monday morning to listen loudly to a conversation between two civilians on a military airwave.

'Get me on the air! Locate the poultry, fast!' The lieutenant shouted instructions.

A superior officer whispered to the cadet seated behind the switch table.

'The Pentagon!

Stupid Abramo! I should have taken them out with the biological that first chance. Imbeciles! Now they are dreaming global dominance, toothless Wolves! When I take up the armored affairs of the Union it'll be their end, mad pigs!' The Lieutenant boomed.

'Get lost, rabbits!' He bellowed at incoming cadets officers.

'Sir, the signal is coming from the west of the Atlantic,' a cadet reported dutifully standing alert.

'Sharrup! Sit-down!' The Lieutenant barked angrily. 'What do you know? It's Americans! They're scheming, they're on it. You recruits have a lot to learn; got to think fast.' He lamented and walked away briskly into his office.

'American-African, African-American, nonsense, am I right?' he asked his C.G.S waiting in his office.

'Negroes, that's all we see on the battle field, monkeys!' He concluded and settled heavily on the arm-chair, his breath impaired.

* * *

Ifashanu sat back leaning against the short fence of the roof. For the first time in three sober days, he discovered he was grinning. He deliberately heaved a sigh of relief.

'It's over,' he breathed. That was a brilliant, crazy idea from Jane, he thought with a steely expression on his face. He had always strongly believed that she had the will to kill a guy, but he never imagined she has the heart to organize mass assassination. Maybe when these elders and chancellors are all gone, he could bring the people together to lead a modern life and abandon ancient and ancestral beliefs. He could make his kingdom look like the United Kingdom, like the Roman Empire, like all those great places. He must form an army, organize a strong system of trade and marketing, and outlaw the current trade by barter. He would construct an airport, bridges and tar the dusty roads.

Ifashanu closed his eyes and hung on to his imagination. The pleasure from his dreams filled his heart. He gave a short hollow laugh and eased up aiming for the front edge of the roof overlooking the villages. Midway, he gave up the idea with a flip of the hand, returned to the radio set instead and closed the case. He removed his T-shirt and laid it gently on top of the machine to reduce the effect of the sun on it. He wanted to sit and rest for a while, but he remembered his mother and wondered what she was doing at the moment. He wondered what she would make of his plan. His thought sank with emotion and his love for his mother overwhelmed him. He thought of her love, how she had always been there for him from the beginning till this final moments. How could he ever show his appreciation to her for raising him from poverty to riches, and instilling in him a sense of culture and leadership? Perhaps, he could show some appreciation to her by holding a banquet in her honour after the ordeal is over; and together they would rule the kingdom as long as she lived. As for his wife Idunnu, she would have to learn to be contended. What difference did it make anyway, whether she was a princess or a queen?

Interestingly, the thought of his son, Jimmy, crept into his mind. Could Jane really be serious, he pondered. Even if she was not, this definitely was not the time for fact-finding thoughts. Briskly, he walked to the stairs and started to descend, heading straight in the direction of his mother's bedroom. He knocked gently on the door and turned the knob, slipping inside quietly.

The queen was lying in bed wide awake and fully dressed except for the head gear that lay across the bed. She was staring unseeingly into space. Ifashanu came over and sat gently on the edge of the bed.

'I have just come up with a possibility; it's rather difficult, but it's possible. It's a plan that might change things in everyway,' Ifashanu said casually. The queen's expressionless face split into a warm smile.

'And what is that you plan to do?' she asked. Ifashanu braced up sitting a little more comfortably. He unloaded the entire radio conversations he had with Adam and Jane without leaving out a word, except the news of her possible grandchild. When he finished, his mother took control immediately. Curiously, she frowned her face, swung out of bed and began to pace around the room.

'Do you think this is right?' she challenged icily. 'You cannot sell the legacy of your ancestors and the future of our children.'

'But mother, what do I do? I don't know what is right from what is wrong anymore, there's no way out,' he complained with spread arms. The queen shook her head in despair.

'You mean you really want to gather 100 elders and 50 permanent chancellors and kill them all at once like that? Have you thought of what will be the future of the kingdom thereafter? Don't you know that a nation without elders is a barren nation? How do you want your story to be narrated in history if your plan comes to be?'

'Mother,' he called emphatically moving towards her. 'Do I have a choice? There can be only two sides to a coin.' He touched the coin around his neck to indicate the two sides. It's either you do away with me or you do away with them. You must decide?'

'What do you want me to say, Ifashanu?' she asked compassionately.

'I want you to decide whether I should go ahead with the plan or put my plan to a halt. As you know I am in a closet, sealed in a calabash. And don't forget mother, you always say that a flood does not pass through the forest without bringing down trees.' He coaxed softly, looking his mother straight in the eyes. A hush filled the room as the queen's face changed to a mournful expression. A moment later, she realized she could no longer restrain her tears and allowed them to flow down her cheeks uncontrollably. After a while, she wiped her face and stared at the roof. His question was a straightforward question but difficult to answer. She seemed to be caught up between two things that mattered most to her, two events that kept her life rolling. It was a calamitous, a terrible development, to have to choose between her two worlds.

She shifted her attention away from the roof and gazed into her son's eyes, his handsomeness was striking. She gazed further down to his bare shoulders and touched his wound lightly. Her gaze rose to the coin around his neck. She held and fiddled it for a while, and then she looked up into his eyes.

'If you decide to sell the legacy of your ancestors and the future of the born and unborn children, it's left to you. There is little I can say, it's your kingdom. Do as your heart tells you to do, but remember that for every action there is a consequence. Think very well before you act so you don't make a mistake. Any mistake shall be costly,' she said in a soft voice that betrayed her doubts, and then she hugged him.

CHAPTER TWENTY-FOUR

Two hours later, Ifashanu called for an impromptu meeting with the palace interns. He sat on the king's throne dressed in his favorite blue shirt. He was facing over 100 workers standing in rows. Most of them were guards and the rest servants. On Ifashanu right hand stood the head of the royal guards and on his left was his personal assistant. Behind him was his soul mate. He hated the idea of a soul mate. His mother got the edge on the issue. She said it was tradition that someone must die and be buried along with him in order to serve him in the grave.

In his composed speech, Ifashanu commanded the head of the guards to cut down security in and around the palace to one-percent. He imposed a compulsory one week break to all his servants and remaining guards. His reason was that there was going to be a spiritual meeting of the elders and chancellors at 11:00am the following day.

'But Your Highness who will serve your guests?' asked the chief servant, a man of moderate height who all along had been taut with amazement and conflicting feelings.

'Eti,' Ifashanu called him by name. 'Don't worry yourself. I've arranged that with the family members. They will take care of it and all that may follow. Understand?'

'Forgive me for questioning your highness,' Eti apologized, putting his case to rest.

'Ayok,' he called silkily. 'Blow your trumpet around town. Pass the houses of the Chancellors and elders. Inform them that the Prince and Queen of Odua call for an important meeting tomorrow at 11:00am. All eyes and legs must be present.' The trumpet leader bowed respectfully.

'It's done your highness. All shall be informed without exception.'

* * *

Meanwhile, outside the palace premises the news of Chief Balogun's mysterious death had spread like wild fire. His body was discovered by his teenage son who had brought him the day's breakfast from the farm. Immediately the news broke, the elders and Chancellors organized themselves for a meeting. They elected the deputy defense chief, Hasamoha as their new leader. However, the decision to raise a violent insurgence against the royal family caused division among them. There were those who felt a spade should be called a spade. He who killed by the sword should die by the sword. There were the liberals who called for dialogue with the royal family. They argued that conspiracy against the royal family was a great offence in the land.

It was the majority that later carried the day. It was resolved that the twelve cult members reduced to ten by the death of the priest and the defense chief were to be assigned the sole responsibility of eliminating the prince who had brought calamity to the land, and degradation to the norms and traditions of their ancestors.

'As I stand here before you today,' Hasamoha said in his final speech. 'I'm gripped with complete sadness, the same sorrow that you all feel. Let everyone return to his house and announce to women and young men of understanding, that our land has been deprived of it future. That the two strongest men, men of timbre and caliber, might and influences have departed our land forever to the place of our ancestors.' He took a deep sorrowful breath, shook his head in despair and continued. 'The information has reached me that a palace meeting has been announced. Let us all be there with the two bodies carried shoulder high and let Ifa-Eledumare be consulted before them. You and I know what they have done, and there's no two ways about it. Before them, the dead shall speak and the gods shall make their request of blood, the blood of he that perpetrated our current predicament. It is their blood that we must use to cleanse and appease our gods,' he said with a grimace.

'For the peace of our kingdom, the queen and her bastard child must be bled,' a furious voice injected. Hasamoha passed him a glance that was full of approval.

'I thank you all for your uncompromising concern to uplift the culture and tradition of our great land. May our ancestors be with us all and deliver us from further calamity, pain, and sorrow. I thank you all for the confidence you have bestowed on me. May the gods of our ancestors see us through,' he concluded in a voice laden with grief.

* * *

Ifashanu returned to the roof at 10:30pm carrying a torch. There were over twenty security lights mounted above the palace walls giving it a partial brightness. The six permanent guards around there had been displaced from their positions. Ifashanu had also personally inspected the evacuation of his extended family and wife from the palace. They were moved to the old palace on the east coast. The few he could not get rid of were three servants, his soul mate, and the queen. The atmosphere was so calm that the tension within him could be felt only by those advanced in spiritual prowess. But all in all, his arrangement went on smoothly and secretly uninterrupted.

Ifashanu dimmed the torch and lay sprawled on the cemented floor in silky blue shirt-sleeves, which he folded up to the elbows. No word yet from Adam. He was anxious. Over the years he had come to hate delay and love promptness and immediate gratification. Now that everything had reached a fever pitch, he was desperate to hear from Adam to change his moody and unsettled look to that of a fulfilled revolutionist. No successful revolution occurred without a fierce struggle, suffering, and bloodshed, he thought with strong conviction.

* * *

At fifteen minutes past twelve, the machine began to buzz and beep. Ifashanu rose hurriedly from where he had sprawled hopelessly. He keyed in some numbers on the set.

Gradually, the signal sneaked through and Adam's voice came on and off.

'Pearl, Pearl, Texas calling over.'

'Copy, loud and clear,' Ifashanu muttered breathlessly.

'Christ! Where're you? I've been trying to get you for over an hour!' Adam barked.

'I've been here hoping you'll call,' he replied innocently.

'Alright, I've got good news for you. Listen, don't talk,' Adam said pacing forth and back in a warm secret service office in downtown Houston. It has been twenty-five years since the lone star flag of the old republic was lowered, making Texas become a state of the union. In the following year in 1846, Anson Jones who succeeded Sam lowered the flag once again at the capitol in Austin, putting an end to the republic and in the process annoying some die-hard Texan veterans, including his father Mark McCarthy, a loser in all ramification. But that's all stories now, the war, the ride and the triumph all enclosed in the book of history. As he moved around the cozy office sipping thick hot coffee, he's in Texas to get rich, the same area in Houston where his father must have died penniless.

Ifashanu took a forced breath; he did not know whether to cry or laugh.

'I'm listening,' he said.

'Good, listen carefully, it wasn't as easy as I thought but I met them anyhow and they agreed.' Adam paused. 'The operation is termed Candle Light. Their code is 167/761/671 Ex-KAT. They are ten in number, all paratroopers. They'll move in on you through the west wing of the palace. They'll land at destination at around 2:00am and it will take them less than an hour to plant the candles. They demand that the gold and diamond be presented before implantation and they warned that you should not play smart. They'll soak you up before your people do. Do I make myself clear, over?'

'Very clear,' Ifashanu replied nervously and tried to comprehend what he just heard. To him, it was like a leap of faith into the uncertainties of life. One moment his enemies seemed to be gaining the upper hand, and the next moment he was an inch ahead of them.

'Hey you, Talk! You have no time.' Adam pierced his short trance. 'Alright, I'm going to lose you now. I have to return to London immediately. Give me a call tomorrow at the zero hour. Pearl,' he called emphatically. 'I must warn you. Be kind, be straight, and be gentle with your visitors. They are ruthless!'

'I will keep that in mind.'

'You'd better,' he said. 'And one last thing, be very careful. 3,500 candles will grope the building to its foundation; don't be anywhere near.' There was a click and the machine went off. As Adam was dropping the phone in Texas, Scotland Yard was busy monitoring movements of people in and out of Leeds.

* * *

Ifashanu's head swelled with hope as he descended the stairs, taking it two at a time. He headed for his mother's room and entered without knocking. She was seated on the floor with her legs folded under her body and holding a beaded stick that resembled that of the priest. There was a small pot beside her that oozed thick black smoke. She seemed preoccupied, far away in the spirit world.

Ifashanu turned away swiftly; he did not want to interfere. He closed the door behind him and rushed to his bedroom in search of binoculars. He ruffled through the twelfth section of his wardrobe until he finally found what he was looking for in a small handbag with his name on it. Inside, the device lay on top of some books. He examined its lenses and then looked through its eye pieces. He nodded impressively viewing the enlarged image of his room. The small rock chair and other furniture were magnified a hundred times their normal size. Powerful, he thought delightfully. He went and stood before the mirror and noticed that so much had changed about him since he left Europe. His physique had not changed much, but his ideology had. He was now hot and dangerous.

It was exactly 2:00am when Ifashanu returned to the roof. He sat vigilantly on some piles of bricks with his legs stretched to their full length. He was exhausted, yet his mind remained completely alert. A nagging suddenly arrested his attention, prompting him to go downstairs outside the palace and make a final inspection of his environment. But his inner mind which did not often mislead him took control dissuading him. A moment later, he rose to his feet facing the west with his binoculars glued to his eyes. The distance appeared blurred and deserted; he saw nothing, except tall trees and rustling bushes. He looked east, south, and north, everywhere was calm. Still nervous and confused, he let the binoculars drop on his chest. Then he thought with alarm, could Adam be playing games with him? It all looked too good, like fiction: A rapid reaction force in the heart of Africa within twenty-four hours!

He slid both hands into the hip pockets of his jean and his eyebrows arched inquisitively. Thoughtfully, he glowered down at the machine disappointedly. In a sudden fit of anger, he pulled off the rope of the binocular around his neck and smashed the device on the floor, grinding the lenses with the sole of his shoe. Minutes later, as he sat in trance sweating in the breezy atmosphere, a beep sounded. Within seconds, the beep sounded the second time. Ifashanu bumped into life and froze when he noticed the red light glowing on the machine. The beeping sound repeated itself a couple of times before a rough voice came through.

'Candle light! Candle light! Candle light! We request you to quote the codes.'

That was their voice, there was no mistaken the American accent, Ifashanu thought frantically. He engaged his microphone and quoted the codes Adam gave him.

'Where are you?' he blurted.

'We are next door! Three of ours are down! Call your guards to order! Slack security! I repeat, slack security!' The voice repeated and went off.

Ifashanu rose to his feet and hurried downstairs feeling both shaky and delighted. He turned the long key of the treasure room thrice to the right and the massive iron door opened. The treasures were arranged in sections. He extracted six crates each of diamonds and gold, and placed them outside the iron door. He turned the key thrice again, relocking the door. Highly charged, he scurried along the passage into the grand hall facing the west side. He flung open all the double doors on the west side, which led to the palace garden. He got hold of a chair and sat at the centre of the hall, facing the distant entrance. He looked straight through the six doors ahead, obviously more nervous than before. His eyes were crystal clear at 2:30am. He could not but hope that this was not a dream.

Woefully, he gazed at his wristwatch for a moment. Breathless, he raised his head and noticed a movement. A shadow slid over the smooth wall and flipped to an angle. Urged by his curiosity, he moved into the shadows and stood akimbo by the giant door. He was aghast when the shadow spoke.

'Quote the code,' it said and Ifashanu did so. Within minutes a human image stepped into the pathway. Another followed, and then another, till they were seven. They marched towards him in rows, the shortest being about seven feet. They wore bullet-proof jackets over green khaki jumpers that had large pockets and sleeveless black tops. As they moved closer to him, he discovered that three of them were black and the others white. Each tied a scarf around the head, and their faces and arms were painted with charcoal. They had sophisticated guns hanging from their shoulders and silenced pistols on their waists. Each carried a green pouch on his back. Their appearance looked dreadful, and they could be mistaken for death itself.

Ifashanu stretched out a hand to the first person on the row. The soldier held his hand firmly. As he felt the hardness of the man's palm through his polyester hand glove, he wondered how many souls that hand must have taken. He shook the others and motioned to them to step inside the hall.

'Where are the stones?' asked one of them who later introduced himself as Dave.

'They are ready.' Ifashanu replied, wiping off perspiration from his face.

'Can we see them?'

'You're welcome,' Ifashanu nodded. Earnestly, he took them to the passage and showed them the twelve crates. They examined them and were satisfied with what they saw. Dutifully, they began implantation. All seven were split in and around the palace. They took their job very seriously. Not a word was spoken, but from time to time they communicated with signs, their heads and their fingers.

Much later, they all converged in the grand hall. Ifashanu returned to the centre of the hall and sat in their midst. He watched with a feeling of accomplishment as they pressed wire into every corner. He was forced to salute the excellence of white men and their craftsmanship in the area of plotting evil. In forty-five minutes, they were through. The man Dave eased himself up and started towards Ifashanu.

'Fixed, they are breathing,' he announced.

'Thank you very much,' Ifashanu shook his hands and managed a smile.

'It's nice dealing with you. Thank you for being honest,' he said in a squeaky tone as if his throat was tied with ribbons around his neck. 'Sir, these are first grade explosives, and the result will take your breath away. Explosion time is set for 12:30pm on the dot, not a second later. He raised a firm finger. 'Finally sir, make sure by 12:10pm you're out with all that are dear to you.' He took two steps backward, stood alert and gave the Prince a military salute.

'Thank you for coming,' Ifashanu smiled into his painted face and stood watching as they hurried down the pathway till they were all out of sight. Ifashanu glanced at his watch; it was 3:15am, so he thought it necessary to take a short nap. At 8:45

in the morning he reluctantly rose to the gentle tap of his mother. He mumbled and grunted. Weak to the bones, he could have slept through the explosion had he not been woken.

'Must you sleep in the hall? What happened to your room?' she asked brusquely.

'Its okay mother, I was so damn tired. I thought it makes no difference.' He rubbed his face with both hands. With sleepy and dazed eyes, he noticed his mother was fully dressed in her favourite attire. He lay resting on his hand.

'Is everything going as planned?'

'Yes mother, they were here and it's all set. The timing is 12:30pm exactly. We ought to be out by 12:10pm.'

'When will the meeting commence?'

'By twelve noon.'

'Alright make sure you leave no stone unturned,' she said turning her burning eyes away from him. She knew the gravity of his plot and what would become of a palace stocked with explosives. Above all, she was convinced that the moment of decision making had come when the living shall meet face to face with the dead. She tried restraining the tears threatening her eyes, but it was a futile effort. Ifashanu struggled to his feet and embraced her warmly for a long moment. She sobbed quietly with her face on his shoulder, hoping his plan was a step in the right direction. After a while, she stepped back gently and dabbed her face with a handkerchief.

'I must see members of the family at the old Palace. I shall be back before the meeting starts,' she said flatly and turning to her heels before he could say a word. He escorted her outside into the garden. Just as they were stepping into the green grass, a guard emerged from nowhere, ran towards them and prostrated. Breathlessly, he reported the death of twenty-six guards on the west bank. He said some of their bodies were found floating in the pond. Ifashanu's reaction was immediate.

'All bodies should be removed and kept in the Palace in preparation for a decent burial later in the evening. No word to anyone. Anyone, I repeat, understand?' he emphasized with a finger raised. The Prince looked up to the sky and cursed the day he was born. He swore at the Chief guard.

'Glorious bastards,' he mumbled and his mother looked on bewildered. Quickly, he kissed her on both cheeks and bade her goodbye.

CHAPTER TWENTY-FIVE

At 11:00am, the stage was set. The Prince watched from the roof as the Elders and Chancellors filed through the Palace gate. Many faces bore anger and were chanting war slogans, while few looked indifferent. However, what stunned Ifashanu most was the two dead bodies carried shoulder high by selected members among them, dressed in white mourning garb.

'Shit!' Ifashanu cried. He rushed downstairs into his room, sipped a glass of concentrated palm wine, and adorned his fa-vourite traditional attire with a cap fashioned into two large ears. He wore his beads in both hands and around his neck, and then slipped into footwear made of a lion's skin. He dashed out into the passage and headed for his mother's room. She was ready and adjusting her headgear when he entered. Unlike him, she seemed more composed. She went to the bed side, got hold of her white fur and laid it gently on her left shoulder. She then picked up her beaded stick and shook it vigorously in the air a couple of times.

'Ifashanu, come over here and kneel before me,' she said with a voice full of sudden concern. He pierced his mother with a curious gaze, and then he answered in brisk tone.

'Very well mother.' He knelt before her. She waved her beaded stick randomly in the air and held it to his forehead.

She began to mumble incantations under her breath. Her face was steely, like someone distraught.

'Your life and destiny are restored. All curses upon you shall not be yours. Any evil fashioned against you, now or in the future, shall not prosper.

Omo owo kin kuloju owo,
Omo ese kin kuloju ese,
Omo adoran kin kuloju adoran.

You will live long to carry on your ancestral respon-
sibility by the permission of those whom Eledumare gave
the control of night and day…'

When it was over, she ordered him to stand.

'We shouldn't keep them waiting for long. We must go now,' she said. Ifashanu eased up and followed the queen behind.

There were sunrays coming through the top ventilation hole of the passage as they moved towards the double giant doors of the grand hall. The Prince opened the door with both hands and looked unsteadily around the hall. Once they noticed his presence, they stood and prostrated.

'*Kabiyesi o!*, long live the King!' Ifashanu smiled and was quick to notice that those who prostrated were just a handful. He took a swift glance at them and was shocked that they were countable. Majority sat still, a calamity totally uncultured and unheard of. Those who refused to prostrate looked up in mock horror at those who did. Ifashanu's eyes shifted to the centre. He could see that the centre table was filled with fruits of different types and fresh kegs of palm wine. As he walked to the podium side by side with his mother, he whispered to her.

'I've loyalists among them.'

'I can see that,' she replied quietly.

'So what should I do? I can't let them waste.'

She smiled indolently. 'Discretion is a better part of valor, your forefathers were brave warriors, need I say more, use your discretion. Issue a proclamation on your authority and separate your friends from your enemies,' she said firmly.

'How?'

'By the power bestowed upon you, it's left to you to decide,' answered the queen as she sat on the edge of the podium. By tradition, Ifashanu could not address the elders and Chancellors while seated on the King's throne as he was yet to be officially crowned. So he sat beside his mother.

Almost everyone was fidgeting, grumbling and cursing. It was a tensed situation that left Ifashanu without any option than to consider his mother's suggestion. Through the corners of his eyes, he noticed his mother rise and the noise in the hall died down. Then there was the final silence, a dead silence. The strain on the queen's face was visible as she spoke softly.

'I, the Prince of Odua and members of the royal family welcome you all to this important gathering.' She paused without much conviction. 'Before the meeting commences fully, the Prince of Odua will wish to issue a proclamation.' She said.

'You see? You see what I mean?' said a voice from the crowd, belonging to a controversial elder statesman.

'Bastard! He never wants to play by the rules. Always creating his own nonsense!'

'The gods can never decide on anything that is incorrect,' said another voice.

Ifashanu rose to his feet like a jump pole. He was face to face with the rumbling and angry crowd that sigh and rattled like a thundering storm.

'Please give me your attention,' he implored with a hand raised in the air. 'My people,' he called emphatically with panic beginning to spread over him.

'Who are your people?' echoed many voices. Ifashanu pretended and continued undeterred.

'Culture and tradition are simply about the nature of humanity, it's height and depth. In our land, our tradition good or bad has become an integral part of our kingdom's heritage. As you're all aware that I have spent many years abroad, it's human nature that I should go through some cultural shock and misunderstanding before finally adjusting. It's good to know however that if I can survive in the white man's land where scores had failed, why shouldn't I survive in the Kingdom of my ancestors regardless of…'

'What is this? Why the history! Are we here for this?' a wrathful voice shouted in the crowd. If you don't have an agenda, we have a lot to show you. Shut your mouth and listen to us and listen to the dead. The dead wish to address you!'

'Listen to the dead?' Ifashanu mumbled under his breath, he glimpsed at his wristwatch. It was 11:45am. He swallowed deeply and continued earnestly.

'Before we proceed on any issue, I'll like to point out an important observation,' he frowned. I can see a sense of division and misunderstanding among us all. There are those of us who still consider me as their future King and there are those of you who think otherwise and have chosen the path of hatred.'

'Yes!' The crowd shouted. 'You are very correct! Yes, we despise your conduct!'

The acting defence chief, Hasamoha rose to speak.

'There are thousands of us with thousand of reasons for hating you and hopefully today disposing you of the honour bestowed upon you by our ancestors. You have brought shame, sorrow and calamity into our noble land!' He completed, looking straight into Ifashanu's eyes.

The Queen on the other hand sat petrified. She had never witnessed such confrontation. Ifashanu glanced at his watch making it obvious this time around. It was 11:55am. He felt his sweat on his forehead and wiped it swiftly with a hand.

'Right now I want to know by raising your hands those of you that believe and subscribe heartily to my leadership and optimism as your future King.'

The gathering began to murmur with bewildered expressions on their faces. They lashed out abuses and swearing at their Prince in vernacular. Reluctantly, the loyal ones raised their hands and Ifashanu counted sixteen of them, mostly elders. They were old men, not a single Chancellor. He moved away from the podium and walked slowly through the crowd with his hands clasped behind him.

'I can see that things have really fallen way apart. Out of one hundred and fifty Chancellors and prominent elders, only sixteen are loyal to me at this trying period.'

'I will never conspire against the King!' One of the loyalists shouted. Ifashanu returned to the podium with a saddened face.

'I'm left with no other option than to subject myself to the wishes of the majority,' he said.

'Now you're talking, mysterious child,' a voice in the crowd cried sorely. Ifashanu's eyes were blazing from fear of the explosives, rather than the ugly comments being thrown at him. He glimpsed his watch again.

'Before hearing your grievances, I'll want to have a word with my loyalists, in confidence.'

'You bunch of betrayers!' Hasamuha barked, standing tall in the crowd. 'Go ahead with him and advise him from your foolishness. But I can assure you that whatever conclusion you arrive at, it shall do you no good. What will be will be, and what will be we already know. Go, shameless goats!' He beckoned. Ifashanu bent and whispered to his mother.

'It's time mother. Let's get going, move it!' The Queen felt oddly disoriented.

'Go ahead of me,' she said simply.

Ifashanu glanced at his watch: 12:15pm. Fifteen minutes left, he whispered the time to his mother and turned away briskly.

'Please spare us a few minutes,' he said to the seated crowd and motioned to his loyalists. He ushered them hurriedly to the exit door of the Palace. One of the elders asked in dismay.

'Where are we going, Ifashanu son of Jajaha? Is everything alright with you?'

'I'm fine Baba, I'm cool,' he said. 'Look,' he gestured to them to stop on reaching the end of the passage. 'I appreciate your genuine trust in me. I want to put that trust to test by making a request from you right away.' The old men looked on with obvious amusement, and then shock.

'Any request you make shall be granted right now.' One of them said looking less amused.

'Okay, I want you all to return to your houses and bring me a lamer or duck; everyone, just an animal for sacrifice.'

'But, Ifashanu son of Jajaha, a lamer is not used for offering in our land. We can each bring you a cow if you so desire.'

'Baba, I said a lamer; no buts, no cows. Do as I say in order to justify your loyalty to me. Move! Move! Bring me the lamer on time.' He dismissed them all, almost pushing them out.

'Your royal subjects bid you well, your majesty.' They all greeted hurrying out along the passage.

Relieved by their unceremonious exit, he checked his watch and became alarmed: 12:23pm.

He hurried back to the passage. The door into the grand hall was closed; he could only hear uncoordinated voices. He snooped, held his ears glued to the door and heard his mother addressing the gathering. There were shouts and booing at intervals.

'Mother! Mother! Mother!' He cried aloud, ignoring the fact that he might be heard. He did not however notice the shadow with a bulging belly slip through the adjacent door unseen. Indeed the Queen could hear her son calling, as she stood at the center addressing the gathering, and holding them down. She had decided twenty-four hours before that like others decreed to die; she would follow to offer explanations to their ancestors in order to save the name of the royal family in the book of history and before Eledumare.

* * *

Meanwhile, Ifashanu was becoming restless at the other side of the door. He knew if he should venture opening the door, he would forfeit his plot. He made another attempt, almost screaming.

'Mother! Mother! Mother! Mother!' He called four times. Soon, it dawned on him that his mother was not going to respond to his calls. He dashed up the roof and opened the machine. He began to press the buttons in quick succession. He flung away his attire to reduce his perspiration. The machine beeped in seconds and he grabbed the microphone.

'Adam, do you read me? Do you read me?' he barked. His Princely voice came alive inside the Squadron stationed on the Mediterranean Sea. The rapid response team was just waking up from slumber in their cabin when they heard the plea through the four speakers hung at the edges monitoring the operation. The ship captain raised a brow at agent Dave.

'I'd call that a farewell message, the last wish of a dying man,' he grimaced.

At the other end, Adam gently picked the receiver in his office and froze.

'Pearl, is that you? Can't pick you well, why the panic? Where are you at the moment? Where are you speaking from?' he smiled ironically.

'On the roof, I'm on the Palace roof!'

'Fuck! What are you doing up there?'

'I want the explosives detonated,' Ifashanu blurted across the line. 'I want the plan aborted. I must stop it now! My mother's in there! She's still there!' He shouted and wept profusely.

'Jesus! Fuck the shit! Fuck it!' Adam shouted; his face drained of blood like a fading rainbow. 'You've got fifty-five seconds nigger, or your whole life will be blown to pieces,' he said, grounding his cigar in the ash tray. Uneasy, he stood straight and husked into the microphone. 'Pearl, when the bush is on fire, the grasshoppers don't wait to say goodbye to one another. Get the fuck out of there now or you'll be roasted!' He slammed down the phone and the line went dead. As he did so, Scotland Yard was sealing off all entrances leading to Leeds station, where Adam was. His arrest warrant had been signed 24 hours before.

Abruptly, Ifashanu ran towards the stairs one last time and called aloud for his mother in such a way that it mocked the occupants of the grand hall. The Chancellors and elders were puzzled. They eyed the queen enquiringly for an answer, an answer they never got. Ifashanu walked back and forth on the roof indecisive and looking up at the sky. He noticed that the clouds had fully obscured the sun. He glanced at his watch and discovered he had less than fifteen seconds. His inner mind told him that his mother wanted him to live and keep the royal family intact. He was convinced that she heard his calls. Even then, it was all too late. He counted the remaining seconds as he ran in desperation to the front edge of the roof and leapt into space. The bang was mighty, loud and clear. He experienced it in flight and was propelled higher by the wave of the force as the building rocked with a thunderous blast and lightening, splitting the clouds into patches.

* * *

Spontaneously, an assemblage of a quarter of a battalion of British soldiers arrived in ships and speed boats at the shore of the ocean and was stunned to see the French army already docked and advancing. The good people of the kingdom were running helter-skelter as confusion set upon the land. The brave ones ran towards the Palace hoping to save the remains of their monumental pride.

Amidst confusion, Ifashanu's body had landed far from the palace. He was not sure if he was alive or dead. Everywhere was smoky and there was grave silence. He raised his head slightly and somehow he could recognize the face, a soldier's face, starring down at him. It was probably a spirit he thought. As dazed as he was though, he looked surprisingly at the soldier whom he now recognized. It was the American who introduced himself as Dave, pointing a riffle right at his head.

In seconds, Ifash refocused on the area where the smoke was mostly concentrated before returning his blurred vision to the gun.

'What is this? What do you think you're doing? Are you out of your mind?' he asked the soldier.

'One more word and I blow out your brains!' Dave warned.

'What?' Ifash managed to shift, bone-wrecked.

'I hired your sorry ass to do a job and you turn around backstabbing? Damn it, I should have known better,' he said and struggled to his knees with the riffle still pointed at his forehead. 'Damn it!' He swore again.

'Ifash Gordon, that's the name?'

'How did you know my name? How did you know I'm Gordon?' Dave drew back the riffle and offered him a hand.

'Up you go,' he said and lifted Ifashanu out of the mud with a strong right hand. Covered with mud, Ifash leapt as the soldier whisked him away to a safe path. The pounding in his head must have deafened his ears to the bomb shells blasting away at various ends of the land. When he finally picked up sound, he turned to the soldier and demanded forcefully.

'Where is that sound coming from, will you tell me what's going on here?' The soldier urged him on.

'We can't stop, I'm sorry,' he responded. 'The Zulu, the Mandingo and the Arabs up north have joined forces with the French. Our priority is to get you safely to the shore. The British are on ground resisting them. If we hurry up and you display more courage, we might just make it.'

'But, I don't know these people. Why would they want to attack us? I can't leave my people in disarray.'

'I guess now you know them, and they are not after your people. They're after you, you're the prime target.'

'How did you know so much?' The soldier grinned hurrying ahead energetically.

'You can say I'm a world class mercenary and for the spirit of comradeship, I mustn't let down my contractor. You are not meant to die in the blast, or afterwards. You've been generous to the team. It's pay back.' The soldier named Dave said.

There were loud massive gun fire and explosions intermittently, setting the forest aflame and tree trunks and bodies flying in all directions. After a long trek through the thick forest, Ifash was quickly pushed into a military van, headed for the Squadron, shadowed by heavy gun shots from hard fighting British soldiers. As the van bumped and tore through the bushy pathways, the smell and sound of gunfire was sucking the air out of Ifash's lungs. He could not comprehend what had suddenly become of what once was a very peaceful land.

The British ground commander, Lieutenant Hopkins read the nasty situation and realized that the fire power of the French and their accomplices were telling heavily on his men. Effortlessly, he signaled to the young soldier with the radio and the quest to link up with London began in earnest. Amidst bomb blasts and razor bullets, the British were fast reducing in number at the same time they were retreating to the shore until the London network line came alive and clear. The Lieutenant snatched the phone and held it with a shaky hand. He lay flat on his belly, sheltered by his men.

'Lieutenant, can you read me? Can you read me, over?' The aging General at the military headquarters barked frantically into the mouthpiece. He was nervous and unsettled.

'I read you clearly General! We are outnumbered! Soldiers are down, we are desperate for reinforcement! The wall cannot hold, they're in collab.! We need to reinforce now, over!'

'Come off it Lieutenant! You know that's not possible, it could take a day or more!'

'The largest of the white squadron is on high sea,' the Lieutenant shouted back at the General. 'Talk to the Americans.'

'That's not also possible! What's wrong with you Lieutenant? You know the rules, damn it! You know how we do it!'

'General Thomas" he called his name as he watched four of his men go down. 'With all due respect, bend the fucking rules! We're flat and will be out any moment. The squadron is our best bet General, over.'

General Thomas Brad paused for a moment, he could hear soldiers shouting instructions and raving gunshots as if the action was across the street from where he stood.

'Okay Lieutenant, I'll do as you wish but don't count on it,' he emphasized with a raised fist. 'And if you don't get back-up in 3 hours, cease hostility and raise the Union Jack. We will meet you at the other end. You know how we do it. Good luck Lieutenant, over and out!'

Hopkins checked his watch; they should expect back-up in 15 minutes rather than three hours mentioned on line. He hoped they could hold them back a little longer.

Inside the Squadron, rocket launchers and fighter jets took their turns for the air. Ifashanu sat at a corner wrapped in a blanket. He wished God would see the horror in Odua and come straight down in a fury against the invaders. He waited, there was no miracle of such and he resigned his thought, peering through the freezing glass window, he watched disdainfully with a total sense of loss as Europeans rip apart the continent for territorial dominance.

* * *

On land, the battle continued fiercely, the great warriors of Odua having read the situation, matched-out charging and smoky. They snarled, fought with all their might and spiritual endowment against their enemies till their very last drop of blood.

And eventually, within three days, the French and their allies fully retreated to Port-Novo, while some injured soldiers among them camped at the border of Lome. Later on, the Union Jack was raised high at the market square, plunging Odua into Colonial rule which King Jajaha dreaded and prevented for so long.

* * *

Three months later, Ifashanu and Adam stood in the dock facing Lord Anderson of the British high court. They were charged with the murder of the queen of Odua and one hundred and thirty-four African chiefs. It was a highly publicized trial dubbed 'Genocide'. Jane could not bear to attend the session, but her son did. Jimmy was accompanied by Aunt Romana. And behind them on the last row, sat the duchess of York. In her usual elegant manner, Kemberly sat calmly, leg-crossed, her hat shading off half of her face. She was convinced that no matter the strength of her influence, Gordon's boy won't get less than 25years at Robin Island.

* * *

A similar scenario unfolded in Houston Texas, U.S.A. The seven surviving soldiers were court-marshaled inside the Liberty Barrack, by eight superior officers. The C.I.A hastily destroyed all records and knowledge of the operation. They took the path of justice, leaving their own to be feasted upon by the law that clearly defines the rules of engagement.

THE END

Lightning Source UK Ltd.
Milton Keynes UK
13 March 2010

151300UK00001BA/57/P

9 781606 938225